Texas
Bad Boys

Texas Bad Boys

ROSEMARY LAUREY

KAREN KELLEY

DIANNE CASTELL

BRAVA

KENSINGTON PUBLISHING CORP.
http://www.kensingtonbooks.com

CONTENTS

IN BAD WITH SOMEONE

Rosemary Laurey

One

"Now then, you just sign your name on each one, honey. Right here now, where I've marked it, and we'll all be set and ready."

Honestly! Pushy and patronizing didn't begin to describe her grandfather's lawyer. Did he really think she'd sign the lot, unread, just on his say-so? The man was barking! Juliet ffrench started reading, frowned at the second line of the first document, skimmed the rest of the pages, and looked up at the white-haired lawyer. "There is one immediate difficulty, Mr. Rankin. You've misspelled my name on every single document."

"Now, wait a minute!" Gabe Rankin's bushy eyebrows shot up toward his receding hairline. "Mildred doesn't make mistakes like that. Here it is." He stabbed his finger on the front page. "Juliet Amanda Felicity French."

"ffrench is spelled with two small 'fs.'"

That earned her a dropped jaw. "I suppose we can redo them if it really matters."

It most certainly did. It was her name and he'd better get it right. "I don't mind waiting."

He conceded the point and sent Mildred scurrying to

correct and reprint them all. "You know," he said, as he sat back down in his swivel chair, "I don't think your grandfather was aware of the strange spelling."

"Given he barely acknowledged my existence until three months ago, hardly surprising." Acerbic, yes, but after a transatlantic flight to Austin and driving miles in a wretched hired car, all on a flimsy promise, the least they could do was get her damn name right.

"Would you like more tea while you're waiting?" Gabe Rankin asked.

"No, thank you." She'd welcomed the offer of "tea" twenty minutes earlier, parched and in dire need of a good cuppa, but a glass full of ice and cold tea with a slice of lemon floating on top was not what she had in mind.

Mildred reappeared surprisingly quickly, handing her a sheaf of papers before nipping back into her office. Juliet read each page carefully, ignoring Rankin's obvious irritation. "It's all fine, nothing to worry yourself about."

"My mother always told me never to sign anything without reading it twice," she replied, with a deliberately sweet smile. Hell, if Mum knew she was dealing with a Maddock, she'd have said twenty times.

"Well, you just go ahead and read them, then."

Interesting reading it was, too. She'd known the gist of it before she left home. The actual reality was impressive: enough dosh to keep her going for a long time and ownership of a building including a bar and four apartments. The Ragged Rooster suggested something out of a Monty Python version of Texas but she could live with it, or change it. She was the owner now.

The money was several times what she'd earned a year managing an art gallery in South Kensington, and living here couldn't match London expenses. True, she had to stay in Silver Gulch for three years, but, heck, it was worth a try.

She'd squirrel away as much as possible and nip back home if it got too much.

She'd give it bash, she told herself as she signed her name on half a dozen dotted lines.

"Well now, then," Gabe Rankin said, as he straightened the pages and clipped them together after giving her copies. "We need to find you somewhere to live. There's a nice bed-and-breakfast down on the river and I'm sure Mizz Jones will be happy to accommodate you."

"Why would I go to a B and B when I own a block of flats?" A purposely bland smile met his pop-eyed stare. "They are unlet, aren't they?" They certainly weren't producing rent.

"I think the manager is living in one, made an agreement with Old Mr. Maddock."

"Good, I'll move into the other." She stood, shoving papers into her bag and picking up the bundle of keys.

"Well, now, I'm not sure about that. . . ."

"I am. No point in paying for a B and B when I own property."

"The Ragged Rooster isn't exactly the sort of place for a lady to spend the night."

Fascinating! "Is it a brothel?"

She almost saw his tonsils. "Good heavens! No! Nothing like that in Silver Gulch. It's just a bar. A bit rowdy on weekends and when the Astros win but . . ."

"I'm staying there, Mr. Rankin, and meanwhile, I think I'll pop over to The Ragged Rooster for lunch."

"She has the look of Drew," Mildred said, coming out of her office as Rankin closed the door behind Juliet ffrench.

"It's that red hair."

"Not just that, she has his eyes."

Couldn't say he'd noticed, but Mildred should know after all the talk linking her and Drew Maddock years back. "Maybe."

"Where's she gone?"

"To look over the Rooster and move into one of the spare apartments."

"She what!" Mildred laughed until she coughed. "You going to call over and warn them?"

He shook his head. "Won't hurt young Carter to get taken down a peg or two. Might just stroll on over later and see if he survives."

Juliet left her hired car parked in the shade behind Gabe Rankin's office and stood on the opposite corner, slap in the middle of the town. If you could call it a town, but "village" didn't quite describe Silver Gulch either. She slipped off her jacket and let the afternoon sun warm her bare arms. At least the weather was a distinct improvement from London.

Curious about the place she was going to be inhabiting, at least for a few years, Juliet turned left and wandered down the surprisingly wide street. The town looked prosperous enough, in a slightly worn way. Several shops lined both sides of the street. There were a couple of empty premises, and on the opposite side from the Rooster was a brick building that looked like a boarded-up hotel.

At least she'd inherited a viable business, not an old ruin.

Odd that after all these years of neglect, her grandfather had thought of her on his deathbed. Most propitiously, as it turned out. She still savored the look in Alistair's eyes when she told him she'd be out of the country for a while—she'd just inherited property in Texas.

True, she'd done absolutely nothing to correct his misapprehension about an oil well, but that was his avaricious mind at work. Serve him right for dumping her for the skinny brunette with boobs and a rich daddy.

The bitchy satisfaction of knowing he believed he'd blown it did a lot to ease her wounded pride. She would not admit to an aching heart over the specimen of humanity named Alistair Winton-Jones.

Why even cloud her thoughts with him? She was in Texas and the sun was shining on a blissfully warm April afternoon. So much for blazing heat, arid land, and tumbleweed. Silver Gulch was surrounded by green fields, rolling hills, and a fast-flowing river. With a bit of a stretch, it wasn't that different from the Home Counties. Not that she'd ever come across a sheriff's office or a shop selling cowboy hats at home.

The little cluster of men holding up the wall between the hardware and the clothing store were not the sort one encountered in a London pub, either. One, in particular, was eyeing her as if he'd bought a ticket.

In a different frame of mind, she might even have returned the stare. He wasn't half bad-looking, sexy even, with tousled brown hair and dark eyes that she was not going to meet. She was so utterly not in the mood for anything even vaguely resembling male bullshit. Gabe's "little lady" patronage had used up her last shred of tolerance.

She crossed the road and headed for the Rooster. Might as well find out if she'd inherited more than a headache along with the money.

After the outside warmth, the air-conditioning came as a bit of a shock. Ignoring the goose bumps on her arms and the chill of the cold air, Juliet shut the door behind her. Heels echoing on the wood plank floor, she walked toward the wide counter. On her right, a row of booths filled the wall, and to her left were half a dozen pale Formica-topped tables. One was occupied by a trio of white-haired ladies. As she passed, she noticed two men in one of the booths; their dark suits didn't quite fit the ambiance. Businessmen on their way to somewhere else perhaps? The only other person in the place besides herself was a waitress, who barely looked up from wrapping cutlery in paper napkins.

Juliet sat down at the counter on a round stool, the twin, she'd swear, of one in a Norman Rockwell painting, and smiled at the waitress who turned and asked, "What can I get you?"

"Do you have a menu?"

"Sure." She pushed over a laminated card in a springy metal stand and Juliet noticed the name Mary-Beth pinned on her overall pocket. "The chicken and fish are finished, but Lucas can fix you a burger or a sandwich."

"Thanks." Juliet scanned the menu. "Basic" and "unimaginative" were words that sprang to mind. Six versions of hamburger, a variety of sandwiches, and that was pretty much that. Definitely not a ewe's-milk cheese or sun-dried tomato establishment. Still when in Silver Gulch . . . "I'll have a bacon cheeseburger, please."

"Want fries or onion rings with that?"

"Onion rings." Why not?

"Lettuce and tomato?"

"Please."

"American or Swiss?"

Now she was losing the thread. "I beg your pardon?"

"Cheese," Mary-Beth repeated, as if to a slow child. "You want American or Swiss?"

Interesting options. Who knew ordering a hamburger could be so complicated? "Swiss."

"Want tea with that?"

Not if it resembled the liquid Gabe had produced. "No, thank you. Water would be lovely."

"Okay." She turned and called the order through a hatch behind her. Moments later, the sounds and aroma of meat sizzling wafted in Juliet's direction. Mary-Beth turned to lift a rack of glasses and Juliet took the opportunity to survey her property.

Clean, reasonably well cared for but definitely needing redecorating. Lack of money perhaps? Not if the money in her bequest was anything to go by. Gabe had mentioned a manager and the stipulation of keeping the current staff as a condition of inheritance. Mary-Beth seemed industrious enough, and Lucas, the cook, was audibly clinking plates and dropping something into hot fat. Seemed the only slacker in the team was the invisible manager.

Mary-Beth brought over a misted glass of water. "Anything else I can get you? Need a straw?"

"Yes, please."

Reaching into a pocket in her apron, she pulled one out and laid it on the counter by the glass and lingered. "Australian are you?"

Juliet paused in the middle of ripping the paper covering. "I beg your pardon?"

"Australian, right? You sound just like Russell Crowe. Heard him on Oprah one afternoon."

"Actually, no. I'm English." Juliet put the straw in her glass and tried not to stare at the woman. Being likened to Russell Crowe was definitely a first time in her life experience.

"All sound the same to me, honey," Mary-Beth replied, with a shake of her impossibly blonde, bouffant hair. "You from England then?"

"Yes. What about you? Are you a native Texan?"

"Sure thing. Born right here in Silver Gulch. My mamma never made it to the hospital in Pebble Creek. I left for a while when I married a man from Shreveport, but once that didn't work out, I came right back home."

And she bet Mary-Beth was a font of local knowledge. "Have you worked here long?"

"Seven years. Rod hired me right after he took over running the place. Me, Betty, and Lucas, the cook, all started the same time." She wiped an invisible spot off the counter with her cloth.

"I bet it's not always this quiet."

Mary-Beth laughed. "You're right, there! That's why I work daytime shift. I'm getting too old to cope with the evening rush. Tips are good then, but see this place on a Friday or Saturday night. . . ."

Juliet intended to.

A call from the hatch into the kitchen distracted Mary-Beth, who reached over for a plate piled high with jumbo-sized onion rings and the largest hamburger Juliet had ever seen. "Here you are." Mary-Beth put the plate in front of Juliet. "Want ketchup with that?"

"No, thank you." Even if she'd wanted any, she doubted the plate could hold even a dab more of anything.

"On your way to San Antonio, are you?" Mary-Beth asked as Juliet unpeeled the napkin from her cutlery.

"Actually, no." Now came the denouement. "I'm staying here in Silver Gulch for a while. My name's Juliet ffrench." No reaction. Shouldn't have expected name recognition. "I'm Pete Maddock's granddaughter."

That raised Mary-Beth's plucked eyebrows. "Drew Maddock was your father?"

For whatever good it had done her. "Yes."

"You inheriting the old man's estate?"

"Some of it. I gather there are three of us." That was obviously news, by the look on Mary-Beth's face, and would no doubt be over the entire town by teatime.

"You got the ranch."

"No." Thank goodness. A bar she could handle; a ranch was beyond her.

Mary-Beth caught on fast. "You got the Rooster?"

"Yes. Part of the agreement was I keep on all the current staff who want to stay." No point in letting her worry about her job.

She didn't look relieved. "I see. Well, I have to nip out back. If you need me, just holler."

Rod Carter was enjoying downtime with Lance Colby. Wasn't often the foreman of Pete's old ranch got into town, and crime in Silver Gulch was little enough that John Snow could always take a few minutes from law enforcement to join them. They'd been buddies since their days on the high school wrestling team, and apart from a few years Rod had spent in the military and John had been down in San Antonio, they'd pretty much stayed together. It was a fine afternoon, and having a sexy redhead walk past just added to his day.

"Nice ass there," Lance said, giving her a look that bordered on prurient.

"Tits are even better," John added. "Think that red hair goes all the way down?"

What was with them? "Look somewhere else you two. She's mine." She certainly wasn't going to be theirs.

"How do you figure that one?" Lance asked, all casual-like. "Put your name on her, have you?"

"She's going in the Rooster. My territory, boys. That makes her mine." And why not? He liked the look of her, admired her self-confidence and her very nice legs and certainly appreciated the way her hair shone in the sunlight, ignoring John's presumptuous speculation, sort of. She had class. What was a woman like her doing in Silver Gulch? It was up to him to find out. He wanted a closer look at her. A much closer look.

"Maybe we should toss for her," Lance suggested, ducking as Rod took a playful swing at him.

"Nah!" John shook his head. "Better let Rod have her. Unless you want to share with us, buddy," he added, grinning at Rod.

Brother, did they have a twisted sense of humor. "Bugger off. She's mine." Whoever she was. "John gets to keep the ones he arrests, Lance gets any who go out to the ranch, and I keep the ones in the Rooster." Made good sense to him. Not that the others appeared to agree. "Come on, for Pete's sake, what else is happening round here?"

"I heard Gabe tell Reverend Wallace that he looked to settle the Maddock estate soon. Seems that Drew left three daughters," John said.

"Beats me how they can administer a will when we don't know for sure he's dead," Lance said. "Never found the body."

"Bet it's in the Gulf by now," Rod said. The Wrangler ran fast and deep this time of year.

"Didn't need to declare death," John replied. "Seems it was some sort of trust he set up a few months before the accident. Just divided chunks of property. Some went to the women and some were to be sold off. There were a few other arrangements. Said the old man wanted to sort out his affairs early. Just as well as it turned out."

Rod smiled. Yes! That had to mean he got the Rooster clear and unencumbered. Hot damn! The old man had promised him the bar on his death if Rod made it profitable. He'd done more than that. The place was a miniature gold mine. Sweated labor and long hours paid off. Sad about old Pete's drowning, but at seventy-five, he'd had a darn good run for his money. Rod was a little curious what the granddaughters got, and which chunks of Pete's property were to be sold, but none of that mattered to him. "Well, boys," he said, "looks like we're due to have a big party celebrating the new ownership of the Ragged Rooster."

"Sure thing. When?" Lance asked.

"Better pick a night I'm off duty," John said, giving Rod a thump on the back. "So I can share a pitcher of beer with the rest of you."

"A pitcher? Hell! We'll have free beer all night!"

Through their laughter came the squeak of Rod's cell phone. He flipped it open. Mary-Beth calling? What was wrong?

"Rod," she said, in her usual no-nonsense manner, "better get your skinny ass over here on the double!"

"What's the matter?" Things looked quiet enough from this side of the road.

"The new owner of the Ragged Rooster is sitting here munching on onion rings and a bacon burger with Swiss. Thought you might want to know."

Two

Anger, shock, and a touch of fury propelled Rod across the road with just a quick "Gotta go!" to his buddies. He pushed open the door and looked around *his* bar. What the hell was Mary-Beth playing at? The two suits were getting ready to leave. Maude Wilson and her cronies were playing rummy, as they did most afternoons, practicing character assassination as they bet for nickel points. The only other occupant was the sharp-looking redhead he'd noticed earlier walking up Center Street.

Her perky little butt was poised on one of the counter stools while she ate . . . he walked closer . . . a burger and onion rings. A bacon burger with Swiss.

Cold rage at Pete's double-dealing clenched Rod's gut. Still not quite believing, suspecting some twisted joke, Rod met Mary-Beth's eyes. She shifted them sideways to the redhead.

Shit! Okay, deep breath here. He could hardly yank her lovely butt off the stool and slug her one. His mamma had taught him better than that, but dammit, what did she think she was doing claiming his bar as her own? Might as well find out.

Giving Mary-Beth a warning glance to stay cool, he took the stool nearest Madame Bar Snatcher. "Hey, there, Mary-Beth. How about pulling me a nice, cold beer."

"I'm sorry. Excuse me," the redhead said and moved her pocketbook, giving him a glimpse of deep green eyes before she turned back to her onion rings, cut one into four, stabbed a piece with the fork, and chewed carefully.

A snob and prissy. Nice boobs, though. Not that it was likely to do him any good. Her hair was something else, though: the color of new pennies, and cut short in a mass of curls. He itched to reach out and let a strand of hair curl over his fingers. Pity it came with a bar snatcher attached.

"Here you are, Rod." Mary-Beth set his glass down with a thud . . . and a smirk. "Anything else I can get you?"

"Fine, thanks. This is just what I need."

She rolled her eyes and proceeded to refill Miss Prissy's ice water. What exactly Mary-Beth had done to earn that wide smile he'd like to know, but her turning to look up at Mary-Beth did enable him to catch Miss Prissy's eye.

"Howdy!"

"Good afternoon," she replied, with a little nod.

"Enjoying Silver Gulch?" he asked before she had a chance to chop up another onion ring.

She paused as if weighing up whether to snub him or not.

"It's interesting. Smaller than I imagined but"—she gave him the oddest look as her mouth twitched at the corner—"definitely fascinating."

"Here on a visit or just passing through town?" he asked, nicely casual, as he lifted his glass and took a drink.

She smiled, almost chuckled. Her green eyes crinkled at the corners as she looked him in the eye. "I'll be staying, Mr. Carter."

Rod almost spluttered his Hefeweizen all over himself and the counter. He grabbed his handkerchief and wiped his mouth, thanking heaven he didn't have beer running out of his nose. Damn her! Damn the smug little smirk on her pretty face! And double damn Mary-Beth for setting him up like this!

"It wasn't Mary-Beth, so don't give her the evil eye like that."

Read minds, could she? "How did you know who I was?"

"An educated guess, Mr. Carter. Gabe Rankin told me your name. Minutes after I identify myself to Mary-Beth you appear off the street, where you were chatting. How many 'Rods' are there in a town this size?" While he digested that, she held out a slim, long-fingered hand. "I'm Juliet ffrench. My grandfather left me this building and the business."

"We'll see about that!"

He felt her green eyes watching him as he stormed out. Gabe Rankin had some explaining to do.

After twenty minutes cooling his heels waiting to see Gabe and an acrimonious ten minutes face-to-face, Rod learned Old Man Maddock had done him dirty and given away the Rooster from under his feet.

"We had a deal!" Rod protested.

"I know you did," Gabe replied, shaking his head. "He knew it too. Said he had only three parcels of property and they had to go to his granddaughters. Said he'd make it right with you."

But the old codger had upended his fishing boat before he could. "So what now? I get kicked out after building up the business?"

"Now, calm down, Rod," Gabe went on. "It's not too bad. Part of the agreement was Mizz ffrench keep on all the employees." So he was an employee now, was he? "If you ask me, she'll not hang around long, whatever she's saying right now. You mark my words. Give it a couple of months and she'll be back in London and you'll be running the Rooster just like always."

Not quite like always. He'd no longer be working for himself but prissy Mizz ffrench. "What if I just quit?" There was an idea!

Gabe waved his hands palms outermost and shook his head. "Now don't you start making hasty decisions, Rod. Why not bide your time and see how things go? The Rooster wouldn't be the same without you." It wouldn't be anything without him and Gabe damn well knew it. "You just hold on a week or two. See how things work out between you and Mizz ffrench."

Fat lot of help Gabe was.

Rod was even more steamed when he walked back into the Rooster, ready to hash out a few details with the new owner.

Who wasn't there.

Neither was Mary-Beth. Lucas, the cook, was standing in at the bar. Where the hell were they? Off doing each other's hair? And he'd been stupid enough to think Mary-Beth was on his side.

"Don't look so sour, boss," Lucas said.

"Where the hell is Mary-Beth? She's got two more hours of her shift."

"She took the new owner on the tour. Say, is she really Old Man Maddock's granddaughter?"

"Yes, Rod, we were wondering that." Old Maude and her cronies swooped on him like the furies. "Is it true? And Pete left her the Rooster. How nice!"

It wasn't nice and it got worse. Two days later, Juliet ffrench had settled in. There was no stopping her.

She could have stayed in the comparative comfort of Sally Jones's B & B, or even the hunting lodge just outside town, but Miss ffrench insisted on moving in. Since the other apartments were boarded up and uninhabitable, she moved into his. After a night on the lumpy sofa, she drove into Pebble Creek, and within hours, carpet and furniture were delivered and she spent the afternoon hanging drapes and unpacking, as she staked her claim on one of the empty rooms. His final objection that there was only one functioning bathroom was met with a bland smile and the unblinking assurance not to worry, that she promised not to use his razor to shave her legs.

A weaker man would have given up.

Rod Carter braced for survival. He'd outlast Juliet ffrench and be a gentleman about it.

"So, you wanted to see the books," he said first thing the next morning. At least first thing for him. He'd worked until the bar closed.

She was sitting at a table in the corner, drinking coffee and browsing over—off all things—paint and fabric samples.

"Yes, please," she replied. "It would be helpful." Helpful for what? To elbow him out. Not a chance. Not if she stood by the terms of the old man's will.

"Whatya doing?" he asked as she scooped up a pile of papers and the samples and put them in a manila folder.

"Planning some repairs. The plumbing is archaic. The bar needs redecorating. So does the entire upstairs. The bathroom needs ripping out and redoing."

"The place suits me just fine!"

"I'm having an architect come and look over the entire upstairs," she went on, as if he hadn't said a word. "The closed-off part and the attics too. Something needs to be done about the roof." He wouldn't deny that but even so . . . "Obviously my grandfather wasn't much on repairs."

Might as well reinforce that he, not the old man, ran the

place. "He had a lot to take care of at the ranch and left me to run the Rooster."

She raised her eyebrows as she twisted her wide mouth in an odd little smile. "Well, Mr. Carter, I hope you did a better job of the books than you did with the building."

Damn her smug little attitude! Let her try fixing the roof on a shoestring. He'd poured almost all his savings into this building, for what? To have it whipped from under him by a prissy redhead. A prissy redhead with one fantastic ass. Right, better elevate his mind a bit. His survival and sanity were on the table here. She might not be able to fire him, but she could sure get on his case and niggle him into quitting.

No damn way! He'd follow Gabe's advice about outlasting Mizz ffrench—and why did she spell her name that silly way? Meanwhile, he might as well enjoy the view of her long legs and swinging hips.

The crowded office seemed dingier and messier than ever with Juliet standing in the middle of it. Her red shirt was fastened with tiny pearl buttons and tucked into her chino skirt. Even her shoes were neat—brown leather sandals with narrow straps around her slim ankles—and her toenails were polished with pearly pink lacquer.

She was all that was cool and dignified and his office was unmitigated chaos.

"The books, Mr. Carter?" she asked, a little smile twisting her full lips.

Damn, he'd been ogling her toes. "Yeah, let me get the program up. It's all on the computer. You're okay with that?"

"With a computer?" Her eyes gleamed even greener when she smiled. "We do have computers in the UK. I believe I can manage yours."

She did a lot more than "manage." Two minutes after he had the machine booted up, she was scrolling screens, compiling reports, and printing out page after page. Mizz Juliet ffrench darn well knew her way around Quickbooks.

"Anything in particular you're looking for?" Rod asked. Might as well help get her out of his chair so he could get to work.

"Right now, I really want just an overall picture of how things are. I'm sure I'll have questions."

He didn't doubt it. "Okay then, I'll leave you to it. If you need more paper it's under the printer." Might as well leave and do something constructive with his day. Watching her put too many ridiculous ideas in his head. He'd always had a weakness for redheads and it seemed this one was going to herald his ruin if he wasn't very, very careful. "See you!"

As the door closed behind him, Juliet leaned back in the oak chair and let out a heartfelt sigh of relief. Thank the heavens he was out of her space. Getting on her nerves was far too mild for what Rod Carter did to her. Okay, he was good-looking and sexy in a rough-edged almost dangerous sort of way. All right. Who was she trying to fool? The man was bedworthy in the nth degree but his resentment of her definitely put paid to any possible attraction. He was obviously one of those macho males who hated working for a woman. Just her luck! They were as big a pain here as in London.

So what? She had more important things to consider than Rod Carter's ego difficulties.

Leaving the printer chugging away—a new one would be a good purchase, for this one was close to antique—she nipped into the Rooster, gave a quick hello to Mary-Beth and Rod, and poured herself a mug of coffee before returning to the office to study the Rooster's finances.

Three

"She carries on as if she owns the place!" Rod muttered to his coffee as the door swung closed behind Juliet.

"I've news for you, boss, she does." Okay, it was true but did Mary-Beth have to add the smirk to the smart-ass comment?

"You women always stick together!" Unfair and unjust but, heck, he was feeling sour.

"Okay, Rod, the old man did you wrong. That's hardly her fault. She never even met him. And seems to me she's got good plans for the old Rooster. She wants to redo the building, and fixing up the bathrooms is a major improvement, in my opinion. Will be nice to sit down without worrying about plaster dropping on my head."

"Redecorating!" he snapped. She would. No doubt she was putting pretty flower wallpaper in the can. They'd be having lacy curtains and pink toilet paper next.

"About time, too," Mary-Beth replied over her shoulder, as she went to the far end of the counter to take Gabe Rankin's order.

"How things going, Rod?" Gabe asked, as Mary-Beth

called his order of three fried eggs, sausage, fries, and gravy to Lucas.

Rod shrugged. "Not too bad." That was a lie if there ever was one! "Getting things sorted out. Right now, she's going through the books."

"Nothing to worry about there, lad! You kept them straight."

Damn shame his emotions weren't in the same condition. "Wish I knew what the hell she had on her mind."

"I guess right now she just wants to check out what she has. Nice-looking girl, isn't she?"

The best answer he had to that was a grunt.

By midafternoon, Rod could stand the suspense no longer. He was even debating the pros and cons of carrying in a cup of coffee to give him a reason to check up on her. He drew the line there, settling for checking on her minus coffee.

Juliet looked up as he opened the door. She had a stack of papers in front of her, the file cabinet was open, and several folders were spread over every clear surface.

Helped herself, didn't she? Mary-Beth's words echoed in his skull. Right!

Then Juliet smiled.

Her green eyes sparkled with an almost blue light, crinkling just a tad at the corners, and her wide mouth curled up, showing teeth that, if not perfectly straight, were white as pear blossoms. Her blouse was a little rumpled from sitting and it gaped over her breasts.

He couldn't quite make out the color of her bra. Pink was it?

Sheesh! Better elevate his mind a bit.

"Rod, glad you came in. I was about to come and look for you."

"Yes?" He made a point of lifting his eyebrows and not smiling more than he could help.

"Just have a few questions." She reached for a sheet of paper and creased her forehead as she scanned the columns. "There's a few things that don't quite make sense."

"Oh?" What was she nitpicking about? "The accountant okays the books every year for the tax returns."

"I noticed. The books are fine. It's just there are some missing expenses. What about insurance and taxes?"

"Pete Maddock covered taxes and insurance."

"I see." That he doubted. "I'm also a bit mystified by your salary. You're the lowest paid person on the staff. Even with the occasional draws from the profits and given you live rent free, it seems skewed."

Rod shrugged. "Doesn't bother me."

"You put in a chunk of money when you took over the bar."

What next? His file of bank statements was sitting open on the table. Had she gone through everything? "Pretty little snoop, aren't you?"

She went stiff from the chest up and glared. No other word for it. "I'm checking the books. I was curious where the major influx of money came from. Your bank statements were in the filing cabinet along with the business ones. There was a notation on the business bank statement that the money came from your personal account. It seemed a large sum, so I checked."

"So, I invested money in the Rooster. What are you going to do about it?"

"Pay you back, I presume."

Like hell she would! He crossed the crowded office, planted his hands on the desk, and leaned toward her. "I bought my share of the Rooster fair and square. You're not buying me out!"

Her bright eyes met his. Her frown deepened as she leaned back in the chair and thought a minute. "Tell me, Mr. Carter, what was the arrangement you had with my grandfather? 'Manager' doesn't seem to cover it."

Since she asked . . . "Simple, really. I put my savings into the place, built it up—it was a real dump when I took it over. Our agreement was I'd get it profitable and keep it going and he'd leave it to me when he died!" There! He'd done it! Felt good to spew his resentment off his chest. Except for the shock on her face. Did she think she was going to lose her precious inheritance?

"So," she replied, after a few seconds' pause, "the old man was as big a liar and as worthless as his son." Her voice was sharp enough to cut glass. Astounded at her reaction, Rod thought a minute how to reply. In the silence she muttered, "Fuck the pair of them!"

The profanity sounded almost genteel coming in her precise accent, but the look on her face was anything but lady-like. She looked ready to cause injury. Rod almost backed off.

"Sit down!"

Rod wasn't about to argue when she used that tone. He pulled up the spare chair and sat down, well beyond slugging distance, and watched her scowl.

"So," she began, "let me get this straight. Pete Maddock agrees that if you invest in the bar and build it up to a going concern it's yours when he dies?"

"Yeah!" That pretty much summed it up.

Another thoughtful pause. "The bar or the building?"

Good question. "I guess both. We agreed over a handshake. Heck, the rest of the building isn't up to much. Next door has been empty for years."

"That doesn't matter. This side was run down and you fixed it up. All upstairs needs is new plumbing, wiring, and a bit of redecorating. I bet next door is the same."

And her point was . . .

She shook her head. "I wonder what the hell he thought he was doing."

"You mean Pete?"

"Yes. He gets me over here with promises of money and property and, to do that, yanks the rug from under you, so to speak." Another thoughtful scowl. "Why? Do you have any idea?"

"Beats me, lady!"

"I think a nice little chat with Mr. Rankin is in order."

"Save your breath. I went over there the afternoon you arrived. It's all signed and sealed. Nothing can be changed."

"Really? Bugger them then!"

"What do you want to do? Give me back the Rooster?" All this outrage was well and good, but how did it help him?

"Not yet." She grinned.

"What the hell do you mean?" Damn, she had him swearing now.

"Listen," she said, resting her elbows on the table and leaning forward, "you were promised the Rooster if you put in money and effort, right?" Okay, that was already established. "Then, out of the blue, I get offered money and property. From, I might add, a man who'd only seen me once in my life for about twenty minutes. A man who lied every bit as well as his rotten son."

She was a bit tough on old Pete but . . .

"Why do it?" she went on. "If not to cause some sort of trouble, discord, or unpleasantness? You spoke to Mr. Rankin about it, right?"

"Yup." For what good it did.

"What did he say?"

He told her.

Didn't make her any happier. "A lying double-crossing old bastard!"

For a nice British lady, she sure had a potty mouth. "But he wasn't! Pete was always straight as a die." She gave a disgusted snort. "Ask anyone. He bought and sold property around town for years. Traded livestock. Made loans. Everything was done on a handshake and I don't remember anyone ever saying he broke his word."

"Maybe not in Silver Gulch."

"Where then? Don't know if he ever left the state." She exhaled twice. Slowly. Seeming hesitant to go on. "You know something otherwise about him?"

She nodded. "Maybe his reputation here, in Silver Gulch, mattered to him but"—she gave another slow exhale, the crease reappearing between her eyes—"I met him once. I was ten, maybe eleven. It was in Dallas." She paused and he waited. "My mother was an opera singer. On tour. I usually traveled with her. Pete Maddock came after the show one night, said he was my grandfather, gave me a big doll—it was quite beautiful but I was getting a bit past dolls—and took us out to dinner. I fell asleep in the booth, I remember, but later Mum said he'd promised to make sure Dad paid money for me.

"Dad never had despite Mum writing several times. We weren't starving or anything, but only the big stars in opera are really well paid and she had the cost of taking me everywhere. After my so-called grandfather promised money, Mum said it meant she'd be able to pay for me to go to boarding school. Didn't fancy the idea much, and between us, I was glad the money never arrived. Mum and I managed fine. I liked moving around and going to school on a very sketchy basis."

Maybe, but it seemed an odd way to bring up a kid. "What about getting through high school? Going to college?"

"I didn't."

"But how did you get a job?" Okay, this was getting far too personal, but frankly, she had him fascinated.

"I was nineteen when Mum died and I knew I had to get a job somewhere. A friend, Max Goldberg, offered me a lowly job as a dogsbody in his art gallery. It was pretty menial, unpacking exhibits and making coffee and running things back and forth to the printers, but I knew the business. I'd spent hours since I was quite small wandering through just about every major and most of the minor art galleries in Europe and both Americas. I studied a lot on the side and soon got an assistant's job in another gallery. Three years later, Max wooed me back as manager and there I stayed until I came here." She shook her head. "I don't know why I'm telling you all this."

"Because I asked?"

"Yes, you did. So now you know my life history and I know nothing about you other than my grandfather did you wrong."

He laughed. "My life history fills about three sentences. I was born here in Silver Gulch. Joined the army after high school. Came back. Couldn't find a job until Pete Maddock offered me the chance to take on the Rooster."

"That's four sentences."

Before he could tell her she was too picky to be real, Mary-Beth put her head around the door. "Boss, the soft-drink delivery is here. Want to sign for it?"

"Coming." He stood. "I'll be back," he told Juliet.

She watched the door swing shut behind him. Why the hell had she spilled her guts like that? Because he'd asked and he'd listened. Right! No doubt to use it against her some day. Or maybe not. He'd been cheated, yes, but there was no way knowing that her father and grandfather had neglected her could help him get his investment back.

Something inside her burned at the thought of the harm this darn family perpetuated. She half toyed with the idea of handing over the bar to Rod, taking the money and running. But to get all the money and keep it, she had to stay three years, and what could she do here for three years? Open a gallery?

She laughed aloud at the idea before looking at the wall that separated the office from the closed-up part of the building. Why not? The space was unused and would be rent free. Okay, the market would be different from London. Very different, come to that. Maybe there were local craftspeople and artists. She'd ask Mary-Beth. She knew just about everything that went on in the town.

First she needed to check on taxes. Presumably her grandfather kept records.

Rod was back in fifteen minutes and she asked him.

"The old man's papers? Records for the Rooster he kept in his office across the hall."

She followed him across the dark corridor to another, even dingier, office. A glass-doored bookcase looked packed with papers and a rolltop desk stood against one wall. "He kept everything in here," Rod said.

He'd also left everything locked.

"I'll call Rudy Johnson. He's the local locksmith," Rod said. "Seems a shame to force the lock. It's an antique."

"No need to," she replied, nipping back into Rod's office. She rummaged in the desk drawer until she found a heavy-duty paper clip. It was rusty but it would serve.

She straightened it out as she walked back into her grandfather's office.

"What are you doing?" Rod asked.

She couldn't resist grinning. It never hurt to surprise a man. "Opening the desk." It took her a couple of minutes. The lock was old and didn't want to budge, but soon she felt the tumblers shift and rolled up the top.

Four

"Where did you learn to do that?" Rod looked, and sounded, shocked.

She didn't try to hold back the smile. "A porter at the Grand Hotel in Montreux showed me. It's really quite easy when you know how."

"I hope, for your sake, we don't have a spate of house break-ins anytime soon. Might look suspicious."

"Door locks are much harder. I can open only the really cheap ones. Drawer locks and suitcases are easy peasy." Enough of teasing him. Even though it was fun. "I'm in here now. Might as well go through things."

"Need any help?"

She looked up from working on the top drawer. They were all locked and she bet the bookcase was too. "I'm assuming you can't pick locks."

He shook his head. "Hot-wiring a car was as far as I went with potential crime."

Rod might almost be worth the trouble, at least when he relaxed and stopped looking at her as if she were something the cat brought in. The next lock gave and she pulled the drawer open to find stacks of yellowing papers. "If you have a spare dustbin I could use . . ."

"Dustbin?"

"Yes. I think most of this needs tossing."

"Oh! A trash can. Okay." He was out the door and came back with a big plastic one from the kitchen, just as she clicked the next lock in the desk. "Here you are. Want some help sorting it out?"

She looked down at the papers spilling out of the pigeon-holes and drawers. It would take her days to get through it all but . . . "Maybe later on. Let me see how long it takes." Right now she didn't want Rod breathing over her shoulder, giving her some really bad ideas. "I'll tidy up the papers in the other room so you can have your desk back. Then I'll start in here."

She was still sorting well into the early evening, when she heard Rod clomp upstairs. The Rooster was still busy but he deserved an evening off once in a while. She now had two empty drawers; a small stack of pertinent papers, mostly bank statements, insurance policies, and tax documents; and a half-filled rubbish bin. She hadn't even started on the stuffed-tight cubbyholes, the deep bottom drawer, or the stacked shelves behind the locked glass doors.

The old man had filed by rubber bands, most of which had perished over the years, so stacks of papers ended up shuffled together in the drawers. Would take days, if not weeks, to sort it all out. Might be a good move to toss the lot and be done with it.

Except she was driven by a need to find out exactly why the old man had cheated Rod. Why she was bothered, she had no idea. The man irritated her, but if his tale was true, he'd been skewered royally. Given the Maddock family propensity for lies and broken promises, she really had no difficulty believing Rod.

Tired and sore, she stood and stretched and saw a face

peering in the window. A face that disappeared as she crossed the room to peer out in the darkened alley. Drat! Who could it be? Curious, she ran out of the room, down the corridor, and out the back, through the kitchen.

The alley was deserted.

"Something wrong?" Paul, the night cook, asked.

"I thought I saw someone peering in the window." Sounded pretty soppy, said out loud.

"No one there now," he replied.

True. Maybe she had imagined it. She was weary. A day sorting dusty papers wasn't exactly intellectual stimulation.

Might as well call it a night. It would still be waiting in the morning.

Rod flipped the top of the second beer but absently put it aside after tasting it. Things were getting out of hand if he couldn't be bothered to drink a beer. Who was he kidding? They were already way out of hand.

Damn!

What the hell was he supposed to do now? Learn to live and work with Juliet ffrench?—Okay, it was a silly way to spell her name, but somehow it suited her. Seemed fitting to add a little extra to an ordinary name. She was different from anyone he'd ever met: smart, sexy, good-looking, with a wicked smile that promised wildness when the door was closed. If she were anyone else on the planet he'd have hit on her, but no way was he getting involved with the woman here to ruin his life!

Okay, not deliberately ruin it. Wasn't her fault old Pete turned out to be a double-crosser. By the sound of things, she'd had more than her share of backhanding from the Maddock family. And her story was true, at least enough of it to convince him of the rest. He'd done a few Google searches after she'd shut herself in Pete's old office, and sure enough, Margarite ffrench had sung halfway across the world in second- and third-string opera companies, and The Tolliver Gallery in South Kensington (wherever that was exactly) still listed Juliet ffrench as manager. Rod wondered if she still checked e-mail at the address on the Web site.

She must have left pretty suddenly. Come all that way to claim her inheritance and oust him.

He picked up the bottle and, this time, tilted it to his lips and drained it.

He reached for the remote and flicked channels. Nothing caught his interest. He was fixating on Juliet, the bar, Juliet, what the hell to do about everything, and Juliet, pretty much in that order.

He considered driving into Pebble Creek, finding a bar, and picking up the first willing woman, but the idea held no appeal. Casual sex had never been his thing, and right now he knew an anonymous fuck would do nothing to ease his mind.

Maybe he should just drive into San Antonio in the morning and reenlist.

That would solve the immediate problem.

By running away? No solution whatsoever! Rod caught the end of a movie he'd already seen. Watching justice, fairness, and decency prevail on the screen gave him the opportunity to pretend it just might in real life.

He watched the credits roll, then stared at an inane commercial suggesting the best beer was produced in a Yankee state way up North. Thinking of beer, he realized that the last one had run right through him. Flicking off the TV, he stood and ambled down to the bathroom. He'd left the light on again. Still thinking hard about what to do about the Juliet question, he was unzipped and aiming straight at the china monster before it registered that the shower was running behind him.

Not quite believing his ears, he looked over his shoulder, then turned in horror.

Standing under the shower stream was a very wet, utterly naked Juliet.

And boy, was she a sight to see! Firm breasts, high and lovely and just the right size to fill his hand. Her skin was all over pink from the warm water. Her hair plastered on her head only made her look sexier. He longed to sit her between his thighs and towel her curls dry, and while he was at it, he'd take good care of the sassy little auburn triangle between her legs.

"Good evening, Mr. Carter," she said, her voice so cold it was a wonder the shower didn't freeze up.

The atmosphere was frigid enough to bring him to his senses. "Christ almighty, Juliet! I'm sorry!" He shoved himself back in his pants and zipped fast. "Didn't realize you were here!" he said over his shoulder as he raced out, realizing, as he closed the door, that he hadn't stopped to flush. Well, damn, he wasn't going back.

Juliet stared at the slammed door. If it weren't for the seat still up, she'd believe she'd imagined the past thirty seconds. First thing in the morning she was buying a shower curtain and a bolt for the door, if she had to drive all the way to San Antonio.

She turned the water off so hard that the ancient plumbing protested, grabbed a towel, and pulled on pajamas before she was properly dry. Skipping teeth cleaning—gum disease being very low on her list of worries right now—she grabbed her clothes and all but raced down the corridor to her room.

Shutting the door behind her, she dragged a chair across the room and wedged it under the doorknob, à la all the best adventure stories she'd read as a child. She slumped on the bed, heart racing and breathing fast, and as she looked across at her barricaded door, she burst out laughing. As if Rod was likely to come barging in. He'd made it pretty clear he couldn't stand her.

Not that she altogether blamed him after what she'd learned this afternoon. Made her ashamed to have the old man's blood in her veins.

With that thought, she crawled under the covers and slept really badly.

Rod dragged himself out of bed late, after one of the lousiest night's sleep of his life. He growled at Mary-Beth when she bumped him as he made his way to the coffeepot and snarled at Lucas for no good reason other than he was smiling.

"Had one too many last night, boss?" Mary-Beth asked, folding her arms on her chest and eyeing him in a way that bordered on insubordination.

"Hell no! I'm just . . ." Good question. "Couldn't sleep last night." Impossible with a boner but that was definitely information he had no intention of sharing.

"There was a program on TV the other night about sleep deprivation," Gabe Rankin said, obviously getting into the spirit of pestering Rod.

Given Gabe's role in the current situation, he was lucky all he got in reply was a grunt and a grudging nod.

"Yeah, right. I got work to do. Can't stand around gabbing." He added cream and sugar to his mug and asked as casually as he could, "Juliet anywhere around?"

"She left early. Gone into Pebble Creek. Said she had some errands to run," Mary-Beth replied.

Thanking Providence for that small mercy, Rod shut himself in his office and wondered what the hell he was going to do next. Apologize to her? Why? *She'd* been in his shower. Shit! No! *Her* shower since she now owned it. Crap!

Damn it all! He'd lost sleep dreaming about Juliet's pale skin and bright red hair in all the right places. He was not wasting the day repeating the torture. Might as well do something productive instead. Filing sales tax returns was a good mind-numbing way to pass a few hours. Days. Weeks. Months. Not that he'd be able to stretch it out quite that long. Sooner or later he'd have to face Mizz ffrench and how the heck was he to handle it? Apologize? Pretend it never happened? Good try, Carter! Just thinking about her had undone the efforts of the prolonged cold shower he'd indulged in earlier.

She took her time. He should be thankful for that, but come back she did. He heard her laughing as she called out to Mary-Beth and then ran upstairs, her feet echoing on the uncarpeted boards. As she descended about half an hour later, he held his breath, praying she wouldn't come near him. Ever. He was convinced he'd never be able to look her in the eye again and he was going to have to, for the next how many years?

His groan reverberated in the high-ceilinged room and came back to mock him.

Then the door opened and the object of his agony and lust put her head around it. "Rod, have you been in the other office this morning?"

What was she getting at? "No! I've been here all morning." When he wasn't eating lunch or getting a second cold shower so as not to scandalize Maude Wilson and her cronies.

"You think someone else has?"

What was she getting at? "Don't see why. No one's been back this way."

He watched her face as she thought that over. Did she doubt him? Did he care? "Sure?" she asked again.

"What's the matter?"

"If you're certain, then we have a poltergeist or a peculiar burglar."

She sounded perfectly serious and just a tad worried. "What do you mean? Show me." He stood up. "Certain?"

She drew her mouth up in a way he guessed she meant to be disapproving but ended up sexy. "Come and see for yourself."

He followed her into Pete's old study.

"Look," she said, pointing to the back table. "I had everything in two stacks. Things I wanted to look at right away, and stuff that could keep. The rest I'd been tossing. That stack there"—she indicated a heap of dusty manila files—"was in the bottom drawer last night. It's all years old and I decided to leave it for much later. I was concentrating on the recent records and skipping the ancient ones."

If she was right, and she seemed certain enough, something odd was going on. "Want me to talk to the night staff?"

"Why would they be going through things?"

"No reason I can think of, but they might have seen or heard something."

"Would you mind asking them? I bet they think I'm nutters after last night."

"What happened?" He reached to touch her and stopped himself just in time.

"Nothing." She shrugged. "Well, not really. I was down here going through things and saw a face peering through the window. Odd. In the dark it looked framed with wild-looking white hair. I rushed through to the bar and into the kitchen and out the back door but the alley was deserted. Whoever it was ran faster than I could."

"And had no business poking around our back alley. I've half a mind to mention this to John Snow. He might as well do something to earn the salary the town pays him."

"He's the police?"

"The sheriff. He can have a look around."

"I hate to make a fuss."

"If I do the asking it won't be you fussing. He and I go back a long way."

"And he's used to you fussing?"

Her grin was verging on wicked and he couldn't help smiling back. "Let's say he'll have a good look and then ask around. Not too much to do for an old buddy who gives him free beer and hamburgers."

She nodded agreement. "A good idea. The looking around, I mean." She frowned at the pile of file folders. "Back to sorting out and, oh"—she looked at him—"I bought a bolt for the bathroom door and a shower curtain." Her cheeks showed a hint of a blush that deepened as he met her eyes.

"Good idea. Got them handy? I'll fix the bolt and hang the shower curtain for you . . . er, us." Assuming there were rings anywhere around.

She shook her head. "Don't worry. I already have."

"What?"

"I installed the bolt and hung the shower curtain. It's done. I wanted to be sure there isn't a repetition of last night."

"Good idea! Yes. Sorry about that." Not really. His nose wasn't growing at the lie but another part of him was definitely stirring.

"It's taken care of now." She sat down in Pete's old swivel chair and edged it over to the table. Time for him to get back to work too. "Oh, Rod," Juliet went on, "thanks for believing me about the face at the window and the papers."

It had never occurred to him to doubt her.

Five

Rod didn't really doubt her but he did head upstairs to check, and there was a heavy brass bolt securely fixed to the bathroom door. The shower curtain, contrary to his fears of big pink cabbage roses, was a plain navy one, hung on a brand-new set of plastic rings. Mizz ffrench didn't mess around.

A quick phone call to Paul confirmed Juliet had searched the alley. Rod had seen the file folders spread out on the table and, for the life of him, he couldn't see why she'd have made it up.

He didn't need to call John. He came in early in the afternoon for a cheeseburger and fries.

"A prowler?" John asked as they sat opposite each other in one of the booths.

"I don't know. Could have been someone passing and just looking in as the light was on."

"Think she made it up?"

"Why? Anyway she didn't imagine the papers moved around. I saw them."

"She could have moved them."

Rod conceded the point with a nod but . . . "She didn't. I'm sure of it. She was genuinely worried."

"You believe her?"

"Yes."

John's mouth twitched. "Falling for her, Rod?"

"Oh, for Pete's sake, John! I'm asking you as an old buddy—and the sheriff of this here town, I'll remind you— to keep your eyes peeled around the building. Is that too much to ask?"

"Okay. I'll keep an eye out and mention it to the deputies. Why don't you check the locks? As old as this building is they might need replacing."

"The ones on this side are new. I put them all in when I took over the bar. Had to for the insurance."

"What about the rest of the building? You could have someone camping out in the boarded-up side and never know it."

Unlikely but . . . "I'll check it out." Wouldn't hurt after all and Juliet wanted to see the other half of the building. He'd put her off so far, but this way she'd be satisfied and he'd make sure they didn't have any squatters or stow-aways. Not that he thought it the least likely.

"Sounds good," John said, looking up as Mary-Beth set his plate in front of him. "Looks good too." He smiled at her and gave his attention to his burger. "Tell you what," he said through a mouthful of lunch, "when I finish I'll go back and have a word with Mizz ffrench. Get her version of things."

Rod couldn't think of any reasonable reason for John not to talk to Juliet. He just didn't want him to. And if John made any off-color cracks about her, he'd wrap his guts around his neck and damn the badge he wore. Deep breath here. He was not seriously considering doing violence to the sheriff and one of his oldest friends over a woman he didn't even like, was he? Or did he really like her but . . . Forget it! At least for now. "Want me to ask her to come out and talk to you?" At least there would be witnesses then.

"I'll go back and look around. There might be clues you civilians missed. Pete's old office you said?"

He had but was beginning to regret it. Why? That question would take some answering. He suspected John had written off the whole business as female neurosis and imagination, but Rod sensed differently. He smiled. If John started patronizing Juliet, he was in for a surprise.

Sneaky of him, but he tiptoed down the back hallway and eased into his own office, leaving the door open. Just in case Juliet needed his help.

He should have guessed she wouldn't. When John left fifteen minutes later, his tread heavy on the bare floorboards, Rod had to restrain himself from rushing across and giving Juliet a high five. He could hardly admit to eavesdropping but he freely admitted (if only to himself) that she had dealt with John with dignity, calm, and a touch of pizzazz.

Smiling, almost whistling, Rod crossed the hallway to Juliet's open door. She looked up. "Everything okay?" he asked.

"I think so. Although I would like to know what it takes to convince policemen here that you're serious. All due respect and that, but he implied I dreamed it or was mistaken."

"I imagine you convinced him otherwise."

Her laugh was loud, sharp, and sexy as all get-out and wobbled her breasts in a fascinating way. "I sincerely hope so. It might not be a crime to peer in windows, but if it happens all the time, I'm darn glad I sleep upstairs."

So was he. Last thing she needed was a peeping Tom.

"Did you need anything?" she asked, a little smile curling up her mouth.

"Not really, except . . . how about we go into Pebble Creek this evening and have dinner?" Where had that come from?

She appeared equally surprised. "You're asking me out?"

Maybe, whatever that meant. "On a date, you mean?" She nodded, a little uncertainly. "Not really. It's not a date or anything, but I thought you might like to see a bit more of the area. Plus it never hurts to check out the competition, and no point in spending every waking moment in the Rooster." All made perfectly good sense from a business point of view, so why was he sweating and his heart racing?

She was quiet for at least a dozen of his turbo-powered heartbeats. "All right. What time do you want to go?"

He had to swallow to ease his suddenly dry throat. "How about seven? After the night shift gets settled."

"Fine."

It was going to be.

After Rod left, Juliet sat staring at the empty doorway. What was that about? Why had he asked her out? And even more pertinent, why had she accepted?

She knew the answer to that one. In spite of all logic and common sense, she lusted after Rod Carter, and darn it, he'd seen her naked, hadn't he? It was now her turn. A nice dinner—she'd even offer to buy a bottle of wine—and then who knows what might happen once they got home.

Of course she might just be deluding herself, and perhaps Rod had not the slightest interest in her, but if that was the case, why suggest they go out to dinner when they could eat for free at the Rooster?

Meanwhile she had a few more cubic meters of paper to wade through. At this rate, it would take her the next five years to sort the lot out. Her grandfather went beyond pack rat, to obsessive keeper of obsolete papers.

As she tossed a stack of receipts that dated back to before she was born, she wondered what sort of person the old man really was.

"Ready?" Rod asked, knocking on her door.

Juliet had decided to wait up there rather than announce to the entire staff and patrons that they were going out together. They'd work out what was going on soon enough (assuming anything *was* going on), but this way she'd be spared the scrutiny of a couple of dozen pairs of curious eyes.

"You look great," Rod said.

"Thank you." Wasn't by chance. She'd spent a couple of hours agonizing over what to wear. She did not want to dress up and give the evening more significance than it warranted, but she wasn't about to slummock off and let down the side. She could have simplified the decision by asking Rod where they were going, but that put more emphasis on the evening than she wanted. Or did it?

She'd settled for black jeans and a royal blue silk T-shirt and gussied the lot up with some of her mother's jewelry: a pair of diamond studs and a gold bangle.

Judging by the look on Rod's face, she hadn't done too shabbily.

Not that he was about to let her down. He too wore jeans, blue ones with knife-sharp creases down the front, and a cream shirt with a narrow leather tie and a silver and turquoise slide. He'd shaved and it didn't take much effort to imagine how the smooth skin would feel under her fingertips. His dark hair was still slightly damp, which must be why he carried his tan hat in his left hand.

She might just have to fight off other women if she wanted him.

Question was, did she?

"All set then?"

She hoped so.

Standing aside like a gentleman and letting her go first gave Rod plenty of opportunity to watch. And what a sight for sore eyes. Juliet's jeans fit perfectly and moved as she did, and the bright shirt, the color of Texas bluebonnets, clung to her curves, not only showing them off, but encouraging his already fertile imagination.

She had style, and class, and made him wish he had something other than an eight-year-old pickup. At least it was clean inside. He'd made sure of that before he dashed upstairs for a quick shave and shower.

She hopped up into the truck as he opened the door for her. He'd half hoped she'd need a hand up, but her strappy sandals didn't slow her one little bit. She had his door unlocked and her seat belt fastened before he walked around to his side. As he got in and started the engine, she gave him an odd, quick little smile. Very odd indeed. Her eyes didn't have quite the same sparkle he'd learned to associate with her smiles. Was she nervous? That made two of them.

What the hell for? He wasn't a teenager heading for the river to park. Why was he thinking about making out down by the river overlook? That was not what he had in mind.

Okay, it might be, but only if she gave the go-ahead. Last thing he wanted was to screw things up.

"What do you feel like eating?" he asked after a few miles of quiet.

"What are my options?"

Stop right here and head for the riverbank? Better slow down a bit. "What do you like? Italian? Steak? Chinese? There's even a fancy French place and a couple of good seafood places. Your call."

She barely hesitated. "Is the Chinese good? I love Chinese."

"It's fairly new. Never eaten there." He gave her a sideways glance. "Shall we give it a go?"

She gave a little chuckle. "Let's!"

Steak was more his taste, but given the company he'd settle for moo goo gai pan.

The Lotus Bowl wasn't just new, and bright spanking new at that—all glistening chrome and shiny dark glass—but if the restaurant business failed, they could use the place as a warehouse. Juliet stared at the vast room as they waited behind a group of men and a rather large family with half a dozen children.

Not an intimate sort of restaurant, so bang went the thought of seduction by candlelight. Maybe it wasn't such a good idea after all. Or was it? She glanced up at Rod's profile. She'd have to be dead and cold in her coffin before he wasn't worth the trouble. Mind you, big question was, would she make a perfect fool of herself if she went for her chance?

They were stuck hip to hip for three years—unless he left or she gave up—and things could get pretty sticky if they didn't work out.

On the other hand, maybe he was thinking the same. He'd asked her out, hadn't he? So far they'd not talked much about the Rooster.

"They're ready." Rod nudged her elbow just before closing his hand right over it. The effect was distracting in the extreme. "They have a table for us."

While she'd been lost in lustful possibilities the crowd in front had dispersed. "Good!"

Probably.

Rod did the gentlemanly thing and held her chair for her. Very nice and all that, but out of several dozen tables in the middle of the room, was it just chance they ended up in a cozy alcove for two? A little alcove with a tiny oil lamp that threw a soft light on the dark blue tablecloth, accentuated the strong lines of Rod's nose and chin, and made his dark eyes gleam with an almost feral light in the shadow of his hat brim.

She made herself stop ogling him and concentrate on the menu.

"What appeals to you?"

"You!" was a bad answer. "I think shrimp toast and twice-cooked pork," she paused, "but I do love crispy duck and pancakes."

"Get all three," he suggested. "I'll have orange beef and we'll share."

They'd be hovering on the edge of gluttony but . . . "All right." Rod looked around to catch a waiter's eye. "We are splitting this, right?" Better get this straight from the beginning.

"Hell no!" His teeth gleamed as he grinned. "I asked *you*. This is *my* treat."

It was on the tip of her tongue to argue but instead she said, "All right then, I buy the wine."

He lifted a dark eyebrow. "Out to get me drunk?"

"You bet. Drunk as a lord, so I can have my wicked will of you!"

His chuckle was as sexy as the rest of him. "Can't wait!"

Pity he was joking. Or was he? Was he wondering the same about her. Was she deluding herself? At least they would have something other than hamburgers or fried chicken for dinner. Still it would be nice to be able to say outright, "Rod, I really fancy going to bed with you." But it would take a stronger woman than she—or one much more brazen.

The food was great. So, come to that, was Rod. Even if he did refill her wineglass with a regularity that had her wondering about his intentions, but in all fairness, he was driving home.

"Why did you really come to Silver Gulch?" he asked, very nonchalantly, as he spread duck sauce on a wafer-thin pancake and proceeded to arrange slivers of duck and scallions before rolling it all up tightly.

He was back at that, was he? If it was going to be open

season . . . "I was rather bored and thought it would be fun to seduce a cowboy and find out if everything really is bigger in Texas."

For a few seconds it looked as though she'd have to do the Heimlich maneuver, but Rod coughed and swallowed and looked at her with bleary eyes in his red face. "You make comments like that and you could end up in trouble!" Part of her wondered if she wasn't already. "Seriously," he went on, "are you planning on settling here?" He gave her a cautious look as if waiting for another wisecrack.

"Honestly? I don't know. I'm sort of committed for three years if I want the money. What I'd like to do is make the whole building pay its way. It's nonsensical to leave more than half of it sitting empty."

"What are your plans?"

Juliet paused as the waitress cleared the empty dishes and brought out the next course. "I want to invest in the property." She helped herself to a generous serving of twice-cooked pork. Might as well keep her strength up. "Renovate the other apartments so they are habitable and let them and do something with the unused retail space. I thought I might open a minigallery with local crafts."

"You know anyone local who makes crafts?"

Back to skeptical was he? Just when she thought they were getting somewhere. "Maude Wilson and her sister make quilts, Mr. Rankins's secretary's brother does exquisite hand carving, and Mary-Beth knows a local leather worker."

"Jeff Williams." Rod nodded. "In a few days you've covered a lot."

"I don't believe in letting the grass grow under my feet."

He reached for the rice. "And what about the Rooster?"

"It's a profitable business. You made it a profitable business."

He nodded, smiled, and raised a dark eyebrow. "I did, didn't I?"

"The current arrangement isn't the best."

"You can say that again. I'd like to know where I stand."

"I think we both would." Both his eyebrows went up at that. Honestly, one of these days they'd disappear up into those dark brown curls but . . . "Could you afford to buy the Rooster? If not now, in three, five years?"

Whatever he'd expected, it wasn't that. Now he stared. "You serious?"

"Just asking. You're good at running it. We'd have to work out some sort of profit sharing but, heck, you've plowed money into it. What my grandfather did was pretty lousy. Mind you, Maddocks excel at lousy."

Rod wouldn't argue with any of that—except the last bit. He was still convinced Pete meant to see him right but circumstances intervened. "You've got to get over despising him, you know."

"*You* don't?"

"He was always straight with me, until the accident. After all, he wasn't too shabby with you."

"I think he got scared when he thought he was getting old. He never much bothered with any of us until now."

"Us?"

"Apparently I have two half-sisters. Seems my father had difficulty keeping his trousers zipped up."

"Who told you?"

"Mr. Rankin."

Well, damn, Gabe should know. "They're coming here too?" What else did old Pete have to hand out? Surely not the ranch?

"One is, in a couple of weeks. She's a photographer and busy on a job right now. Don't know about the other one. Mr. Rankin hadn't heard back from her. Or so he said."

Talk about a petticoat invasion. Better concentrate on his particular petticoat. "Interesting, but back to the Rooster— you really mean that?"

"Yes. It seems the only decent thing to do. Not sure how we can set it up, but we ought to be able to work out something."

So he hoped. "We will." He held out his hand. "Shake on it?"

She looked up at him, cocking her head to one side. "We haven't actually agreed on anything."

"We agreed to agree. Isn't that something?"

Juliet nodded, smiled, and took his hand.

He'd never got a hard-on from a handshake before, but her smooth, soft skin sent everything into overdrive. Her thumb rested over his and he tightened his hold, wanting to keep her hand, and just about the rest of her. He was reacting like a randy youth and didn't give a rat's ass, and when she leaned forward and he caught a glimpse of the swell of her breasts in the vee of her T-shirt, he closed his hand over hers and held on.

She didn't object. Her clasp was strong and steady—until she pulled her hand back. "We'll work it out," she promised. It took him a full thirty seconds to realize she was referring to ownership of the Rooster.

"How about we take a stroll around the big city of Pebble Creek after dinner?" Rod asked.

Six

Juliet looked up from reading the check. As she'd requested, she got the tab for the wine. "Why not? Let's have a wander around the big city. Think it's safe?"

"Honey, I think the worst dangers round here are the mosquitoes."

A few mosquitoes would have added to the excitement but the quiet suited Rod. He parked by the Ben Franklin's on the corner of Main and Austin and together they walked across the square and past the courthouse. "The river's to the left," he said. "The riverfront used to be the local trading center once upon a time. Now it's full of yuppie souvenir stores and overpriced coffee shops."

"Why don't we have a look? Might find ideas for the other half of the Rooster."

Rod could think of better ways to spend a nice spring evening, but since she'd just taken his hand and seemed quite content to keep hold of it . . . "Okay."

It was farther than he expected. He'd always driven it the few times he'd come down to this part of the town. Darker too. In the distance he saw the lights along the river and debated going back and getting the truck. He was getting a bad feeling about this.

Too late.

They came out of the shadows. Two skinny youths, not much out of their teens, in tattered jeans and wife-beater shirts, with malevolence in their eyes.

"Get behind me, Juliet!" She moved out of his line of vision. Thank God she listened. He didn't dare look back to check. His eyes were on the two youths.

"Yo, man!" the taller one said. "You lost?"

"Yeah!" added the other, pulling a knife from behind his back. "We can help ya! What you got to give us for showing you the way home?" If he only had the gun he'd left in his dresser drawer, but maybe all they wanted was his money. "Let's have your wallet, man!"

"Sure."

"Hand it over then!"

"Okay." Rod reached for his inside pocket.

Number one sounded nervous. "Move it!"

A bloodcurdling yell broke the night quiet. The knife flew in an arc. Juliet's leg and then her body leaped between Rod and the punk and landed facing Rod, midway between the two thugs.

"Bitch!" the second one muttered and moved in. She was faster. A sideways jump. A crack of bone, and as he fell, Juliet turned, swift as fire, and her foot caught the other between the legs, lifting him off his feet before he too fell to the pavement with a thud.

In less time than it took Rod to realize what had happened, one punk lay clutching his upper leg, screaming obscenities that made his earlier comment sound downright friendly. The other appeared to have lost his vocabulary entirely and groaned like a dying elephant.

Juliet stood, knees bent, as if ready to spring, arms out and her eyes scanning the street. Seeming satisfied she'd felled all comers, she relaxed, then rushed into Rod's arms. "Are you all right?" she asked, breathing hard and looking up at him with worried eyes.

"*I'm* supposed to do the rescuing!"

She laughed. "They were watching *you*. They'd discounted me as a girl. Their mistake."

She was right, there. "You okay?"

"I think I might have chipped a fingernail. . . ."

"Let me kiss it better." He took her hand in his and kissed the soft pad on the finger she held out. And wanted the rest of her.

She gave a little sigh. "Shouldn't we call the police?"

She had a point. He pulled out his cell phone and punched in 911. Juliet noticed the nonmaimed mugger was trying to get up, so she sat on his back. The ensuing vocabulary was colorful, if monotonous, and got worse once the cops arrived.

Three carloads of them, followed by the rescue squad. Obviously a quiet night in Pebble Creek. Worry over, Rod found himself enjoying the next little while. Juliet had been dead right: people still discounted "girls"—particularly ones with English accents and red hair. Even the female police officer stared and drooped her jaw when she realized it was Juliet who'd felled the felonious pair.

The thugs' insistence that they'd been strolling innocently when they were attacked was instantly discounted when Rod pointed out the knife lying in the gutter. It was quickly bagged, along with a gun they found on number one, after they got him to his feet.

Once he was confined to the back of a cop car, and the other one loaded into the ambulance, Rod and Juliet were invited to ride over to the police department to complete reports. Rod managed to convince them to let him drive his truck, but an officer insisted on riding with them. Ostensibly to make sure they found the way, but Rod suspected it was to make sure they arrived. Not that he minded—a third riding in the cab meant he and Juliet sat very close and cozy.

It wasn't until they stood in the harsh lights of the police department that he noticed how disheveled she was. Her T-shirt had a rip in the armhole and she was barefoot.

"I kicked them off back in the street," she explained. "Strappy sandals are useless when it comes to kicking."

He wanted to kiss her there and then and muss her hair up even more, but they were led off into different rooms to give their reports.

Later, sitting side by side, waiting for the okay to leave, she gave a tired smile. "Honestly, I'm getting fed up. I swear they questioned everything I told them."

"Honey," he replied, "if I hadn't been there, I'm not sure I'd believe you felled those dudes with your bare hands and feet." He stretched his arm behind her and let his hand rest on her shoulder. To his delight, she leaned into him. "To look at you, no one would think you packed such a punch or could kick like that."

She chuckled. "It's called taking the enemy by surprise."

"Not just the enemy."

Another laugh, a sexy, throaty one this time. "Is that why they all sounded so skeptical?"

"Why not? No one expects nice English ladies to lay lowlifes flat."

She threw her head back against his arm and laughed so loud the officer manning the desk looked up from his computer. "Seems to me," she said, "some of you have rather odd ideas about the English."

"Must come from watching too much public television." That set her off on a giggling fit. Rod held her close, suspecting stress was beginning to show. "Want a cup of coffee or a Coke? I could try to get one."

"No, thank you," her voice was tight and tired. "I just want to get home, get in the shower, and scrub myself clean."

She reached out her hand and he grasped it with his free one. "We'll be home soon. They can't keep us here all night." He hoped.

Twenty minutes later they were back in the truck, heading home. She sat close, even though there was space to spare. Not that he was about to complain. If she needed the contact, he was more than willing. They drove home in near silence. He thought she'd fallen asleep several times until she moved or snuggled closer, or one time reached out her hand to squeeze his.

At least the Rooster was dark and shut up when they eventually arrived. He parked in the alley and turned off the engine. "Back home," he said, "and since you saved me, you get first dibs on the shower."

She made a sound like a cross between a choke and a cough, muttered something he didn't quite catch, then sniffed. She was trying unsuccessfully to hold back tears. He caught two with the pads of his thumbs. "Hush," he said, his mouth in her hair. "It's okay, Juliet, we're home. It's okay, Juliet."

She grabbed him, rested her head against his chest, and sniffed again. "I know. It was so scary." And she started shaking.

Doc Sherman would mutter about delayed shock. Rod just knew he wanted to pulverize those two punks. Although *she* might make a better job of it. "Honey, you did good and fixed their wagon. What you need is a hot shower and a good stiff drink." And his arms around her all night, but that last he kept to himself. He was not going to push anything on her while she was so torn up.

He carried her to the door—she was barefoot after all— stood her close to him, keeping his arm around her, while he unlocked the door, and once he had it closed behind them, took her upstairs and down the hallway, ignoring her halfhearted protest that she did have legs, even if they were wobbly. He went straight to the bathroom, with the new shower curtain she'd put up that very morning. Hell, seemed like three weeks.

Setting her on her feet, he got the shower going, then helped pull the ripped T-shirt over her head. This was going to be torture, but she needed TLC right now, not fucking. Seeing the red, lacy bra did not make anything easier. Her breasts were perfect: just big enough to fill his hands. Not now! He got her jeans off and found, to his delight, she wore matching panties. Something about red lace against her fair skin had his body way overreacting.

"Okay now?" he asked, knowing *he* damn well wasn't. "I'll throw this lot in the dirty laundry and get you a drink to help you sleep. What do you want? Bourbon? Rye?" She shook her head. Thinking even that much seemed beyond her. "I'll get you something. You get yourself in the shower."

She nodded and he closed the door behind him, lingering outside a few moments while his fertile imagination pictured her sans all that red lace and wet under the shower spray.

Better do what he'd promised. He put the dim lights on in the bar—no point in drawing attention, although he didn't doubt news would spread within twenty-four hours—and reached for the Rock and Rye.

He gave her plenty of time in the shower. When he got back upstairs, she was wearing a long, cotton nightshirt and drying her hair.

Her smile was the most incredible mix of nervousness, bravery, and sheer outright sexiness. "Thanks," she said as he held up the glass. "I'll drink it in bed. You're right—I'll need something to knock me out tonight."

Unable to stop himself, he followed her into her bedroom, telling himself all he wanted to do was tuck her into bed and turn out the light.

He even managed it, leaving her sitting up in bed, sipping Rock and Rye while her hair gleamed like polished copper in the light from her lamp.

He headed for the bathroom. She'd taken most of the hot water but she was entitled to it. A cold shower was a better idea right now anyway.

Her light was still on and her door ajar when he passed. "Rod?" she called.

She looked pale in the dim light. Pale and shakier than before. He sat on the edge of her bed and held her hand. "I'm sorry to be so wet and feeble," she said. "I'm getting the heebie-jeebies at being alone."

"No problem. I'll stay close until you get to sleep."

He slipped under the sheets and kissed her forehead when she turned toward him. "Thanks, Rod."

"Honey, you saved my life. Reckon I owe you."

She went to sleep holding his hand. Just as well she wasn't closer. That way he could keep his erection to himself.

Seven

Juliet woke early, aware of a warm body in her bed. A warm Rod. An aroused, warm Rod if the bump in the sheets was anything to go by. The previous evening replayed in her mind at warp speed. What a fiasco! And to top it off, she'd slept through the night with the sexiest man in the Western Hemisphere mere inches from her and she'd snored the opportunity away. That Rock and Rye stuff of his was potent in the extreme. Like him, she didn't doubt.

But she was awake now.

He was still dead to the world. Okay, he had driven both ways and carried her upstairs—a treat she'd been too far gone to fully appreciate at the time. Now she was bright eyed and ready for him.

Seemed downright rude to actually wake him, so she settled for snuggling close and resting her head on his nicely naked chest. How had she missed it last night? It was broad, warm, and covered with just enough dark hair to tease her fingertips as she rested her hand over his nipple. Hearing his steady heartbeat in her ear was the cream on the cake.

She shut her eyes and prepared to doze off.

Rod shifted a little and a warm arm wrapped around her shoulders. "Doing okay?" he asked, kissing her forehead. She smiled at him and nodded. "So am I."

That was patently obvious. Seemed a crime to waste such a glorious opportunity. "Are you awake?" she asked.

"Almost."

Good! She'd hate to deprive a hard . . . working man of sleep. Taking full advantage of his arm holding her very close, she nestled into his warmth and strength and stretched her leg over his.

"Honey," Rod said, his voice still a little raspy from sleep, "do you have in mind what I think you do?"

"Yes, please."

His chest vibrated as he laughed. Even better, his hand cupped her breast, then smoothed over her nightshirt to stroke her other breast before finding the opening and sliding inside. As his warm fingers came skin to skin, she gasped. His touch was magic, incredible. As he brushed her nipple with his fingertips, her pussy responded. She was aching for him and they'd barely started.

He'd better not change his mind!

To make sure, she trailed her fingertips down his chest, not stopping when she reached the elastic of his boxers, but sliding her hand inside to his splendid erection.

If only last night had gone differently, but Juliet suspected Rod was worth waiting for. She closed her fingers over him and smiled at his hoarse groan. She stroked his cock down to the root and back again.

A louder groan. "Juliet, my love, give me a break! I'm about to lose it!"

She eased her hold just a wee bit. "Sorry. Couldn't resist the temptation."

He reached under the sheets and took her hand away but kept a tight hold on it as he kissed her fingertips. "I can't think of a better way to wake up, but are you sure about this?"

"Rod, if I wasn't sure, I'd have woken you up by pushing you out of bed." Just to emphasize her point, she pulled her hand away and slid it slowly south, relishing the look in his eyes as her fingers trailed down his chest and hesitated over his belly.

"I get your message," he said, grinning so hard he showed almost every one of his perfectly straight teeth. "Give me five minutes, sweetheart. Gotta get us some protection." He sat up, lifting her along with him, since she made a point of not moving. Staying close was infinitely preferable. "Won't be long, I promise, but first . . ."

He held her head in both hands, tilting her face up to him, looking into her eyes for several long seconds before lowering his mouth to hers. His lips were warm and confident, leaving not the slightest doubt of his intentions. She smiled under his lips and he took the advantage and opened her mouth with his. Her heart snagged as he pressed his lips. Hard. She gave a little sigh and parted her lips completely, wanting him, needing him, yearning for his kiss. He didn't disappoint. Holding her head steady, he possessed her mouth. Wild sensations raced through her. She wrapped her arms around him, not wanting him to leave, hoping he'd never stop. As his tongue moved against hers, she took over the kiss, pressing deep, caressing and feathering the tip of her tongue against his until he groaned and gently eased his mouth away. "Juliet, my love. I'll be back!"

She didn't doubt it and suspected she had a rather soppy grin on her face as she watched his delicious posterior dart out the door.

Hoping his five minutes was a gross exaggeration, Juliet yanked off her nightshirt and pulled the sheet up to her chin. Giving Rod a nice surprise could only work to her advantage.

He was back in far less than five minutes, a glint in his

dark eyes, a grin on his face, and a box of condoms in his hand. And he'd shed those cotton boxers.

Good heavens! Things *were* bigger in Texas! She'd never much bothered about a lover's cock, believing the man it was attached to mattered far more than the dimensions of a few inches of flesh and muscle.

She was fully prepared to revise that opinion.

As he walked toward her—cock hard, proud, and ready—Juliet sat up and stared, not wanting to miss one single second of the sight. The sheets dropped down to below her waist, but she barely noticed, her attention riveted on Rod. She licked her lips, her mouth watering in anticipation. "Oh, my," she whispered as she looked up at him and caught an almost worried look in his eyes.

"You okay, Juliet?"

She probably was gawking like a virgin but . . . "Oh, yes! I doubt I've ever been this okay." She swallowed.

He was standing by the bed now, smiling down at her. Her obvious admiration was having its effect, when she'd already decided it wasn't possible for him to get any bigger. He was . . . stupendous. All it would take was a stretch of her arm and she'd have his power between her fingers.

But Juliet had a far, far better idea. Swinging her legs to the side of the bed, and pushing aside the sheets tangled about her knees, she stood and let her gaze take in every inch of him, from his gleaming eyes to his strong chest, his flat stomach and . . . here she had to grin. Why look any lower? Why just look?

She dropped to her knees and as slowly and as deliberately as she knew how, she ran her index finger down the side of his erection and back.

"Juliet!" he muttered.

"That's okay," she replied, as much to herself as to him,

and ran her finger up and down the other side before look-ing up at him and smiling. "Got a condom to spare?"

"Sweetheart, I brought a whole damn box."

"One at a time will do." She held up her open hand. Seconds later, she had the foil package ripped open and po-sitioned the rolled-up condom on the silky smooth head of his cock. Then she did what she'd practiced for ages some months back—she rolled the first inch or so of the condom down with her mouth.

Rod grabbed her head and gasped, "Sheesh! Juliet!"

He was not distracting her now. Not when she'd waited for months to do this for real. Placing her hands flat on ei-ther side of the base of his cock, to keep his dark nest of curls free of the condom, she slowly unrolled the rubber. Once satisfied she'd done it right, she eased her mouth off him, knelt back on her heels, and admired her handiwork.

Rod sort of gasped. "Where the heck did you learn that?"

Might as well tell the truth, after all they were both naked here. "I saw it in a naughty film once and practiced."

He went very still. "Practiced?"

Maybe this hadn't been the right moment for the truth. Too late. "Yes, on a cucumber. I always wondered if it worked in real life."

He looked ready to say something else. But she wasn't in the mood for conversation. Kneeling forward, she wrapped her arms around his thighs and circled the tip of his cock with her mouth.

This was the moment that always flipped her mind into overdrive and sent her libido roaring. With his cock be-tween her lips, he was utterly vulnerable. She could bite, in-jure, or maim, but instead she'd pleasure him as completely as she knew how.

She flicked her tongue across and around the rounded head of his lovely cock, teasing the rim with the tip of her tongue and fluttering it around and under, flicking it gently over his frenulum and, then, with a swift move of her head and neck, swallowed him to the root.

He groaned, his knees wobbled, and both hands grabbed her head. His fingers tunneled in her hair as he held her close and muttered, "Hot damn, Juliet, you're incredible!"

She looked up at his half-closed eyes and his parted lips. As their eyes met, his opened wide. They seemed darker than ever, more intense and lovelier. She smiled around his cock and eased her mouth back up. Slowly. "Thank you," she said and swallowed him deep again. He rewarded her with another long, drawn-out groan.

With deliberate, teasing slowness, she ran her tongue up one side of his cock and down the other, her body responding, her need growing. She'd be content to stay like this, adoring his cock with her mouth, kneeling here all day, spending hours celebrating his erection until she climaxed from the sheer pleasure and power, but he eased her head off him.

"Juliet, love," he said, "we'd better change tack, if you want this to last. Keep this up much longer and I'll shoot my wad before I even get you going."

She looked up at him and laughed. "Rod, I'm going quite nicely already!"

"Honey," he said, closing his hands round her upper arms and lifting her to her feet, "you wait until you see what I can do!"

He picked her up by the waist and all but dropped her on the bed. As she bounced on the mattress, he moved fast and ended up kneeling between her legs.

"Lovely," he said, smiling down at her. "You are utterly and totally beautiful."

"I could say the same," she replied, leaning up a little to

rest her hands on his chest and slide them toward his belly, playing with his nipples and navel on the way down.

"My turn!" It was almost a growl, as he grabbed both wrists and held them to the bed on either side of her. "You had your fun, now I get to tease you."

Very, very slowly, he licked up from her navel to between her breasts. While her little whimpers of pleasure were still fading, he blew gently up and down on the damp skin and set her off again. She was still trying to catch her breath from that little trick when his hands tightened on her wrists and he leaned forward and did the same from nipple to nipple.

He hadn't been kidding about teasing.

"How's that?" he asked.

"Wonderful!"

"This will be even better." As he spoke, he closed his mouth over her left nipple, his tongue circling and teasing, as if mimicking her movements of a few minutes earlier. Once she let out a little sigh, he moved. To her right nipple.

He went back and forth, teasing each one just enough to get her wriggling and moaning before switching. At least she had her hands free now, and she used them to full advantage, holding his head; running her fingers through his dark, and now disheveled, hair; stroking up and down his back; even scratching with her nails until he muttered, "Trying to leave your mark on me?"

"It's a thought."

He lifted his head and looked her right in the eye. They were so close she could have counted his eyelashes. Darn long, thick, and luxuriant they were, too.

"Better stop you thinking then, hadn't I?"

"You can try!"

With a deep, sexy laugh, Rod slid down the bed, grabbing her wrists on the way down. Once again, he had her pinned to the mattress. A sharp thrill rippled across her mind, sending a rush of desire right down to her pussy. Her heart raced, her mouth went dry, and all he'd done was hold her wrists! Not quite all—he was looking at her spread legs as if he'd never been that close to a woman before. Something she soundly discounted, given the last few minutes.

"Yes," he said, a note of pent-up excitement in his voice, as he let go of her hands and gently opened her vulva, "let's see if you can think through this!" His mouth came down on her.

She gasped, then groaned aloud as the flat of his tongue teased her from fore to aft and back. While she recovered from that bit of excitement, his tongue got in closer, flicking over her ready flesh, back and forth and round and round, just skipping her clit every time.

She wanted, needed his tongue on her most sensitive spot and he was deliberately avoiding it. She grabbed his head, trying to hold him where she needed him most but he was not about to be led. Not now. He had her spread and needy and was playing it for all it was worth, ignoring her groans and cries. He was wicked! Wonderful! Incredible! And she couldn't stand being strung out any longer.

"Rod! Please!" She was about to implode, explode, or . . .

"Since you asked so nicely, my love." He moved faster than she could have credited, kneeling up between her legs, pushing her thighs wider, and grabbing hold of her hips. Lifting her up and pulling her closer, he pressed the head of his cock to her ready opening and with one swift movement entered her. Deep and hard.

He was so big, so immense inside her, that she cried out, lost in a wild rush of sheer and wondrous pleasure as sensation bombarded her brain and she roared with delight.

He paused a moment or two, as if giving her a chance to catch her breath and accept the vast cock sheathed hard and deep. She was invaded, possessed, taken, filled. Her head sagged back on the bed and she let out a long, slow keening sound as the reality of his wondrous size and power swept over her mind.

"Okay, love?" When she gasped out her assent, he began to move. Slow and easy at first, waiting until her body accepted his rhythm.

She sighed with the sheer joy of his presence inside her, and as her hips began to pick up his tempo, he quickened his pace and the depth and force of his thrusts.

His power, size, and strength drove her arousal higher and faster. She was lost in a wild eddy of sensation as her body responded to his cock, and her mind zapped out. She couldn't think. Had no need to. Ever. All she wanted was to be joined with Rod, to feel his male power, and to receive his strength and love.

She was yelling, the words making no sense, but it seemed he understood, driving even harder and faster until her cries became shouts that echoed in the room, and sensation flooded her reason and her will. She was climbing the peak now, spiraling up to a climax, soaring higher and faster than ever. Her entire mind, senses, and reason focused on Rod's cock and the pleasure he gave her. In the distance she heard shouts and grunts, as her mind whirled upward in a wild rush of joy and she climaxed. Again and again and again. Until Rod gave a loud shout and together they collapsed, sated, sweaty, and contented, into a tangled mass of hot, slick bodies and limp arms and legs.

Juliet couldn't move. She couldn't think. Was a darn good thing breathing and heartbeat were reflexes or they'd have shorted out, too. Her pulse pounded in her ears and somewhere near she heard Rod's racing heart. Shifting slightly she curled into his wonderful body, draping a limp arm over his chest as she felt his damp skin against her face. Turning her head, she kissed the nearest bit of Rod's flesh—his arm, perhaps?—and tasted salt.

"That," she said, with great effort and concentration, "was incredible!"

"Yes, sweetheart, you sure are!"

She meant to say something more, but her fogged brain couldn't find the words she needed. She closed her eyes, to help her think, and was asleep in seconds.

Eight

Juliet awakened to an empty bed but her memories were as clear as the morning sunlight pouring through the window. The room smelled of lovemaking. Rod might have left, but his presence remained along with a wonderful ache between her legs and a glorious feeling of lassitude. As she rolled over and stretched, a sheet of paper rustled under her hand. A note from Rod. She grabbed it and sat up. "Darling, hated to leave so soon but it's my turn to open up the Rooster."

Back to reality with a thud. Not that she was about to complain about her current reality. She and Rod did have to sort out the future of the Rooster but they had time.

She showered fast and headed downstairs for coffee before attacking the desk and filing cabinet again. She took the last few steps at a skip and pushed open the door into the Rooster. Seeing Mary-Beth was busy, Juliet leaned through the serving hatch to ask Lucas for a sausage biscuit before helping herself to coffee. She was topping it up with milk, when Mary-Beth looked her way and smiled.

"Morning. Has it been busy?" Juliet asked.

"Not too bad," Mary-Beth replied, breaking into a grin. "You look relaxed and happy. Date with Rod went well?"

Not quite what she'd expected over her morning coffee but no doubt the word had spread via the police. "We had a wonderful Chinese dinner at the Lotus Bowl."

Mary-Beth gave an earthy chuckle. "Honey, it's written all over your face. You had way more than spicy fried noodles last night."

Blast! Was it really so obvious? Going by the heated flush spreading up from her neck, yes. Twenty-eight should be far too old to blush, but unfortunately it wasn't and Mary-Beth didn't miss a thing. And now Lucas was leaning through the hatch expectantly.

"One sausage biscuit coming up! Looking good this morning! The boss came in humming. Something put him in a real good mood!"

All right, meet fire with fire. "Yes!" Luckily there was no one sitting at the counter. This might be a bit too much for old Gabe Rankin. "Must have been the all-night, wild, monkey sex!" She gave them the sweetest smile she knew how, picked up the plate and her coffee, whirled around, and headed for the door.

She never made it.

"Mizz ffrench, Juliet?"

It was Rod's cop friend, Sheriff John Snow. She was tempted to ignore him, but he was a policeman after all. Suppressing a sigh and her irritation, Juliet turned back just as Mary-Beth roared with laughter. It obviously took her a few seconds to process the monkey sex confession. "You got me good there," she said, still laughing. "Good luck!"

Looked like she might need it. The sheriff was coming toward her, a worryingly intent look on his face. "Morning," he said, "you all right?"

"Of course." *He'd* better not make any comments about how she looked contented and relaxed this morning.

"I spoke to Rod a while back. He told me what happened last night."

How dare he! She bit back the temptation to emasculate the lawman with hot coffee and then grab the full carafe and look for Rod. "He did, did he? Interesting, was it?"

"Astounding! Quite impressive, I understand."

Damn Rod Carter and every breath he took! Mortification had her blood thundering in her ears. "Indeed?"

"Of course, I'd already heard about it." How the hell? "First thing when I came in at seven, I got a call from Joe Watts over in Pebble Creek. The whole force is talking about how you took out those two punks."

"Oh, that!" A minor incident that faded into insignificance compared to the true splendor of the evening or, rather, early morning.

Another odd look; this time it was pretty much justified. "Do that sort of thing every evening in England, do you?"

"No!" She shook her head. "I most certainly don't! First time in my life and I hope the last."

"Don't blame you," he replied. "Mind you, the guys over in Pebble Creek more than owe you. Seems when they brought in the punks' car, the backseat was littered with wallets and pocketbooks, some from as far away as San Antonio. That pair was a regular two-man crime spree. They're nailing them with upwards of a dozen jobs."

"I'm glad to hear it." That sorted out, she wanted to find Rod.

"Got a black belt in karate, have you?"

"No, a brown belt in kung fu." Nice pause while that registered. "If you'll excuse me, I have some work to do."

Rod wasn't in the back anywhere and his truck was gone. No point in languishing in his absence. Might as well toss another couple of bin bags of old papers. She opened the door to what she now thought of as "her" office and almost trod on a file folder lying on the floor, its contents spilling out on the threadbare carpet.

Remembering two nights ago, Juliet looked around for

other signs of tampering. Other than a desk drawer slightly open, which she might have done, everything else appeared untouched, but how the dickens had this file ended up on the floor halfway across the room?

She should have bought a lock for the door when she got the bolt for the bathroom.

But right now . . . She bent over to gather up the scattered papers and noticed the handwriting on a yellowed sheet torn from a memo pad. It was a handwriting she'd become quite familiar with the past couple of days.

There were other notes, most of them stapled to printed sheets, and a few loose letters in envelopes with foreign stamps: France, Italy, even Hong Kong. A letter, in a different handwriting, fell out of one of the envelopes. It was the name signed at the end that caught her eye: Drew. Her father's name. Okay, nothing unusual in a son writing to his father, and it was hardly out of the ordinary for a father to keep those letters. But stapling a canceled check to it?

She opened the letter and read. Ten minutes later she was sitting on the floor, papers spread around her. Her coffee went cold and the biscuit sat untouched. The contents of the folder were far more engrossing.

An hour later, she stood. She'd just made an incredible discovery and needed someone with whom to share it. There was still no sign of Rod, and much as she liked Mary-Beth, this was not something she was ready to tell her.

It was just going to have to stew a while.

How this particular file ended up on the floor mystified her. Had it been Rod? Had hearing her gripe about her father and grandfather caused him to leave this file in her path—literally—so she'd learn the old man had *not* neglected her? He'd sent money for her keep, school fees, holidays, and even a pony for a birthday one year. Only the money never reached her. Every check sent to her father for

her use and her mother's support went straight into her father's bank account and stayed there.

Seemed, if the rough notes were accurate, her grandfather had discovered the truth only after his son's death.
This recent bequest had to be his attempt to right a wrong.
Certainly changed her opinion of the old man. And made
her wonder, yet again, what sort of specimen of humanity
her father was. He'd written repeatedly asking for money
for her and even supposedly a deposit for a house for her
and her mother, and not a single penny of it ever reached
them.

And if he'd done it for her, what about her two half-
sisters? She rooted through every drawer, searching for
folders labeled with their names—Nina and Lillie, she remembered—but didn't find a trace. Or maybe Rod still had
them. After all, it had to have been him who'd left it out.
Although why he took such a roundabout way was beyond
her. "Hey, Juliet, I think you ought to look at this file" would
have been considerably more direct.

Thinking of Rod, where was he?

Nine

Rod was sitting in a booth at the Rooster eating lunch with a man who looked vaguely familiar. While Juliet had been shattering a belief held since her earliest childhood, Rod had been munching on beer-battered onion rings.

He had his back to her and didn't notice her until she was within touching distance. The other man looked up. Rod, following his gaze, turned. Seeing her, he stood up, delight spread all over his face. "Juliet!" In front of the lunchtime clientele, he put his arm around her shoulders and kissed her. Just a gentle brush of his lips on hers, but it woke a tidal surge of physical memories and, she suspected, was registered and mentally recorded in the minds of every single Silver Gulch inhabitant present.

She certainly wasn't about to forget it in a hurry.

"Have a seat," he said, standing aside for her to get into the booth.

He slid in beside her. Very closely beside her. They were hip to hip, thigh to thigh, knee to knee and she was convinced she had a silly smirk on her face and there was nothing she could do about it. Rod made her want to smile.

He also had her wanting to yank him onto the Formica

tabletop and rip his clothes off, but that urge she managed to control. Just.

"Okay?" Rod asked.

Between them they'd rewritten the definition of "okay" quite nicely. "Oh, yes. I'm fine. Made an interesting discovery going through some old papers, but I can tell you about it later." She looked at the man opposite. "Hello, I'm Juliet ffrench," she said and held out her hand.

The wide brim of his hat dipped as he nodded. "Lance Colby." His hand was strong and callused and he didn't get those shoulders working at a desk job.

"Lance is the foreman on your grandfather's ranch," Rod said.

"Mr. Rankin mentioned a ranch and other property. How large is it?"

"Twenty-five thousand acres."

"I've been in countries smaller than that."

"It's a good-sized spread. Many are much larger."

Most likely. What she knew about ranching she could hold in her closed fist. "Sounds pretty large to me. You must have half an army working for you."

He shook his head. "Five."

Yes, agriculture was beyond her. Besides, this was sort of interesting, but nowhere near as vital as what she'd just discovered.

"Want something to eat?" Rod asked.

"Not yet. I have something I need to talk to you about."

After a brief pause, Lance downed the last of his beer. "I need to get back." She hadn't quite meant it that abruptly but . . . "Good seeing you again, Rod, and meeting you, ma'am." It took her a minute to realize Lance was addressing her.

"Yes, it was a pleasure."

He stood. "Why don't you come out to Maddock's Dream one day and look around?"

Was he talking to her, or Rod, or . . . "We'd be glad to," Rod replied and then had the courtesy to look her way. "That okay with you?"

Since she was curious about her grandfather, seeing his home would surely tell her a little about him. "Of course. I'd love to."

"Great. We'll take you around the place." Lance paused as if a thought just struck him. "Can you ride? We could go around in the jeep but . . ."

"I have ridden. It's been a while, but yes."

He looked a little dubious but gave a smile. "Okay, then." He reached for the bill lying facedown on the table. "How about Sunday? Maxine can fix us lunch and then we can take a ride around the ranch."

"Thanks. I'm curious about my grandfather. I'd like to see where he used to live."

"See you both then." He took the bill over to the counter and left with a look back at her and a tip of his hat.

"Didn't mean to scare him off but we need to talk."

"He needs to get back. He was waiting around hoping to see you."

"Why me?"

"Why not you? By now the whole town knows you're a crime-fighting superwoman."

"Then the whole town has gone bonkers. Haven't they anything better to talk about?"

"Not round here."

That was beginning to bother her, but there wasn't much she could do about it. "Hope they enjoy themselves. Now, I have something to ask you."

"Certainly, love," he replied, his arm resting on the back of the seat. "What time? I ought to close tonight but I'd much rather have a long, slow conversation with you. How about it, darling?" Her face must have shown what she thought about the diversion. "Something the matter?" he asked. "I hated to walk out on you, but I had to open up. I left a note."

"Yes, you did. That's not it." Heck, she might as well say it since, according to Mary-Beth, it was written all over her face. "Last night was wonderful! Utterly fantastic and thank you very much."

"I could say the same and you're welcome." His free hand took hers and he squeezed his leg much closer. "Okay for tonight then?"

She'd be a fool to say no, but first . . . "Just explain one thing. Why exactly did you leave that file out where I would find it? Couldn't you have just told me instead of rooting through the desk drawers?"

"Are we switching subjects here—from telling me 'you were fantastic' to accusing me of messing with your files? I haven't touched anything in that room. Haven't been in there."

Either he was a brilliant actor or he had no idea what she was talking about. "Bear with me, Rod. Please, I want to believe you, but you're telling me you did not take out a file and leave it on the floor so I couldn't miss it?"

"No, Juliet, I didn't. Why would I?"

"Because it held information that radically changed my opinion of my grandfather." It hadn't been Rod; he looked more perplexed than ever.

"Honey, what are you talking about?"

She told him.

"And you found this on the floor?"

"Yes, looked as if it had been dropped there and left for me to find."

"Well, sweetheart, it wasn't me."

"Then we're back to the poltergeist. A very selective poltergeist, it seems."

"A poltergeist that opens drawers and finds specific papers. I don't think so." A crease appeared between his eyebrows. "Obviously someone has been in and out of your office, and that means someone's been in and out of the building."

"Who?"

The crease deepened. "That I intend to find out."

"How? Have Sheriff John round up the usual suspects?" Personally she'd start by asking Gabe Rankin who else had keys.

A flicker of a smile twitched the corner of Rod's mouth. He picked up his almost empty glass of iced tea. "Here's looking at you, kid!" Heavens! A man keyed on to *Casablanca*! "I think I'll start looking closer to home and . . . while we're on the subject, think this might be the start of a beautiful friendship?"

Heavens, he did know the movie. "I hope so, Rod, I really hope so."

"You and me both, love. You don't still think I was messing with your papers?"

"No. Not now. Didn't really but couldn't think who else might and it irked me, though, to think you'd been there after last night."

"Yes." His eyes went all thoughtful. "Last night." His lovely mouth curled into a wide smile. "It was incredible wasn't it?" He wasn't talking about the mugging.

She meshed her fingers with his. "Yes."

"Tonight?" he almost whispered it.

"Yes, please."

"Anything else I can do for you, love?"

"Actually, yes. Can you turn on the electricity in the closed-off part of the building?"

He shook his head. "Don't think so. We'd need to call the power company for that. Hasn't been used since before I took over."

"I'd like to look at it. Rod, I'm serious about wanting to make it habitable."

"You're not planning on moving out?"

"No. I thought I'd set up a luxurious love nest for us." She had to be getting soppy on him but his sexy laugh got a definite physical reaction and it wasn't in her toes.

"That all?"

"That's a start. Eventually, I'd like to make all the space usable and I'm serious about the minigallery. If you're running the Rooster, that can be my bailiwick." After she worked out who was poking through her papers. All right, her grandfather's papers.

"Makes sense. I'd have done it but fixing up the Rooster took all I had."

And there her grandfather had done him dirty. Maybe there was more to that as well. "Where is he buried? My grandfather, I mean."

"He wasn't."

"He was cremated?"

"Neither. They never found his body."

News to her. Come to that, what did she really know? All Rankin had mentioned was money and property. She did need to talk to him and now was as good a time as any.

Juliet deflected Gabe Rankin's comments about crime-fighting Amazons. They were, after all, marginally preferable to his "little lady" approach, but other than that, a twenty-minute wait netted her nothing new. Her grandfather had no grave because there was no body. Her "How did you know he was dead?" earned a pained look. She'd take it up with someone else. As for keys, she apparently had the only set in existence. "I think I'd better have the locks changed, then" resulted in soothing platitudes and exhortations to avoid being hasty.

Five minutes after leaving him, she was back in the Rooster, grabbing the heavy phone book from under the counter and hauling it back to her office. Relieved there wasn't another mysterious file left for her attention, she called Rudy Johnson, the local locksmith, and arranged for him to come out as soon as possible and rekey all the locks. Monday was the soonest he could come. She'd make do with that. She also called an office supply place and ordered a filing cabinet with extra strong, supposedly unpickable locks.

Satisfied she'd done all she could right now to foil whoever was doing this, and wondering why she wasn't more worried, Juliet leaned back in the swivel chair. Who was it? Rod was the obvious one but he swore he wasn't and she believed him. Of course that could be hormones overtaking her brain.

And right now, the inspiration for her hormone surge was filling the open doorway.

"Learn anything from Gabe?"

"Not a dratted sausage! There are no keys except the ones he gave me. He didn't exactly say I was hallucinating but . . ."

"You're not, Juliet. Someone's been in my room, too."

She was out of her seat and across the room to him. "What?"

"Silly really. Just like in your room, it was a paper moved. Come and see." She followed him across the hall. "I haven't been in here since yesterday," he went on. "Opened the bar this morning, was busy there, ran out to pick up an order that was delayed, then Lance came in. Just got back in here ten minutes ago and this was lying on my desk."

He picked up a sheet of lined yellow paper and handed it to her.

She recognized the writing immediately. "My grandfather wrote that."

Rod nodded. "Seven years ago. Go ahead and read it."

She scanned it and soon caught the gist. It set out pretty succinctly, and in the terms Rod had claimed, the promise her grandfather had made re the Rooster. The handwriting left her in no doubt at all.

"If I'd seen this yesterday, I'd say it was just more proof that my grandfather was a no-good, selfish old man who wasn't worth his word, but after what I found this morning . . ." She sighed and handed the paper back to Rod. "I suppose the most pressing issue is who the hell is getting in the building and making free with our private papers? I assume this was filed away?"

"Yes." He put the paper back on the desk and frowned at it. "It was in a folder with my birth certificate and my Social Security papers. They're still there. I checked."

"Let me think," Juliet said. "Give me a minute." He gave her several, even offering her the battered desk chair, but somehow, standing helped her brain turn over.

"Bear with me, Rod. This is a proper pig's ear. All right"— she counted off on her fingers—"someone is moving our papers. Presumably because they want us to read them. We agree it's not either of us. So, who is it? How are they getting in? And why?"

"All good questions," he replied, "but I have another. We could stop whoever it is by changing locks and installing a security system but do we want to?"

He was nutters! "Of course we do! We don't want anyone breaking in."

"But are they? Seems whoever it is knows their way around and has no trouble coming and going."

"You don't think it's one of the staff?"

He thought about that a minute. "Don't see why they would."

"Why would anyone?"

"You changed your mind about your grandfather after reading that file."

"Yes, and you had it rubbed in that he went back on his word. They rather cancel each other out." He picked up something small off the top of his desk and squeezed it be-tween his fingers with an oddly familiar crackling sound. "What's that?"

"This?" He opened his hand. "Just an old candy wrap-per. The old man sucked mints as if they were going out of style. Dropped the damn wrappers everywhere. We'll most likely be finding them for the next twenty years."

Yes! "There were heaps in my desk before I cleaned it out."

Rod stood. "You wanted to go over the closed-off part of the building. Let's do it now. Heck, we could have a fam-ily of squatters up there and not know it." That thought gave her the creeps! "Let me get a couple of flashlights."

He came back with two heavy-duty torches from the storeroom. "We keep them in case the power goes out," he explained, handing her one. It was heavy black rubber, threw a wide bright beam, and would come in handy if she ever needed a murder weapon. "The stairs are old, and who knows what the floors are like," he said. "Let me go first and keep your distance. There may be places that take one person's weight but not two."

"When were you last back there?"

"Four, five years ago. I thought of expanding but it was too run-down and I didn't have the money to take on such a major project. You've got the keys?"

"I'll get them."

They were where she had left them, in a cubbyhole in the rolltop desk. The lock on the heavy door was old and stiff but Rod had it unlocked on the third try. He opened the door, and they stepped through.

The place was filthy, bare patches on the walls showing where plaster had fallen. There were damp marks on the walls and the smell of mice was everywhere.

"It's worse than I imagined," Rod said. "It'll cost you a small fortune."

"It so happens I have a small fortune."

He gave a grunt and walked down the corridor. All right, he'd taken umbrage but it was hardly her fault her grandfather left her money.

The main shop was large and lofty and a good bit of the ceiling was still intact. The place was dark, with the windows boarded up, and the walls were covered with cheaplooking white imitation paneling. "There's been some work done here," she said. Just not quality work—a corner of a panel came up in her hand and an army of cockroaches poured out! "Ugh!" Something tickled her leg, and as she looked down she saw an immense cockroach heading for her knee. She hit it off and jumped back.

Rod pulled her away. "Better be careful—there could be worse."

"What's worse?"

"Snakes!"

"Lovely!"

"At least a couple of snakes will mean there are no rodents."

"I suggest we make a lot of noise and scare them all off."

That was easy enough going up the uncarpeted stairs and tramping through the four large rooms. There was rudimentary plumbing, and the water heater and the old stove belonged in a museum.

"It needs a heck of a lot of work," Juliet said. Rod nodded. "Thanks for not saying 'I told you so'!"

He smiled. "Are you really serious about this?"

"Definitely, Rod. I have the money. This way, I'll have my shop and you'll have the Rooster. I can redo the apartments."

"You don't want to stay with me?" He'd taken a step closer.

"Do you want me to?"

"What do you think?" They were close, close enough for her to feel his breath.

"I wouldn't ask if I knew."

"Hell yes!" He grabbed her, pulling her against him. "After last night you're not certain?"

"I'm certain. Didn't know if you were."

He muttered something that sounded vaguely like "damn this"; let his flashlight fall; and, with both hands, pulled her to him and kissed her.

It was like drowning in sweetness and heat. For a second, his lips just brushed hers; it was enough. With a little whimper, she pressed her mouth on his, wrapping her arms around him to draw him closer. He responded by opening her mouth with his lips and teasing her with the tip of his tongue. He traced the outline of her lips, then gently tapped her tongue with his. It was not enough. She pressed her tongue against his, seeking to share his passion and relish his maleness. She was leaning hard into him now. And he was hard. For her. No mistaking it. Rod Carter was hot for her. Brilliant!

His arms tightened around her, one hand smoothing down her back to cup her bottom and press her against his erection. She rubbed and rocked against the glorious hardness under his jeans. It wasn't enough; she wanted his skin on hers. Needed him inside her.

Her pussy all but throbbed, her nipples ached, and little sharp moans were coming from somewhere inside her head.

Rod moved, backing her up so she was against the wall, his erection pressed harder into her belly, and now he was yanking her shirt from her waistband and unhooking her bra. Both hands were on her breasts, and her shirt was now up under her chin.

And it wasn't anything like enough!

Her moan came deep from her heart as she lifted her right leg and ran her foot up and down his calf.

He groaned.

And deepened his kiss, his hands stroking her breasts

until she felt her pussy wet with need and beads of sweat ran down her back.

Pressed hard against the wall, she ground her belly toward his hips and lowered her hands to cup his butt and press him into her.

Her heart was pounding inside her ribs, his breath tight and ragged, when he looked down at her.

"Juliet, my love, I want you. I want you sweating for me, needing me, gasping for me. I want to fuck you until you cry out with pleasure, like you did last night. I want to make you mine forever. Will you marry me?"

Ten

Juliet's heart snagged for a second, then raced until blood echoed in her ears. She was not hallucinating. Her mind was not fogged out with hormones and passion. She had not dreamed his last four words. One look at his face, the heat and light in his eyes, the flush on his skin, and the bead of sweat over his upper lip, and she knew he was as aroused as she was. He'd spoken wildly, his brain scrambled by lust and hormones.

"Rod," she was surprised how steady and clear the word came out, "a minute ago we were arguing about living together, now you ask me to marry you?"

"It would settle the matter, once and for all. You'd have no choice. You'd have to live with me."

"Rod, I hardly know you."

"I'd say we've *known* each other pretty thoroughly." In the Biblical sense perhaps but . . . "I'm serious, love." He pulled back a little but she was only too aware of the heat of his body. "I want you and I want you forever. I'm not having you running off to London. I'm keeping you here."

"It's too fast!"

He shook his head. "The morning I first saw you on the

street, I thought you were the sexiest, most beautiful woman in the world. Okay, I admit, finding out who you were and why you are here threw me for a day or so, but damn it, Juliet ffrench, can you look me in the eye and tell me you don't want me?"

She actually opened her mouth but the words wouldn't come out. They couldn't. How could she look into the eyes of the man she loved and lie? Love? Her mouth went dry. It was too much too fast and . . . "How about we just live together for a while? Just to be sure."

"Hell no! Why delay?" His hand stroked her breast as he kissed her gently. "Say yes and I'll take you into my bedroom and make your wildest dreams come true."

She tilted her head to one side. "I thought you did that last night!"

"Honey, I'll do it every night for the rest of our lives."

"What if I'm saying yes just for the sex?"

His fingers tightened over her left nipple. "Sounds like a darn good reason to me."

It did to her too, right now. "But that's not all there is to getting married."

He let out a sharp tsk. Getting irritated, was he? Well . . .

"Look here, Juliet. I love you. You love me." Presuming a bit but she wouldn't argue with that statement. "We're attracted to each other, we're great together, and we have shared life and business goals. Seems we have all the bases covered. We could go to Reno for the weekend and make it official if you like."

"Can't. We're going out to my grandfather's ranch on Sunday and that, Rod, I really want to do."

"Next weekend then?"

Persistent wasn't the word but, oh, he was so wonderful. Was she a fool to hesitate? When in her life had she ever met a man like Rod? She knew darn well she'd never find another. This was far, far too fast but . . . "Not next weekend. I'd like to get the place habitable first." There, she'd done it. Said yes. Sort of. It was insane. She was insane. Nuts! Bonkers!

His eyes lit with a fire of happiness. He grabbed her by the waist and swung her around, whooping with joy, before setting her on her feet and positively plastering his mouth on hers. She met him, open-mouthed, and kissed back as hard and as well as she knew how.

Between them they stirred enough heat to raise the temperature in the unheated room. Or maybe it was just the desire between them. He drew his mouth away, giving her a chance to catch her breath. "We won't wait for the damn renovation. That could take months, years. How about Labor Day?"

He was talking about their wedding day. "When's Labor Day?" Come to that, *what* was it?

"First weekend in September. That give you enough time?"

"Plenty! Five months to practice to have perfect sex on our wedding night."

"If perfect sex is the only requirement, might as well go ahead this afternoon."

"You did promise we'd do 'it' if I said yes."

His lovely mouth widened to a spectacularly sexy smile. "I did, didn't I? Better keep my promise." He grabbed her hand and headed out the room and down the long corridor to the stairs.

"Hold on!" she said. "I think that door"—she pointed to one behind them—"is right over the one near the bathroom. If it is, it's a shortcut. And here"—she dug into her jeans pocket and held up the bunch of keys—"let's see if one of these works."

Liking the idea, he snatched them out of her hand and tried several in quick succession. The third or fourth worked, and after a bit of a push, the door opened.

Onto a wide landing.

They both stood and looked around. Ten feet or so across the landing was a door, presumably the one they'd been aiming for. On the right was another doorway, this one blocked and papered over with faded, sludgy wallpaper.

To their left, a stairway led up to the attics and down to . . . "Damn," Rod muttered, "that's how sneaking Tom got in!"

Light came through a glass-paneled door at the foot of the stairs and a narrow chink all around it.

"They broke in." Juliet was down two or three steps before Rod stopped her.

"Better go carefully."

All right, the banister was wobbly and the stairs rickety and . . . "Think they are still there?"

"Doubt it. Too many people here, but just in case"—he stepped around her—"stay behind me." He ignored her irritated sputter.

Since she had just accepted his offer of matrimony, this time she'd do as she was told. He'd better not expect it again anytime soon.

Pity she was so wound up at the discovery she failed to fully appreciate the view of his broad shoulders and nice firm arse.

At the bottom of the stairs, the decor was, if possible, even grungier than upstairs. Paper hung in tatters from the walls, the floor covering was threadbare and ragged, and there were several footprints in the dust on the floor. Footprints that led across the hallway to a door in the far right-hand corner.

"Does that lead into the Rooster somewhere?" Juliet asked.

"I guess so," Rod replied. "We'll find out in a minute." He was intent on the knob and lock on the outside door. "Someone oiled this so it would open easily, and it must have blown open, or maybe they left in a hurry and didn't latch it properly behind them."

"We can take care of that easily enough with a good bolt."

"Yup, that'll take care of them."

"Did you know this door was here?"

"I'd forgotten about it and it's hidden pretty good." He opened it wide. A foot or so away stood the bulk of an industrial rubbish bin. "The Dumpster hid it. Bet that's how the 'face' you saw disappeared so quickly the other night. He slipped behind the Dumpster. Could have even gotten inside the door. In the alley all you'd see would be the Dumpster."

And have no idea there was a door behind it. "Let's make sure it's sealed for good. I don't want anyone else sneaking in."

"Don't worry, I'll see to it they won't. Let's check out the rest of his route." The far door wasn't even locked, and it opened into a cluttered storeroom. "Damn," Rod muttered, "I'd forgotten about this place."

They were in a large room, packed with enough cast-off and battered furniture to open a junk shop.

"Where is it?"

"It's behind the storeroom. I shoved all this in here when I took over. Hated to throw out the stuff, as technically it belonged to Pete, so I left it all here and locked the door."

The door that was now unlocked and, yes, opened into the small room where they stored cartons of toilet paper and napkins and catering-sized tins of beans and fruit.

"He had an easy way in and out," Juliet said, "but also had to know his way around. How many people know there is a back door behind the Dumpster?"

"Not many. Let's worry about that after we make sure they don't get in again." She gave him a hand moving a tall bookshelf that Rod angled against the bottom stair so it made an effective barricade. Then, just to be sure, they locked all three doors. "The storeroom should be locked anyway," he said. "I keep it locked!"

"Not a problem if our intruder had keys," Juliet pointed out.

"Which, by all accounts, isn't possible," Rod muttered. "But he obviously does."

"We'll take care of that on Monday," Juliet said, and it couldn't be too soon. "You know"—they were in the corridor now, heading for her office, or maybe his—"why would someone go to all that trouble and risk being seen just to get us to read certain papers?"

"Changed your perception of the old man, didn't it?"

True. "But it underscored he'd done the dirty on you!"

"I'm not sure about that." Rod stopped and turned, pressing her against the wall, his hands flat on either side of her head, surrounding her with his presence. "Pete always said he'd see me right. I think he has. I'd rather have you than the Rooster."

"Rod Carter, that's the most romantic thing you've ever said to me!"

"Honey, I'm just starting with romantic. Didn't we make plans just before you decided to explore behind locked doors?"

She decided? Yes, she supposed she had. Besides, there was no point in splitting hairs. Not right now. She could think of far more interesting things to do. "I've finished exploring for today." She rested her hand on his chest and slowly trailed her fingers down until she cupped his fly and grinned up at him. "On second thought, perhaps not."

His mouth was still; his eyes weren't. "What about third thoughts? Are they naked thoughts?"

"After all that rooting around in the dust and dirt, I think they should be naked-in-the-shower thoughts."

His smile suggested he agreed completely. "Good idea. You look great naked in the shower."

Okay, so he'd had an eyeful. "It's my turn to see you wet and soapy."

He dropped a kiss on her forehead, nose, and each corner of her mouth. "Wet and soapy, eh? It's going to be a tight squeeze, two of us in that shower."

"We'll manage—trust me."

He kissed her chin. "Honey, we're going to manage fine, for a long, long time, and now it's time to give you a proper welcome to Silver Gulch." He swept her up in his arms and headed for the stairs.

RUN OF BAD LUCK

Karen Kelley

One

"Damn, I could've been in a nice air-conditioned room surrounded by naked men this morning. What the hell am I doing here?" Nina Harris grumbled.

Her front tire hit a pothole, throwing her off balance. She righted herself, glaring at the dusty dirt road stretching in front of her.

"I am so not enthused with Texas." And apparently she was losing her mind since she was talking to herself. "Not good," she mumbled.

She slowed as she came to a cattle guard with a half-moon wooden sign hanging over it. *Maddock's Dream,* she read.

"Ah, there is a light at the end of the tunnel."

This was it. Her grandfather's spread. Probably more like a nightmare, but it was her nightmare now. He'd deeded her the place right before he'd died.

She'd never even met the man.

The little red convertible she'd rented bounced over the metal bars of the cattle guard, almost jarring her teeth loose. Up the road and around a bend, a sprawling two-story house came into view. A cluster of outbuildings, a couple of pens, and a large brown barn dotted the landscape of the Texas hill country.

No, not a nightmare. From what she could see, damn nice. One thought kept running around inside her head: Why had he deeded the place to her?

A group of men lining one side of a wooden fence caught her attention. She supposed they were cowboys by the way they were dressed: cowboy hats, chaps, boots.

Her interest peaked. Real cowboys . . . hmm . . . The magazine she freelanced for needed a centerfold. Maybe some of these bronco riders still had all their teeth. Her gaze swept over them again.

A bowlegged cowboy glanced her way, then returned his attention to the pen. Too old and obviously bent out of shape. Another cowboy spit a stream of brown juice on the ground.

She gagged, forcing herself to swallow past her nausea. She wasn't *even* going there. Okay, the third one down the line had a nice butt. Maybe him?

She parked near the pen to see what they found so interesting on the other side of the fence and grabbed her camera off the seat as she climbed out of the car. She rarely went anywhere without it.

The lawyer hadn't mentioned any of this, she thought, as she looked around. She'd only scanned the papers before signing them. It was a deed. Nothing that would get her into trouble. Besides the fact she was damn tired after her flight from California.

The men cheered, drawing her attention back to the pen. What were they having? A rodeo?

She smoothed her hands down her beige slacks and wandered over, found an open spot between two of the older men . . . and stared.

Ah, man, why hadn't she come to Texas a long time ago?

Her whole body tingled with awareness, heat spreading down her limbs. This was so not what she had been expecting.

The cowboy sat atop a bucking horse, one hand gripping a rope while the other hand was high in the air. His body jerked and twisted, moving with the animal.

This guy couldn't be real. He oozed raw energy and a lethal dose of sex appeal, and, oh baby, he could park his boots by her bed any day. Her gaze moved over him.

This was good. Really good.

Excitement flittered down her spine. She jerked the lens cap off her camera and leaned between two boards, zeroing in on his face: the sweat beading his tanned skin, the unadulterated excitement, his rugged good looks.

A hot flush washed over her skin, leaving goose bumps in its wake as an ache began to build inside her. Taking pictures had never felt this damn good. She'd been photographing naked male hunks for a few years now, and she had to admit that it had been pretty exciting at first, but after a while it became routine.

This was different. He had all his clothes on and still looked better than any of the men she'd ever photographed. She didn't think she'd ever get jaded capturing this much intense emotion.

No, this was the real thing.

She snapped pictures as the cowboy's muscles strained, the horse dancing and bucking beneath him. The horse grunted, attempting to unseat the man. It was electrifying and damn sexy from where she stood because the cowboy didn't look like he was ever going to give up.

She snapped a dozen or more pictures, then paused for a moment, mesmerized. The cowboy moved with a smoothness that told Nina this wasn't the first lady he'd ridden, wasn't the first lady he'd broken to his will.

He clinched his thighs on the horse's sides, refusing to be thrown off. He rode her hard and fast, moving with her gyrating twists and turns.

Nina drew in a deep, ragged breath. Moisture broke out on her upper lip. Her breasts strained against her shirt, her nipples sensitive and throbbing with the need to feel his mouth covering one, then the other.

The camera whirred as she snapped off more pictures, capturing the man as he tamed the wild horse. The hunger inside her built. She lost count of the number of pictures she took. It could've been ten or one hundred and ten.

The horse's sides heaved when she finally stopped bucking, coming to a jarring standstill, giving in to the inevitable.

Exhausted from the sheer energy it took to watch him break the horse, she lowered the camera, her arms limp at her sides.

The cowboy nudged the horse's flanks, walking her around the pen, letting her settle down completely as he soothed her with soft words, then jumped off to the cheers of the men. Two of them hurried to the center of the pen and took the horse's reins.

He laughed at something one of them said, his smile wide and unrestrained. Nina was transfixed, unable to look away for even a moment.

The small group of men dispersed, apparently going back to their other duties, as the cowboy unbuttoned his sweat-drenched shirt and tossed it across the top rail. She was on the opposite side of the pen, but she had better than twenty-twenty vision and she didn't miss a detail of each sinewy muscle. She was really glad he hadn't noticed her yet or she might not have gotten this delectable display of flesh.

She brought the camera back up.

Her mouth went dry as she moved in for another close-up, watching the way his muscles flexed and relaxed, then flexed again. She snapped off more pictures, practically drooling over broad shoulders, bulging pecs, fantastic biceps, and a six-pack that made her long for a tall cool drink. And as if that weren't enough, his low-riding, faded jeans and worn chaps jealously hugged his lower half.

Her gaze slowly moved back up his torso. She could almost imagine running her tongue over his skin, flicking across his nipples before raising her mouth to accept his kisses. She gripped the camera and drew in a deep breath.

Could her fantasies get any better than this?

He scooped a hatful of water from the metal trough and dumped it over his head, and as the water splashed over him, he slung it away with a jerk of his head.

Oh, yeah, things could get a whole lot better. Lord, she was practically having an orgasm just standing there. She didn't even want to imagine what it would be like making love with him. But, then again, maybe she did.

She took more pictures. Water dripped from his sandy-blond hair onto his chest, over his stomach, sliding inside his jeans. What she wouldn't give right now to be those droplets of water.

When she realized she just stood there, holding her camera in front of her face but not doing a damn thing, she quickly snapped off more pictures, then lowered it once again.

He looked up, seeing her for the first time. Their eyes met and held. His gaze leisurely moved down her body, slowly sliding over every inch of her, caressing her neck with a light touch before slipping down to her breasts, grazing her nipples. He touched her waist, her stomach, a feather-light burning touch between her legs.

His gaze returned to her face, a slow grin lifting the corners of his mouth. He'd seduced her with his look.

And he'd done it very well.

The cowboy reached for his shirt on the fence rail and,

with an easy stride, sauntered toward her, bare chested. God, she couldn't even swallow. He stopped a few feet away, the fence still between them, but it was all she could do to breathe. He nodded toward the camera.

"Tourist?" he drawled, his voice caressing her, touching her in places that turned her body heat up more than a notch.

"Freelance." At least she sounded a hell of a lot calmer than she felt.

He nodded. "Lance Colby. I'm the foreman."

"Nina Harris." Her gaze moved over that very sexy body again. "I'd love for you to take off your clothes."

His eyebrows rose. "Ma'am?"

She jiggled the camera in front of her. "Like I said, I'm a freelance photographer."

"Of what?" He planted a booted foot on the bottom rail and levered himself over the fence, landing on the other side with a thud as his feet hit the packed earth. He stood right in front of her—every delicious inch of his upper body displayed for her viewing pleasure—still not bothering to put his shirt back on.

Breathe!

Okay, this was too much cowboy, a little too much testosterone in her face. She wanted to fan herself but that might just be a little too obvious.

She'd never been this close to a real cowboy. Sexy men, yes, but they were like plastic Ken dolls. She could have as much fun with a vibrator. Not that a vibrator couldn't be fun.

No, this was the real thing. Damn, she'd love to oil his skin, making it slick and shiny, and . . . and take his picture. Yeah, right after they made wild, passionate love. Oh, hell, a little down-and-dirty sex would be perfectly fine with her. Would he mind if she just ran her hands over his arms? She bit her bottom lip, quelling the urge to touch.

"Photographer of what?" he repeated, drawing her out of her tantalizing daydream.

She took a deep breath, cleared the erotic scenes from her mind, and raised her eyes to meet his. "*Bodacious Bodies* . . . the magazine for women. Have you seen it?"

He leaned against the fence and smiled. "Can't say I have." His words held a trace of laughter. "I don't have much time for reading."

She wondered what he did have time for. Wrestling bulls? His biceps were large enough that he could easily throw her over his shoulder and carry her inside the barn, rip her dress off . . . *Yeah. Don't even go there, Nina.*

His laughing blue eyes met hers, making her wonder if he could read minds. Or was he making fun of her job?

She squared her shoulders. "I photograph men with exceptional bodies." She didn't give a damn how clipped her words sounded. She'd been razzed enough because of what she did for a living. She wasn't about to take it from this . . . this cowboy.

"A nudie magazine—but for girls." His grin widened. "Y'all have your rights as well as men, but then I've never much cared for looking at pictures of naked women when I could have the real thing snuggled up next to me."

She chose to ignore the hot flush of desire that swept over her. "It pays good money." She named a ballpark figure and watched his eyes widen.

"That much?"

There, that would make him stop and think. She couldn't help adding another dig and leaned in closer. "If you have the body, that is. Do you want an audition?" She kept her words low and husky.

He laughed. A deep rumbling sound that made her thighs quiver. "Yeah, right, and be laughed out of Silver Gulch." He shook his head. "Real cowboys don't pose naked for magazines."

She raised an eyebrow. "You mean you don't want to fulfill women's fantasies?"

"Who's to say I don't already fulfill them, darlin'?"

Her pulse quickened. She had no doubt he was telling the truth. "Maybe I can help you change your mind about dropping your pants for me." His eyes flared with a sudden spark of desire. "So I can take your picture, that is," she added.

"Will you be around that long?"

"Yeah, I'm the new owner." Her gaze raked over him. "I guess that makes me your boss."

He chuckled. "I still won't drop my pants—for a picture, that is."

He made it sound like he would under other circumstances, though. The ache grew stronger inside her. She might have to see about that later on. Who knows, he might not be cameraworthy after all.

She abruptly turned toward her car, calling over her shoulder, "Come up to the house around six. You can tell me about the ranch."

"You going to feed me, Mizz Nina Harris?"

"I don't cook for any man, but I might be persuaded to throw a sandwich together—if you play your cards right." She opened the car door and climbed in.

"You are so playing with fire, girl," she muttered to herself, but it had been such a long time since she felt a desire to step closer to the flame. How the hell was she going to resist Lance? Did she even want to? No, she didn't think so.

She started the car and drove toward the house. *Do not look in the rearview mirror. Do not look . . .*

Her gaze strayed to the mirror. When he saluted her, she almost ran over one of the hedges that lined the drive. Egotistical ass . . . but, damn, he was gorgeous. Lance would make the perfect centerfold. And she wanted him—to pose, that is—and Nina always got her man.

Her mouth went dry just thinking of him sprawled on his back wearing only a hat and a pair of boots. Oh, yeah, that's what she was talking about. Maybe she could even get him bare-assed naked on a bucking bronco.

Ouch.

No, that wouldn't work. She'd hate like hell if he injured anything on that magnificent body.

She stopped in front of the house, then grabbed her suitcase out of the back. Six wooden steps led to the front porch, where four rockers sat. It looked comfortable. She opened the screen door and went inside. The quietness enveloped her like a tomb.

Then she heard thumping coming from upstairs.

A cold chill washed over her. "Hello?" What if the house was haunted? Her grandfather couldn't be resting too well, knowing that his son had impregnated three women, then left each one to raise her child on her own.

There it was again, coming from upstairs: thump, thump.

Worse, what if there were rats. A shiver of revulsion ran down her spine. She'd rather have ghosts than rats any day.

A door opened.

Rats didn't open doors. She didn't think ghosts did, either, but if she heard chains rattling, she was out of there.

She breathed a sigh of relief when a middle-aged woman came to the top of the stairs and glanced down. The woman jumped, slapping a hand to her chest.

"Lord a mercy, child. You scared the hell out of me." She took a deep breath. "I bet you're Nina Harris. Your grandpa's lawyer called a bit ago and told me you were headed this way. I was just tidying up a room for you." She started tromping down the stairs.

If there were any ghosts, the woman would've scared them off. Rats, too.

For someone who couldn't be more than five feet, two inches and didn't weigh more than a hundred pounds, she walked as loudly as a marching band. She got to the bottom of the stairs and stuck out her hand.

"I'm Maxine: housekeeper, cook, and chief bottle washer."

Yeah, and Nina wondered just how many bottles she'd emptied today so she could wash them. Although she didn't smell any alcohol on her breath.

"I don't stay nights and I'm off every Sunday and Monday. Not that I go to church or nothin', but even so, I believe in God and everything. Sunday just seemed a good day as any to take off since Pete usually had that bunch of saddle tramps over to the house for poker on Sundays. I told him he was goin' to hell . . ." Her face turned a rosy hue. "Meant no disrespect. I'm sure Pete went straight to heaven." She looked down at her feet, then quickly added, "God rest his soul."

How could a woman so tiny hold that much air in her lungs? She hadn't taken one good breath while she was talking. Amazing.

"I'm Nina . . . Nina Harris," she confirmed, then shook the woman's callused hand. "Thanks for getting a room ready."

"That's what I'm here for." She looked pointedly at the suitcase. "Can I take that upstairs for you?"

Nina shook her head. "No, I can manage."

She nodded. "Top of the stairs, second door on the right. I didn't think you'd want to stay in your grandpa's room. His was the first on the right. When you get settled in, come on down and I'll have you a glass of iced tea fixed."

"Thanks," Nina said, as she started up the stairs.

She carried her stuff upstairs, pausing at the first door. Without reasoning why, she set her things down and opened the door. Her gaze slowly swept the room. She took a deep, shuddering breath before stepping inside.

There was nothing really special about it. A typical man's room: heavy ornate bed, two equally heavy nightstands on either side. On a dresser was a jar full of peppermints. Apparently, her grandfather had had a sweet tooth.

She couldn't stop her smile from forming. Maybe they'd had something in common after all. She loved sweets.

"We could've shared our life," she said, sadness etching her words. Just as quickly, she brushed away the silly sentimentality. It had been his choice, not hers.

She stepped from the room, closing the door harder than necessary, and went to the room next door.

Her room was nice. A canopy bed with an old-fashioned quilt for a spread. She dumped her bag on the floor, placed her camera on a red velvet upholstered chair, and looked around. Warm, cozy—it would do for the length of time she planned on staying.

She strolled to the window and glanced toward the barn. Lance had pulled on a clean shirt. Nice. She couldn't force her gaze away. But then, who the hell would know she was staring? She leaned against the window frame and looked her fill.

This was too good an opportunity to let slide. Reaching inside her purse, she brought out her cell phone and speed-dialed her editor and friend, Mica, who answered on the second ring.

"Mica, you're not going to believe this. They have real cowboys here."

"Well, yeah, you're in Texas." She laughed. "What did you expect?"

"Certainly not this." She watched as Lance bent and picked up a bale of hay. His biceps bulged as he gripped the wire and busted the bale. He bent again. Damn, he had a fine-looking butt. Just right for a man. She flexed her fingers.

"Any of them cameraworthy?"

"Oh, yes."

"But can you get one of them to pose naked? Cowboys

have some sort of code of honor. I've yet to have any of my photographers talk one into stripping for the camera."

"I bet I can have him posing before the week is up."

"You're on. I'll give you a bonus if you can get the shot."

"And if I lose?"

"Honey, I doubt you will. You never have in the past. But if you do, you can buy me dinner at the fanciest restaurant in San Diego."

"You're on." She'd always loved a challenge.

They said good-bye and Nina dropped the phone back in her purse. Lance disappeared inside the barn and her breathing returned to normal. Except her throat suddenly felt very parched. She whirled from the window and hurried out of the room. Iced tea sounded really nice right now.

Two

Lance felt stupid knocking on the screen door. Maybe he should've mentioned that a couple of years ago Pete had him move into the main house. Said he didn't like waiting for Lance to get up there when he needed to talk to him about something. Lance just thought the old man was lonely, but he didn't mind. Pete had been like a father to him.

Damn, he missed him.

"Right on time." Nina walked toward him.

Not exactly walked. More like glided. Her hips swaying gently from side to side. His gaze raised to her face and the wisps of dark brown hair that curled around it.

Her sultry brown eyes twinkled with merriment as she opened the door. "Are you coming in or do I make you nervous?"

Kind of mouthy, though.

"I don't know. You got anything to eat? I'm starved." His glance raked over her. It wasn't actually food that he was hungry for right at that moment.

She'd changed into a pair of red slacks and a bright yellow top with little-bitty straps. The material hugged every delicious curve, and if that wasn't enough, her perfume drifted over him, wrapping him in a blend of spices and exotic flowers. Maybe he'd been around sweaty horses and working men too much, but, man, she smelled sweet.

"Maxine was nice enough to fix a casserole."

He cleared his thoughts and met her smile. "She's a damn good cook." He stepped into the house, taking off his hat, and followed her to the kitchen. Yeah, he liked the way she moved. She had the perfect ass, nicely rounded, not too big, not too small.

He still couldn't fathom her taking pictures of naked men, though. It beat the hell out of him why a man would even pose naked. You couldn't pay him enough to strip down to bare skin and have his picture taken for some magazine. Nope, it wouldn't happen in his lifetime.

Making love with her, now that was a whole different story. He'd shed his clothes in a heartbeat for one night wrapped in her arms. She had that look about her. The one that said she liked sex. The hot sweaty kind.

He wondered if she knew they were going to make love. Because they were. He wasn't sure when, but they would. Gut instinct. His was never wrong.

Something occurred to him. Because she photographed all those naked men, she would probably make a lot of comparisons. Not that he thought he was lacking in that department, but he supposed it could make some men uncomfortable.

She opened the oven door and bent in front of the stove as she checked on the casserole. Man, did she ever have a sweet ass. When he realized he was crushing his best Stetson, he smoothed his hand across the creases and set it on a stool.

It was getting really hot in the kitchen.

He went to the refrigerator and grabbed a beer, then remembered where he was. "Do you mind?" Actually, he'd bought the six-pack, so technically he was asking for his own damn beer. That irked the hell out of him.

She glanced at him before straightening and his moment of aggravation subsided. How could he be angry with someone who looked as sexy as she did?

"Only if you'll hand me one," she said.

He reached for another beer, twisting the top off before handing it to her. At the rate he was going, he should pour it down the front of his jeans. Yeah, right, like that would cool him off.

"So, tell me about the ranch," she said, taking a drink before setting her bottle on the table.

He liked the sound of her voice. It had a musical quality to it. Like water splashing over rocks in the Wrangler River on a crisp spring day.

Damn, where the hell were his thoughts headed? The next thing he knew he'd be writing poetry or some other nonsense. He mentally cleared his mind and returned to the subject at hand, and not how Nina sounded. He was acting like a lovesick fool who'd never been off the farm.

Actually, he hadn't been to San Antonio in a while, and Silver Gulch didn't really count since he knew all the women there. Except maybe the new gal, Juliet. She was a looker all right, but Rod had already roped her for his own.

"The ranch?" she prodded.

He cleared his mind. "We do our own breeding."

Her eyes widened and a slight smile curved her lips. "That sounds like fun."

Heat rose up his face. Damn mouthy. He cleared his throat.

She was playing him. He thought of a smart-assed rebuttal but snapped his mouth shut. Hell, the worst possible mistake he could make would be fooling around with his new boss.

Something sour rose inside him. He had a hard time digesting the thought of her running the ranch. The only thing that kept him from walking out was reminding himself it wasn't her fault.

"It's a moderate-sized spread," he began, trying for a serious tone.

It wasn't easy. He sauntered to the table and set his beer down so he wouldn't have to look at the way her eyes danced with merriment.

"Pete ran cattle and horses. It's self-sufficient. We plant our own coastal grass, cut it in the spring, and bale it for winter." He shrugged before picking his beer back up and taking a long, much-needed pull.

"And you're the foreman." She grabbed two potholders and removed the casserole from the oven, placing the dish on a hot pad in the middle of the table.

"I'll take you around tomorrow if you'd like to see some of the land. You could take pictures." It was the least he could do and, he had to admit, he was damn proud of Pete's spread. No, not Pete's anymore. He took a deep breath. It was Nina's ranch.

"I'd like that."

They each took a seat. For a moment an uncomfortable silence hung between them. Hell, he knew what was bothering him. Still, he hesitated, then just said what was on his mind. "Some of the men are worried about their jobs. They'd like to know what your plans are."

"I'll probably sell the place. I don't need a ranch in my life."

It felt as if a knife ripped through him. "I thought as much." He wasn't even close to having enough money to buy the property. When the hell had things gotten so complicated? This wasn't the way it was supposed to be.

"They had to know my . . . my grandfather wouldn't be around forever," she said, interrupting his thoughts.

"They did, but they just thought I would take over after he passed on."

Her forehead bunched. "Why would they think that?"

He set his beer back on the table and met her gaze straight on. Hell, she'd find out sooner or later.

"Because I was first in line to inherit the ranch, that is, until he changed his mind and deeded it to you."

Three

Nina opened her mouth then snapped it shut. Lance would've inherited the ranch if not for her? Lord, he must have wanted to kill her grandfather when he'd deeded the place to her.

Since she'd first laid eyes on Lance, she'd been thinking about jumping his bones. Had he been thinking about burying hers?

She drew in a deep breath.

What if Lance had known her grandfather had changed his mind about leaving him the place? Then killed him, not knowing her grandfather had already signed the ranch over?

She realized the direction of her thoughts and mentally shook her head. Who did she think she was? Nancy Drew?

No, she wouldn't even go there. It was stupid. But she couldn't stop suspicious thoughts from racing across her mind.

"Exactly—" Her voice cracked. She reached for her beer, tilted the bottle and swallowed the last drink, then tried again. "Exactly how did my grandfather die? I mean, the lawyer didn't say. I assumed it was from old age." She flattened out her napkin, ironing across it with the palm of her hand.

He leaned back in his chair. "No one knows exactly. You see, they never found his body. Just an empty boat floating upside down in the water. The Wrangler River swells pretty bad in the springtime from runoff waters." He looked down at his hands. "Everyone just figured he'd drowned."

"But wouldn't they find a body?"

"Not if something"—he shifted in his seat—"we have wild animals in the hills . . . and . . ."

"Ah, I see," she interrupted, not wanting any gory details. She understood perfectly what he was trying to tell her and she didn't want to hear more.

How convenient they couldn't do an autopsy.

What the hell was she thinking? That Lance had actually murdered her grandfather? Damn, she could feel the heat going up her face. She looked at Lance, then quickly averted her gaze.

"I didn't kill him if that's what you're wondering."

"Of course I didn't think that—pfft." But when Nina looked at his face, she saw his doubt. Okay, so maybe she was thinking he might have hurried the old man along. Why wouldn't she? Lance might be downright sexy, but she didn't know the guy.

"I wouldn't blame you for thinking like that. We don't know each other." He stood, taking his plate and glass to the dishwasher. "I liked Pete. He was a good man."

"It doesn't make any difference what I'm thinking. You and my grandfather could've been like father and son, for all I know. It doesn't matter." She cleared her throat. "But I do have to wonder why you aren't really pissed at me because the ranch won't be yours."

He hesitated before speaking. "I was, but I've had time to adjust. When Juliet came to town and claimed your grandfather's bar, I figured the ranch would go to you or the other sister. The fact of the matter is, it was Pete's ranch to do with as he saw fit."

"It was still rotten of him. After I sell the ranch, I can't guarantee what the new owner will do. I'm sorry."

He shrugged. "Who knows, this place might grow on you. You might even decide to stay."

"I'm not the country-girl type." But this proved to her that the Maddock side of her family were real jerks. How could her grandfather promise the ranch to Lance, then give it to her?

"Hey, don't worry about it."

The warmth of Lance's smile made Nina feel a little more at ease around him. Lord, she'd been in the city way too long if she was seeing a killer around every corner. It wasn't inconceivable that her grandfather had fallen into the swollen river and drowned. He must've been nearly eighty.

She placed her dishes inside the dishwasher and closed the door, then leaned against the cabinet. "What time are we leaving on your guided tour tomorrow?"

"We'd better head out before it gets too warm. Around eight?"

An uneasy silence followed his words. It was time to end their evening before she did something crazy—like lean forward, press her lips against his. A shame they couldn't have met under different circumstances. Like her photographing him naked.

A damn shame.

"Eight is fine," she told him. "I'll walk you to the door."

"Actually, I live here."

"I'm sorry?" Surely she'd misunderstood.

"My room is just down the hall." He motioned toward it. "Unless you'd like me to move into the bunkhouse. I'd hate to think you were"—his gaze slowly roamed over her, then touched back on her face—"nervous about having me in the same house."

It took a second or two for his words to sink into her brain. First, she had to get past the stirrings he'd created when his gaze had slid down her body. When his words got past her muddled brain, she frowned. What exactly did he mean by that? Her, nervous of him? "I've lived in California most of my life. Believe me, you don't make me nervous."

"I don't?"

He stepped nearer, his hand going to the back of her neck and pulling her closer. *Resist!* He was about to kiss her only to prove a point.

But the heat of his mouth was so damn consuming. She didn't want to resist, and when his lips touched hers, she automatically opened her mouth. Little earthquakes erupted inside her body as he teased with his tongue. She pressed closer to the heat, wanting more . . . needing more.

All too soon, he pulled away. For a moment she thought she saw surprise on his face, but he quickly masked his expression with a cocky grin, and she was left wondering what exactly she'd seen.

"I don't make you nervous?" he asked again.

She tilted her chin. "Not at all."

His expression said he thought she was lying. "Good night, California girl." He sauntered out of the kitchen and down the hall.

She should say something. After all, he'd kissed her. She usually had a smart-ass remark for everything. A few minutes later, she heard the sound of a door closing and it was too late. Not that anything had come to mind except how the warmth of his kiss had left his brand on her.

She realized she was gripping the counter for support. Not make her nervous? *Yeah, right, let go and see if your legs will hold you up.* She waited another minute before she turned loose.

Damn, he kissed good. No, he was a fantastic kisser. Her body felt like mush. Very hot mush. It was a good thing his room was downstairs and hers upstairs or she might be tempted to jump his bones.

This was just great. She had the hots for the man who'd stood to inherit the ranch if not for her. A cold flush washed over her like a blast from a freezer.

Who might still inherit it if something bad happened to her.

And she was going sightseeing with him tomorrow? All that California smog had fried her brain cells.

She left the kitchen and started up the stairs to her room.

But what if Lance *had* done something to her grandfather?

She gripped the stair rail, stopping halfway up. There'd been genuine sorrow on his face when he'd mentioned her grandfather. Sadness, or was he a good actor?

Another chill ran down her spine. No, she wouldn't even go there. She was not here to solve a murder mystery, just to sell a ranch.

It was odd, though, that no body had been recovered.

Sleep. She needed at least eight hours of peaceful slumber so she could think more clearly.

But when she came to her grandfather's door, she paused. There were so many unanswered questions. Like the fact that she knew nothing about her grandfather.

What had he been like? Why would he leave her the ranch when he hadn't cared enough to want to see her in all these years? Sure, they were blood, but apparently that hadn't mattered when she was growing up. He hadn't even attempted to contact her. So why the turnaround?

Without thinking twice, Nina opened the door and stepped inside his room. Her gaze scanned from one side to the other, looking for some clue that would tell her more about him. Unless she started digging through the night-stands and dresser she was afraid she wouldn't discover . . .

Her gaze swung to the dresser, then the nightstand. Hadn't

the jar of peppermints been on the dresser when she'd peeked in earlier? She stepped farther into the room, taking a deep breath as she did.

The smell of peppermints was strong. Almost as if . . .

She chuckled at her fanciful thoughts, but it sounded a little forced to her ears. She must be more tired than she'd thought.

Or maybe someone wanted to scare her away.

She turned around and walked out of the room. She couldn't stop herself from looking down the staircase.

Someone who might want to get rid of her?

Yep, she was losing it all right. What the hell did she think she was doing? Living a Gothic romance? She was positive Lance was not a murderer. Call it gut instinct or whatever, but she was pretty damn good at judging people. Lance was not a killer.

Shaking her head, she went to her room, but as soon as she closed the door, she turned the lock. One thing living in the city had taught her: better safe than sorry.

The next morning, Nina was in the kitchen by seven. She was accustomed to rising early for shoots, so eight actually seemed a little late. Maxine was already in the kitchen and had a pot of fresh coffee ready. She could learn to love this woman.

She looked around as she poured a cup but didn't see Lance. Before she could ask Maxine where he was, the back door opened and Lance came into the kitchen.

It wasn't fair that a man could look this downright sexy so early in the morning. It wasn't good for her equilibrium.

He looked ruggedly handsome in jeans and a western shirt. His hat sat low on his forehead until he pulled it off and ran a hand through his sandy-blond hair. Even that motion put fire into her blood.

"Good, you're up," he drawled, his gaze sliding over her

before returning to rest on her face. His eyes twinkled, as if he knew a joke that she didn't.

She took her coffee to the table. "Did you expect me to still be in bed? You forget I'm a working woman."

"Photographing naked men, right?"

"Taking pictures of men in the buff?" Maxine turned from the stove, her jaw dropping all the way to her chest.

Nina bristled, casting a glare in Lance's direction. "Do you have a problem with my job?" she asked Maxine.

"Oh, hell no, child. I just didn't know there were jobs like that out there, and I was wonderin' what the hell I'm doing fryin' bacon and cookin' eggs when I could be doing somethin' fun." She shook her head as she turned back to the stove.

Nina smiled, liking Maxine more by the minute.

They ate a quick breakfast, then left the house. Nina walked toward the pickup parked at the side, camera strap looped over one shoulder. The air was crisp and clean with a freshness you didn't normally find in the city. The ranch would be a great place to get back to nature. She knew exactly who she'd want to play Adam to her Eve, too.

"It'll be easier if we take the horses," Lance said, breaking into her Zenful thoughts.

"Easier for whom?" She turned and looked at him, one eyebrow raised. She'd never ridden a horse, had never planned on riding one, and wasn't exactly thrilled about the prospect of climbing onto one right now, either.

He grinned. That slow lifting of the sides of his mouth. The kind of smile that reached out and caressed her, leaving no spot untouched. She drew in a deep, shuddering breath.

"You don't want to bounce around in a pickup all day, do you? Unless you're scared of climbing on."

His words carried a whole different connotation and she had a feeling he'd meant for her to read more into them.

She swung around to where two horses were saddled and bridled, their reins looped loosely over a wooden railing.

"Being on top of anything has never bothered me," she threw over her shoulder as she headed for the horses with more bravado than she felt. It didn't help when he chuckled.

When she got to one of the horses, she had more than a few doubts running around in her head. It looked really high. Besides the fact that she didn't know how to go about getting up there.

"Here, let me help."

Before she could protest, he slipped her camera off her shoulder, his knuckles grazing her arm in the process. His hands were warm through the thin material of her shirt. If the mere touch of his hands on her shoulder could send tingles down her arms what would making love be like?

He set her camera on the porch, then came back. "Turn around," he told her.

"I still don't see why we couldn't take your pickup," she grumbled but faced the horse.

"First, you want to put your foot in the stirrup." He slid his hand down her thigh.

She bit her lip as heat spread through her. Before she could have a fantasy moment, he'd placed her foot in the stirrup.

"Grab the horn," he said close to her ear. So close that the warmth of his breath tickled her ear, sending little tremors over her body.

She didn't have time to protest that she wasn't ready when he placed his hands on her hips and lifted. As she went in the air, his hands slid to her bottom and he boosted her up and onto the saddle. She clutched the horn with both hands at the same time as she swung her leg over the saddle.

And there she was on top of the horse before she even had time to think about being there.

Well, that sucked. She could've explored all kinds of possibilities when he was standing close and even more when he'd cupped her butt, but they'd fizzled away into a puddle of "I don't like heights"!

Oh, crap. *Are we having fun yet?* she thought, with more than a little sarcasm. Being on top of the horse was a whole different ball game from being on the ground looking at it.

"Ready?" he said after he handed her the reins and looped her camera over the saddle horn.

"No."

He smiled. "It won't be so bad once you get used to it. You might even discover you enjoy riding."

"I doubt it," she said, between gritted teeth.

But after an hour in the saddle, she had to admit that he'd been right. Riding wasn't so hard and the horse had a nice easy gait. She'd even managed to take a couple of shots with her camera.

Lance was great about pointing out different things. Like the wildflowers that dotted the landscape with glorious color. The feathery pink basket flower; the bright yellow black-eyed Susan, with its chocolaty center. She'd even captured a jackrabbit when it had poked its head up from behind a splash of red petals. Its ears were almost as long as her arm from elbow to wrist.

Lance kept pointing out different areas of interest until she was dizzy from absorbing so much.

"It's beautiful," she whispered without realizing she'd spoken aloud until Lance agreed.

"Pete loved the land."

"And my father, did he love it as well?" She didn't look at him.

"I only met Drew twice."

She shifted in her saddle. "Twice? But I thought . . ."

"Drew was raised by his mother. She divorced Pete when Drew was young and they moved back to Connecticut.

From the bits and pieces I've heard, she was pretty much the socialite. He came here a couple of times when he was older."

It didn't look like he was going to embellish so she prodded. "And . . ."

He tilted his hat back a little on his forehead. "We didn't get along."

"In other words, you didn't like him."

"You could say that."

"I did say that," she said, with more than a touch of sarcasm. "I never met him," she admitted. "He had a short affair with my mother, promised her the world and all his love. Then when she discovered she was pregnant with me, he took off and she never heard from him again except a couple of times by phone. Drew told Mom that Grandpa wanted nothing to do with me."

Why was she telling him all this? Maybe because she felt like clearing the air a little. Her grandfather might have been a friend to Lance, but he hadn't bothered to get in touch with her or, as far as she knew, her sisters. Which made all this even more puzzling.

"Why did he leave me the ranch, Juliet the bar, and Lillie the hotel? If he didn't care to see us when he was alive, then why would he leave us his property after he died?"

"Guilty conscience, maybe?"

"I'd rather have had him." As if she'd said too much, Nina turned away.

That's when she saw the deer.

"Look," she whispered, raising her camera and clicking pictures. She snapped off about ten before the deer raised her head, apparently caught their scent, and gracefully leapt away.

"Do you look this enraptured when you take pictures of naked men?"

She raised an eyebrow and glanced in his direction.

"Only if the subject warrants being enraptured over. Are you vying for that audition?"

"I'm hungry," he said, conveniently changing the subject. "Maxine packed us a light snack. I've been smelling peanut butter cookies for the last hour."

He nudged his horse nearer to a grouping of trees and climbed down. She had no choice but to follow since her horse had a mind of its own and seemed to follow Lance's horse without question.

When he raised his hands, she waved him away. "I'm perfectly capable of getting down on my own." But when her feet hit the ground, her legs wouldn't hold her. Lance was right there to catch her.

"You could've warned me that I'd be wobbly."

"Your legs will be wobbly," he said.

"Smart-ass."

She turned. Another mistake on her part. Now she was facing him, and for a woman who enjoyed photographing naked men, Lance was just a little too tempting, even with his clothes on. She moved away, hoping she wouldn't make a fool out of herself and fall flat on her butt. Thankfully, there was a large rock nearby. She leaned against it for support . . . and unabashedly stared.

Lance brought the sack out of his saddlebag. "Sure you won't have a cookie?" he offered.

She shook her head. Damn he was sexy. He'd make a great cover model. There was an unpolished look about him. Not every hair was in place and there was a smudge of dirt on his shirtsleeve. She couldn't picture him in a suit and tie. She had a feeling it would stifle him.

Something told her he didn't run with the crowd. He was more of a leader. She wondered if she could capture that edge on film. "Take off your shirt," she said, without thinking.

His eyes twinkled, but behind the humor was a flare of heat. "You just want to have your way with me."

She did, but she wasn't about to admit it. "Surely you're not embarrassed. I mean, you had it off yesterday. It didn't seem to bother you then."

"I will if you will," he countered.

Nina inwardly grinned. She'd never been ashamed of her body. She frequented nude beaches all the time, preferring the freedom of going naked rather than wearing clothes.

She set her camera on the rock and slowly unbuttoned her shirt. "Deal," she said, slipping her shirt off and laying it on the rock. "Your turn," she said as she picked up her camera.

One question ran around in her head: would he or wouldn't he?

Oh, you are so playing with fire, Nina.

Four

Lance choked when she faced him again. Literally.

Yep, Nina knew she was being bad. The fires of hell were licking at her feet, she was so bad.

But it felt oh so good to be so bad.

He tilted the thermos against his lips and guzzled. When he lowered it, he took a deep breath. "Do you always strip at the drop of a hat?" he croaked.

"Only when I'm challenged." She grinned. "Besides, I've never been ashamed of my body."

"Who said I was ashamed of mine?" He frowned before setting everything down. After unbuttoning his shirt, he took it off. "Fine. No problem whatsoever." He tossed it over the nearest tree branch.

She wiggled the camera. "Do you mind?" The need to take his picture was almost more than she could stand. She was like a drug addict who needed her next fix.

"I think you're playing me." His forehead bunched. "Don't expect me to drop my pants."

One of the reasons *Bodacious Bodies* had hired her was her ability to get a man to drop his pants. Lance would be no different. It just might take a little longer to talk him into stripping for the camera, but she had all the time in the world.

"Raise your arm and hold on to the branch above your head," she told him.

He did, looking quite nonchalant as he continued to eat his cookie. How could a man look so blasted sexy eating a friggin' cookie? When he licked the crumbs off his lips she thought she would die. She wanted to be the one to lick them off.

But it wasn't just him eating a cookie. No, it was his muscles shimmering in the shadow and light of the branches and leaves above him, caressing his magnificent body. Hard, tanned muscles tapering down to a slim waist. Nice, real nice.

She couldn't stop her smile when he took another drink and came away with a white mustache.

Got milk?

Slowly, he raised the back of his hand and wiped away the milk mustache, but his eyes never left her face. Eyes that said, "Come get me." They were such a deep intense blue that she forgot for just a moment how much she wanted to capture him on film.

And her legs began to tremble.

He tossed the thermos on the ground and raised his other arm. Oh, Lord, she was growing hotter by the second and not because the temperature was rising. More like her body heat going up a few degrees.

She swallowed past the lump in her throat. "Unbutton the top two buttons of your pants," she told him.

He raised an eyebrow.

"Do I make you nervous?" she asked, regaining just a little bit of control.

"You first," he countered, with a smug gleam in his eyes.

But she'd already known he would throw the challenge back at her and she was ready. She set the camera down and undid the top two buttons of her jeans. Her pants rode low on her hips. She knew part of her scarlet thong showed. Tit for tat. She could live with it—could he?

"Your turn," she told him, wondering if he'd cry uncle. He'd already told her she wouldn't get him to drop his pants. Now they'd both see if he had the . . . ahem . . . balls to go all the way.

He unbuttoned the top two buttons, fanning the sides of his pants out. A thin line of dark hair trailed downward and disappeared. A few more inches and the possibilities of what she could capture on film would be endless.

"Nice," she murmured and snapped off a couple of pictures. She ignored the moisture dotting her upper lip.

"Do you know how damn sexy you look wearing that scrap of lace that barely covers your breasts?" he said, taking her off guard. "Who the hell wears a flaming red bra and panties? If I didn't know better, I'd think you wanted to seduce me rather than take my picture. Is that what you're doing, Nina? Trying to seduce me?" he said, with a slow southern drawl that made her thighs ache to have his fingers caress her, to ease the ache that began higher up.

"I'm just taking your picture, cowboy."

She raised the camera and focused. So maybe he was more than half right. She zoomed in for a close-up of his face. Ohhh, not good. He was giving her that slow, heated look that men had when a woman turned them on. If she were smart, she'd stop this right now.

Why hadn't she paid more attention in school? If she had, she might be a whole lot smarter.

She sighed. What a shame.

"Briefs or boxers?" she asked.

"Thong or bikini?"

"Thong."

"Briefs. I'll show you mine if you'll show me yours."

"But you're not taking my picture," she pointed out. A

tremor of excitement tripped down her spine, curling her toes. *This is a dangerous game you're playing,* she warned herself. Ah, hell, when had she ever played it safe?

She set the camera down and undid the remaining buttons on her jeans. She saw the flare of interest sparkle in his eyes as she wiggled out of her pants and kicked them away.

"You're not a bit shy, are you?"

She shook her head. "Your turn."

He slid his hands down to the last three buttons of his jeans and undid them, but she noticed he took his own sweet time. It didn't matter. In fact, it made her job easier. Raw, sexy maleness oozed from his pores. Maybe because she was standing in front of him practically naked, but she continued to snap her pictures as he undressed. God, these were going to be so damned hot.

Whatever it takes to get the job done, right, Nina? Yeah, like she wasn't enjoying the hell out of this.

"Lean up against the rock," she told him. He surprised her by doing what she asked without a bit of argument. He was so damned beautiful, leaning back wearing only briefs and a cowboy hat.

"This okay?"

She nodded. Oh, it was a lot more than okay. "Now"— she cleared her throat—"take off your hat and run your fingers through your hair."

The sun hit his tanned skin perfectly. It was all she could do to hold the camera as she took shot after shot. The women would drool over him. Lord, she was practically slobbering all over the place herself.

Now, if she could just get his briefs off.

A flush of heat stole over her skin. "Uh . . . want to go for the whole . . . ?" Why the hell was she stuttering? She never stuttered, but then, she'd never taken a shoot this far before. She could usually talk men into stripping with a few heated looks, a few compliments. She cleared her throat. "I mean . . ."

He straightened and ambled toward her. Her throat tightened around her words. She couldn't speak, couldn't say a damn word as he took the camera from her lifeless fingers and set it on the rock.

"Do I want to go all the way with this? Yeah, but it's my turn to call the . . . shots." He rested his hands on her shoulders, then ran a finger under the straps of her bra. "Damn, you're one sexy lady." He pushed the straps off her shoulders.

"I need my camera so I can take pictures." Was that really her voice sounding breathless . . . eager? Probably, since she was both of those things.

His hand slipped around behind her and undid the clasp of her bra. "I want to see all of you."

She watched his face as he removed her bra, saw the way his nostrils flared.

"Damn, you're beautiful." He rubbed her nipples between his thumb and forefinger.

She arched toward him as liquid heat swirled inside her, pooling deep in her belly. He lowered his head, running his tongue across her bottom lip. She opened her mouth, inviting his kiss, but he surprised her by lowering his mouth to her breast and sucking gently on one tight nipple while massaging the other.

Oh, God, this feels so damn good. From the moment she'd laid eyes on him, Nina had fantasized about his touch, what his hands would feel like on her bare flesh.

The restlessness, the unsatisfying relationships in her past were suddenly swept away, the slate cleaned. It was as if everything came down to this one moment. She didn't care that they barely knew each other. There'd been sparks from the moment they'd met. She knew it, and she was almost certain he did.

He scooped her up and set her on the rock. For a moment he only stared at her; then he picked up her camera. She felt a second's apprehension. She'd never been on this side of the lens before, but suddenly she felt like a puppet with no will of her own.

"Lean your head back. Let your hair just brush the rock. Yeah, just like that. Now hold still." He snapped off some pictures. "Your naked breasts really turn me on. The nipples are so damn tight. And the way the sun shines down on them almost makes me jealous."

Her breath caught in her throat as she watched him move around the rock, taking pictures from different angles.

"Yeah, that's the look," he said. "As if you want me to kiss and suck on your nipples. So damn hot that you're almost burning me with that look."

"Then take me," she said.

He shook his head. "Not yet."

He stopped taking pictures for a moment and caressed first one breast, then the other. She moaned and arched toward him, her eyes closing. He brought her hand up so that she cupped her breast, fingernails grazing her nipple.

"Stay right there."

Her eyes were closed, her mouth slightly open. She didn't care that she was in a vulnerable position. That no one had ever photographed her like this. That he'd turned the tables on her and used her camera to seduce her. She didn't care about any of that right now. The only thing going through her mind was the sensations that he'd created inside her. The heat. God, the all-consuming heat.

"Spread your legs some more."

Her eyes flew open. He'd gone too far. She couldn't . . . she . . . no.

"It's just you and me," he said, seducing her with words. Words that she'd used in the past when working with a new model, and damn it, she could feel the barriers around her tumbling down.

He nudged her knees with one hand, opening her legs. The camera whirred. He stopped long enough to tug on the wisp of material, pulling off her thong and tossing it to the side.

"Spread your legs." His voice was raspy, taut with restraint.

Her body smoldered with need. She wanted to feel him buried deep inside her, stroking her, bringing her to climax. But she couldn't open so that he could take her picture. Not like this.

He lowered the camera and stepped closer. "I don't think I've ever met a woman like you," he spoke softly.

Lightly, he ran his fingers up and down the inside of her thighs, coming close to her sex, but not touching. She gasped, raising her hips, wanting and needing more.

"Open for me," he said from what sounded like far away. The thunder of drums inside her head blocked the last of her reservations as his fingers brushed through her curls. She moaned, opening her legs.

"That's it. Just like that."

She heard the whirring of her camera. She didn't care.

"Sweet. So damn sweet," he said.

She bit her bottom lip. "Lance . . . please . . ."

He set her camera carefully on the ground, and through half-closed eyes, she watched him strip out of his briefs.

Oh, yeah, he was most definitely cameraworthy, but right now, she didn't think she could manage to hold a camera long enough to take his picture.

He stepped nearer. "I've never met a woman who was so confident in her own sexuality." He started at the center of her chest and ran his knuckles downward until he came to her mound. With both his hands, he spread her lips.

She gasped, arching toward him.

He didn't disappoint but lowered his mouth. She cried out as spasms of pleasure washed over her. He slid his hands under her, cupping her bottom, bringing her closer to his mouth. He sucked on her sex, running his tongue up and down her clit.

She climaxed against his mouth, crying out. Before the sensations ended he eased her to the ground, using their clothes as a makeshift blanket, and slipped a condom on before entering her.

As soon as she felt him sliding inside her, she clenched her inner muscles, pulling him in just a little deeper, and wrapped her arms around his neck, bringing him into even closer contact, her nipples rubbing against the hairs on his chest.

A light wind rustled through the leaves, tickling her bare skin. She'd never had sex out in the open. God, it was so fucking good getting back to nature!

She gasped when he began to move inside her, slowly at first. *Ah, yeah, just like that.* She closed her eyes, letting the sensations he was creating inside her wash over her in sensuous waves.

In one fluid motion, he rolled to his back until she was on top of him. He'd given her control of the motions.

She did so love being in control.

With her hands braced on her thighs, she raised and lowered herself over him, biting her bottom lip as the intensity increased.

"Oh, yeah, like that," he moaned. "Son of a bitch, that feels good."

She closed her eyes, her body moving to a tempo inside her head. The beat picked up and she went right along with it, her body tightening when the first spasms washed over her. She barely heard his groan as he climaxed, she was so lost in her own pleasure.

Her body seemed to float downward until her head

rested on his chest. She listened to his heartbeat. At first fast, then slowing to a more normal rate.

She'd never had such mind-blowing sex before. A wave of giddiness washed over her. What the hell did they put in the drinking water here? She damn sure felt purified. Okay, so maybe "purified" wasn't the right choice of word, but damn, she felt fantastic. As her world righted itself, she raised her head and smiled . . . and met his look of satisfaction.

Her forehead creased into tiny frown lines. Wait a minute. This wasn't supposed to happen.

"I was taking *your* picture," she grumbled. "Not the other way around. You seduced me with my own camera." She shook her head. "That is so bad."

He chuckled. "No, what we did was so bad, but it was damn good."

"Oh yeah." She laughed for the pure joy of it. So what that he'd turned the tables on her. She'd have him drop his pants and pose for the camera before she left the ranch.

The wind rustled through the trees, sweeping over her, but this time it didn't feel quite so good. Almost like there was a chilly foreboding in the air of things to come. Things she might not like.

She shook off the feeling. Sometimes she could be so demented. She eased away from him and gathered her clothes, knowing he watched her. "I don't suppose you have a washcloth."

He pushed away from the rock and rid himself of the condom. He really was a fantastically built man. Yep, she was going to have to get him to pose nude. Women would go crazy looking at his buff bod.

"I have better than that," he said, scooping up his clothes.

She raised her eyebrows. Had he been so sure of himself?

"I have a bath awaiting, milady." He bent at the waist and waved his arms toward the trees. He laughed when she didn't move. "Follow me." He slapped his hat on his head and grabbed his boots.

Curiosity got the better of her. The view was nice, too. As Nina walked behind him, she watched his firm butt muscles clench and unclench, and as if he were the Pied Piper, she knew she'd follow him anywhere. What woman wouldn't with a flute like his? Lord, she was getting snarky.

They didn't have far to walk. Just past the trees was a river. It wasn't that wide, but the water was beautifully clear. She loved skinny-dipping. And there was a rope hanging from a tree.

Lance started wading out. "The water's great," he tossed over his shoulder, but she wasn't listening to him. She was focused on the rope and thinking what fun it would be to swing out and splash him. That would teach him for stealing her camera away from her.

She smiled to herself and began climbing the small incline. It took her only a few seconds to get to the top. She grabbed the rope and laughed. Lance turned, his grin dropping from his face as she pushed off.

The sound of the rope breaking echoed in her ears. She landed with a hard thud in shallow water. As the water closed over her face she thought how pretty the sun looked as it sparkled down on her. Was this the last thing her grandfather had seen?

Darkness enveloped her.

Five

Nina opened her eyes. The sun was still shining but she was on the bank of the river, Lance hovering over her with an anxious expression.

What happened?

Everything came back to her in a rush. The rope, the rope breaking, dropping into the water like a lead balloon.

Had Lance sabotaged the rope earlier? He *was* next in line to inherit the ranch.

She closed her eyes.

"Nina, are you okay? Damn, I didn't know you'd go for the rope. I should've warned you it might not be safe. That was stupid of me." Concern laced his words.

No, she'd done something stupid. Not Lance's fault. How could he have known she'd climb the small knoll and attempt to swing out and drop into the river? And drop she had. Her plan didn't have the outcome she'd expected.

She could only blame herself. She was a good judge of people and Lance had not tried to kill her.

Great, after all that hot, yummy sex, he thinks I'm a doofus.

"I just got the wind knocked out of me. Other than being embarrassed as hell, I'll live." She gratefully took the hand he offered and pulled herself up to a sitting position. The world swam in front of her. She closed her eyes for a moment. When she opened them again, everything was back in focus.

"So, how about that swim?" she said, knowing her smile came off a little wobbly.

"Are you sure?" he asked.

"Yeah, but I think I'll just walk into the water this time."

Nina had refused Lance's offer to take her to the emergency room. Maxine had even said Nina would be fine after a short rest and gave her a couple of Tylenol.

Maybe they were both right, because when Nina came down to supper after a couple of hours, other than her movements being a little stiff, she looked as if nothing had happened.

She looked damn good, in fact. Lance's gaze swept over her. She'd changed into blue shorts and a sleeveless knit top and had pulled her hair into a ponytail. No makeup—the damp tendrils of hair told him she was fresh from a shower, her face scrubbed clean—and she was the sexiest woman he'd ever seen.

Maybe because the knit top hugged her body and when she raised her hand to brush back a tendril of hair that had escaped, the hem of her top inched upward, displaying just enough creamy flesh that it became increasingly hard to concentrate.

"Are you feeling better?" He took a deep breath as he quickly turned back to the stove, scooped up the home fries into a bowl, and moved the skillet off the hot burner.

"I've had better days, but the Tylenol, and lying down for a while, helped. There are other parts that are sore, though."

He frowned. "From the fall?" He briefly wondered if she meant from sex but refrained from asking. He wouldn't bring up their interlude if she didn't. Women were funny about sex after the fact, but damned if he didn't want her all over again.

"No, from sitting in a saddle most of the day," she wryly stated, rubbing her bottom.

His frown turned into a grin. "Sorry about that. I forgot you're not used to riding. I have some liniment in my room that I'll give you. Just rub it on and you'll feel better by morning." He casually added, "I can apply it if you'd like." For just a moment, he closed his eyes and pictured her lying naked on the bed, his hands sliding over her body. . . .

"I'm sure you could but I don't think I would fully appreciate the gesture. Maybe tomorrow night, though," she murmured.

It took a few seconds for her words to sink in, dispelling the image, but not the damn hard-on his lascivious thoughts had given him and the fact she'd mentioned tomorrow night. Good thing he had a towel tucked into the front of his jeans.

She glanced at the table he'd set earlier. "This looks and smells wonderful," she said, changing the subject.

Pleasure ripped through him that she'd even noticed. He was a pretty decent cook, but on the few occasions he'd thrown a meal together for the men, they'd wolfed it down. He had a feeling if he'd opened cans of dog food they would've appreciated it just as much. It was nice Nina noticed.

"It's not fancy by any means." He shrugged off her compliment. "I sent Maxine on her way and told her I'd get supper tonight. Her canasta group meets on Thursdays."

"That was nice of you. Can I do anything to help?"

He shook his head. "You can grab us a couple of beers, unless you'd rather have something else."

"Beer is fine," she said and went to the refrigerator.

They didn't talk again until the meal was over, but it was a comfortable silence. When she stood, picking up her plate, he took it from her, noticing that she still moved a little slow.

"I'll get those later. Come on, you haven't lived until you've seen a Texas sunset."

He led her to the back porch. It wrapped around the house, with aged cedar posts and a split-log floor. The red plaid cushions in the rocking chairs were just old enough to be comfortable.

"How long have you worked for my grandfather?" she asked after easing into one of the rockers.

He sat in the rocker beside hers, pushing off with the toe of his boot. The sun was just starting to set, casting a blue-tinged orange haze across the western sky.

His first day as a wrangler had ended just like this, except with him and Pete Maddock sitting in the rockers. Damn, he missed the old man. He'd taught Lance what no book, no school, ever could. He'd taught him about human nature, about ranching—about life in general.

"I started working for him right out of high school," he told her.

"You didn't want to go to college?"

He shook his head. "Pete taught me everything I ever needed. He had the best head for business of anyone I know. Not just with the ranch, but the bar and the hotel as well. Not that he had that much to do with the bar. That was Rod's baby. Pete might have bought it, but Rod took it from nothing to what it is today. He turned the Ragged Rooster into something anyone would be proud of."

"Until Juliet took his dream away from him." She looked down at her hands, then at the sunset. "Have you met her?"

"Yeah. She's sexy as . . ." He cleared his throat. "Red-headed, not real tall. She was kind of quiet, but you know it's like they say, the quiet ones are always the ones who fool you. I suspect she's giving Rod hell."

"And you know Rod?"

"We went to school together. Hardheaded. Always has been. But he's pretty decent, most of the time. In fact, they're probably giving each other hell. If you want, I'll take you to the Ragged Rooster to see your sister."

"Maybe in a few days." She stopped the motion of her rocker with her foot and stood. "My head's starting to hurt. I think I'll go back to my room."

As he followed her inside, he wondered if her head hurt because of the fall or hearing about her sister. He knew they'd never met.

Drew Maddock had been a real bastard, but Lance refrained from telling Nina exactly what he thought about her father. Drew was a disappointment to the old man. Maybe that's why Pete had taken Lance under his wing.

Damn, he just wished Nina wouldn't sell out. He swallowed past the bile that rose in his throat. He'd lied when he'd said he'd adjusted to the fact it wouldn't be his. He'd do just about anything to keep the ranch out of a stranger's hands.

As she started toward the staircase, he remembered her sore muscles. "Hold on a second and I'll get that liniment for you." He hurried to his room and grabbed the jar of cream.

She waited at the bottom of the stairs. When he handed it to her, their hands touched. A spark of electricity passed over him, and from the look on her face, he knew she'd felt it, too.

Just one word, Nina, just one word and I'll carry you up the stairs just so I can apply the liniment.

"Thanks." She turned and went up the stairs. He watched the way her hips moved from side to side, the sexy shape of her bare legs in those incredibly short shorts. He closed his eyes, gripping the newel post so he wouldn't be tempted to hurry after her.

It was going to be damn hard sleeping right below her bedroom and remembering how they'd made love that afternoon and how damn much he wanted a repeat performance. This was going to be a cold-shower night.

Nina could feel him watching her. The heat of his look sent small tremors over her body. Had he felt the spark of electricity when their hands had touched? It had taken all her willpower not to fall into his arms.

Are you that desperate, Nina?

She had a feeling she was, but she'd needed a little space between them. She hadn't meant to seduce him. Okay, maybe it had been in the back of her mind, but what she'd really wanted was the photo shoot. She still did. He'd thrown her off balance and she needed to regroup. Mica had challenged her and she'd be damned if she'd lose their wager.

There would still be time for sex after the shoot.

She opened her door and went inside, setting the jar of liniment on the dresser, but she couldn't stop picturing Lance bare assed and leaning against a tall pecan tree. She'd always had a weakness for nuts.

A noise from the next room startled her out of her musings. Her grandfather's ghost? An intruder? She swallowed past the sudden lump in her throat.

A weapon. She needed a weapon. She grabbed the jar of liniment. Yeah, that would make a great club. She set it back down as her gaze flew about the room. The only thing that even came close was her blow dryer. If it was an intruder, maybe he'd mistake it for a gun.

And if it was a ghost?

She'd scream really loud.

Lord, she'd hit her head harder than she'd thought.

She slipped from her room, blow dryer at her side, cord trailing behind her as she crept to her grandfather's door. She listened for a moment. Nothing.

Had she imagined the noise?

No, she didn't think so. Living in the city had made her accustomed to noises. This had been different. She couldn't explain why; it just had been. The sound had been more like someone moving about. Well, the person had met his match!

Holding her breath, she slowly turned the knob and quietly pushed the door open, her grip tightening on the blow dryer. She might not be able to inflict much damage, but she'd be prepared.

She opened the door enough to peer inside. Still nothing. She straightened, pushing the door open the rest of the way and turning on the light. Empty. She frowned, stepping farther inside.

The closet?

Maybe. She crept closer. "Okay, you'd better come out right now," she warned in her toughest voice, knowing she'd crap her pants if someone were to jump out. Her gut told her that whoever had made the noise was long gone.

She jerked the door open, blow dryer raised.

"You don't really think you would hurt someone with a blow dryer, do you?" Lance spoke directly behind her.

She screamed and whirled around, blow dryer raised. Lance caught it in his hand before she could do any damage.

"Whoa, easy now."

"Yeah, right, you're not the one ghost hunting. You've just aged me by at least ten years." She took a deep breath, willing her pulse to slow to something less than 200 beats per minute. When she could breathe a little easier, she glared at him. "What are you doing here, anyway?"

"My room is directly under yours. I heard you moving about and wanted to make sure you were okay. Apparently you aren't. What's all this about ghost hunting?"

"I heard a noise." Had she really told him she'd been hunting for a ghost?

"First rule around here is that if you see or hear anything suspicious get help."

She squared her shoulders. "I didn't need any help. I was only checking out a noise. No big deal."

"With nothing more lethal than a blow dryer?"

"I'll have you know it made a good weapon."

He took it from her. She could tell he was holding back a smile as he tried for a serious look while he examined it.

"Yes, I can see how you might blow someone away with this."

She grabbed it from him and set it on the small oak desk that graced one wall. "Very funny. I heard a noise and I knew if I didn't check it out I'd never be able to go to sleep. Rather than make fun of me, you can at least see if anything has been disturbed."

"Can't help you there, either. I've never been in Pete's bedroom." He glanced around, then frowned. "I'm surprised Maxine hasn't cleaned in here."

One eyebrow rose. "What do you mean?" The room looked fine to her. The bed was made, the pillows plumped.

"Peppermint candy wrappers." He walked over to the dresser and bent down, picking up the clear cellophane.

When he stood, she noticed a sad smile on his face. She had a sudden urge to pull Lance close and comfort him.

"Pete loved peppermints better than anything else. For as long as I knew him, he nearly always had one in his mouth."

Realization came slow. Wrappers on the floor? They hadn't been there before. Or had they and she just hadn't noticed them? And hadn't the jar of peppermints been on the bedside table earlier? No, they'd been on the dresser, then the bedside table, and now they were back on the dresser.

She closed her eyes. Or could she be mistaken? The last few days had been long and stressful. Her arrival in a small Texas town, when she was definitely a city girl, and meeting with a very condescending lawyer to sign legal documents sure hadn't been a piece of cake. She had a sister in town and another expected any time neither of whom she'd ever met. Her grandfather's body had never been found.

Sex with Lance had been incredible, though. But then she'd made a doofus of herself by falling into the river. And how could she have thought Lance might have had something to do with her accident?

And to top it all off, she still had to convince him to do the centerfold.

Stress? Nah, why would she feel stressed?

Okay, time to regroup again. Maybe she'd only imagined the jar of peppermints had been in a different spot. She'd landed pretty hard when the rope broke.

"You okay?"

She drew in a deep, steadying breath. "Fine. I think I'll feel better in the morning. Night." She hurried out of the room.

But when her door was locked and she was burrowed down in bed, everything that had happened that day played out in her mind as if she were watching a movie.

Especially the part about making love.

Warmth spread over her like a wildfire. Heat that was totally out of control as she remembered the way his hands had caressed and kneaded her breasts. The way it had felt when he sucked on them, his teeth scraping across her sensitive nipples.

Good Lord!

She flipped to her side, clamping her legs together. It didn't help. She swore under her breath, but it didn't stop her from remembering what it had felt like when he'd buried himself inside her and began sliding in and out, her moving on top, their thrusts becoming harder and stronger until the very air exploded around her from the intensity of her climax.

She bit her bottom lip and tugged the covers under her chin. Ah, damn, this was going to be a really long night.

Six

Nina awakened slowly. Noises came in through the partially opened window, which also let in a light breeze. They weren't the normal city noises that she was used to. No, these were the sounds of a working ranch. A horse's whinny, the jingle of a bridle, men laughing and talking as they started a new day.

She snuggled into the plush mattress, sighing deeply. A person could get used to this.

No, she couldn't let anything influence her decision to leave. As soon as she checked out the ranch and where it stood financially, her days here would be numbered. It would be back to the city for her. The crowds, the traffic, concrete everywhere you looked.

No, she really did love the city. She did.

But just for a moment, she wondered what it would be like to wake up to this every morning, to be able to photograph more than naked male models. She'd always wanted to take pictures of nature: hills and streams, the animals in their natural habitat. Not something painted on a canvas background with a fake cowboy posing in front of it. She wanted the raw reality of men who actually tamed this wild land.

Like Lance had tamed the horse. Like Lance had tamed me.

The thought flashed across her mind before she could stop it. She snuggled deeper into her pillow—at least he had for a little while. The man did know how to make love. She wouldn't mind a couple of repeat performances before she left.

Damn, the sex had been fantastic. She luxuriated in the memories of making love with him until she couldn't stand not having the flesh-and-blood man in front of her and shoved the covers to the side before jumping out of bed.

She did a quick sponge bath and pulled on a pair of jeans and a green tank top that left half her midriff bare. A pair of tennis shoes on her feet, a rubber band pulling her hair back, and she was set to go.

Grabbing her camera off the chair, she left the room, pausing outside her grandfather's door.

Had she really thought she could face a possible attacker with a blow dryer? That had been so lame.

She bounced down the stairs and almost straight into Lance's arms. A giant condor flapped his wings inside her stomach.

"Good morning," she said, in what she hoped was a normal-sounding voice, then smiled brightly.

"You look like you're feeling pretty good."

"All this country air."

"Told you it would grow on you."

"Don't get your hopes up. I still plan on leaving. I'm thinking of this as a nice vacation. Like all vacations, this one will end, too."

"We'll see."

His gaze moved slowly over her as if to refute her claim.

When he met her gaze he wore a perfectly innocent expression.

She knew better.

There wasn't a thing innocent about him. For which she had been oh so grateful yesterday. He'd scratched an itch that had been bothering her for way too long. Problem was, she was starting to itch again. This wouldn't do at all.

"So, what are your plans today?" he asked.

"I thought I'd go over the finances. I didn't pay a lot of attention when I met with the lawyer. I just glanced through the papers. They all seemed to be in order."

"I have some free time. I can help you if you'd like."

She gave him a grateful smile. She'd never really had a head for business. "Great, but first I really need a cup of coffee." A pot might even be better if she was going to have to do anything more than add two and two.

Half an hour later and caffeine loaded, she stacked the papers from the lawyer on the dining room table. Lance added the ledgers that he'd brought from her grandfather's office and they both sat down.

"Here, slide in a little closer," he told her, without looking up from the papers.

"Why are you doing this?" she asked before moving.

"So we can look through them at the same time. Besides, I like you this close to me."

A warm flush of pleasure washed over her. "You know that's not what I meant. Why are you helping me go over the papers at all?"

He looked up. "Because you looked like you needed a little help."

When he grinned that damn condor flapped his wings again. She tried to concentrate on his words and not his mouth, but it wasn't easy.

"The only one who knows more about this ranch is Pete.

Since I don't believe in ghosts, you're stuck with me." He stared at her for a few seconds before continuing. "Pete meant a lot to me. If he changed his mind, then he had a reason. Maybe it was because you're his granddaughter."

She cocked an eyebrow. "That's why he was so generous to my mother over the years," she said, with more than a touch of sarcasm.

"I don't know the whole story, Nina, but I can't see Pete not helping out."

She didn't want to get into what her grandfather had or had not felt or what he didn't do to help her and her mother financially. They had struggled over the years to make ends meet. From the looks of this ranch, her grandfather could've helped out. The simple fact was, he hadn't. She didn't think she could ever forgive him for that.

"Can you explain exactly what my inheritance entails?" she asked, changing the subject.

"Gabe would've been happy to, you know. He was your grandfather's lawyer for many years."

She frowned. "He was very condescending. I didn't particularly like him." She scooted her chair nearer.

"Gabe? Doesn't sound like him." He picked up the sheaf of papers once more.

Maybe Lance didn't know people as well as he thought.

She glanced over his shoulder at the papers he held. Damn, he smelled great. He definitely knew what cologne to wear that would make a woman want to lean closer. Fresh, clean . . . male. Yum, very male.

He flipped the page. "Mostly legal jargon," he mumbled.

"But I do own the ranch? I mean, the lawyer told me that much."

"The papers list the ranch, the acreage, barn, out-buildings."

He flipped to the next page and was quiet for a long time. She watched his expression. One eyebrow rose, then lowered. His forehead wrinkled. He'd found something. Maybe this was all an elaborate scheme to make a mockery of her so-called inheritance. Then he smiled.

Her stomach rumbled uncomfortably. "What?"

"You can't sell."

She straightened, the roaring in her ears getting louder. "What do you mean, I can't sell?"

He jabbed his finger against the paper. "You have to keep the same employees, and you can't sell for at least three years."

The breath left her body in a whoosh. "That's not fair." She'd been scammed by a Maddock. Just like her mother. She closed her eyes and counted to ten. "Okay," she said, opening her eyes. "I'll just go back to the city, you'll continue to run the place, and I'll sell it in three years. Problem solved."

His smile grew wider as he turned in his chair until he faced her. "You have to live here for the three years. Except for occasional short trips, you have to stay at the ranch."

That wasn't fair. Why the hell had he attached strings? She stiffened her spine and raised her chin. "If I don't?"

"The place is mine."

"Not fair!" She jumped to her feet, her chair rocking precariously back and forth before it came to a stop. "How will I live without money? My savings can't possibly last that long."

He opened his mouth, then snapped it shut.

"What?" Her eyes narrowed. There was something he hadn't told her.

He opened one of the ledgers and turned to a page midway into the book, then pointed to the last number in the column. "That's what the ranch brought in last month."

She glanced down. That couldn't be right. It was more money than she earned in six months. She grabbed the table for support.

"Pete always had enough money in the ranch account in case something major happened. More than enough, in fact. He usually kept the place running pretty smooth. Some of the money goes for general upkeep, of course. We bought a new hay baler a few months ago and that took out a chunk, but you can live pretty comfortable for the rest of your life on what the ranch brings in and still have enough in savings for a lean year."

"And this would've all been yours," she said after the world stopped spinning.

"I have money saved back. In a few years I'll buy my own spread. Don't worry about it. Life doesn't always have to mean how much money you make."

Yeah, right, try being poor sometime. Okay, so maybe she wasn't money hungry, but she did like to know where her next meal was coming from.

"I need a little while to think about all this. Could we finish going over all the papers later?"

He hesitated for a few seconds. "I think you're wrong about Pete. I don't know what went on in the past, but he did mention his granddaughters occasionally and the love he had for you three girls shone in his eyes." He stood and walked out of the room.

A cold shiver washed over her, almost as if Lance had sucked all the warmth out of the room when he left. It was crazy; she knew that.

But Lance was wrong. Her grandfather hadn't cared enough to be a part of her life. Her gaze strayed up the stairs toward his room. "Why are you doing this? Why dangle the carrot only to snatch it back again?"

"You say something?" Maxine asked from the doorway.

Nina glanced up. "What was Pete Maddock like?" she countered with her own question.

Maxine stuffed her cleaning rag into the front pocket of her red apron. "Pete?" She looked thoughtful for a minute.

"A damn shrewd businessman even though he never looked the part. I'd known him since he had coppery red hair. It turned gray over the years, though. He still had the clearest, darkest green eyes I've ever seen on a man." She smiled. "And always a damn peppermint stuck in his mouth. That man sure had a sweet tooth. Never could stand peppermints myself."

Her expression turned serious.

"Your grandpa was a good man. Once, when my daughter was in a car accident, he drove me all the way to Dallas. She wasn't hurt bad, but he told me a mother should stay with her kid.

"Ruthy was twenty-five, but I guess she was still my baby. Anyway, he put me up in a really nice hotel. Fancier than any place I've ever stayed before. Gave me money for food and taxi fare when I needed one. Told me to call when I was ready to come home and he'd come back and get me. The hardest thing I ever had to do was clean his room knowing he wouldn't be coming back. Your grandpa was real special." She dabbed her eyes with the corner of her apron and hurried from the room.

"Then why hadn't he taken care of Momma and me?" Nina whispered.

Her gaze moved toward the staircase again. Maybe it was time she found out the reason. She'd start in his room. See if she could find anything at all that would give her an insight into the man. Anything that would give her some kind of clue why he would do so much for some and nothing, until now, for his own granddaughters.

She climbed the stairs and opened the door, looking around before she stepped inside. She still wasn't sure the noise she'd heard last night had been her imagination.

All clear.

At least the candy jar was in the same place. . . .

Her eyes narrowed. Hadn't it been nearly full? Now it

was down three-quarters. She shook her head. "You're definitely losing it, girl."

She stepped closer, bending to pick up a wrapper Lance must've missed. But Maxine said she'd cleaned his room since he'd died. How had she missed the wrappers? Unless Grandpa had a restless spirit. Goose bumps ran up and down her arms.

She shook her head, clearing it of crazy notions.

Maxine had been tired, under a lot of stress. That was all it was. Of course she'd miss a few clear cellophane wrappers. There was certainly no such thing as ghosts. She tossed the wrapper in the wastepaper basket.

"If your ghost is still hanging around, then why the hell didn't you help Momma when she needed it?" She paused, then realized she was practically holding her breath as she waited for some sign he'd heard. "Definitely losing it, girl." She walked over and opened the top drawer of his dresser.

Socks, boxer shorts—she ran her hand beneath them. Nothing. She didn't find anything in the others, either. Nor the closet, only clothes—jeans, boots and tops . . . a few belts.

There was a bag of peppermints in one of the bedside drawers and a bag of chocolate bars. Maxine was right; he'd had a bad sweet tooth. She went to the other side. There were loose pictures in this one. One was Lance with an older, gray-haired man. She turned on the lamp to take a closer look, turning the picture over and glancing at the back. The names Pete and Lance were scrawled across the back.

She flipped it over again. So, this was her grandfather. He was grinning, his arm across Lance's shoulder. It could've been a picture of a proud grandfather with his grandson. Pete Maddock didn't look like a man who wouldn't care. In fact, he looked just the opposite.

She lightly ran the tip of her finger over her grandfather.

"Why?" But again, silence was her only answer. Rather than put the picture back, she tucked it into her pocket.

Now what? There was only one place she hadn't looked—the desk.

She walked over and sat in the chair, then opened the top drawer: pen, pencils—nothing of importance. The next one yielded the same. She swiveled the chair toward the other drawers and opened the top one on the opposite side. The same as the others. When she opened the bottom one, she pretty much expected more of the same. She was surprised to find a black book.

"Probably nothing that matters," she said, wondering why her hand trembled when she lifted it out.

She crossed her legs and gingerly opened the spiral-bound book. There were only a few words scratched on the first page, but it was enough to make her heart speed up as she read them aloud.

"Diary of Pete Maddock."

Seven

Lance glanced up at the second floor. He'd seen Nina moving around in her grandfather's room, crossing in front of the window. What was she searching for? She already had the ranch—at least as long as she stayed here. That thought brought up a lot of interesting possibilities.

It was a win-win situation for him. He enjoyed her company. He liked the hell out of the way she looked when she took pictures. All excited and everything. He especially liked the way she looked when she made love—all excited and everything.

"So, are we going to be out of a job tomorrow?" Stan asked.

Lance tore his attention away from the house and looked at the bowlegged, middle-aged cowboy. Of course he was worried, even though he tried not to show it. Every man on the ranch except maybe Rowdy was worried. Rowdy was young enough, he could pick up and leave. He was a drifter, didn't have ties to the community, but the rest of the men did.

"No," Lance told him. "You won't have to worry for at

least three years. There was a stipulation Pete added. You're safe, for now."

"Good thing." He hitched up his jeans. "Three years. That's a long time." He eyed Lance.

"What?" He didn't like the way Stan measured him up. As if he suddenly thought he might bring a fair piece of money down at the sale barn.

"She's not bad looking. Filled out those jeans she wore yesterday damned nice, in fact. I saw her taking your picture. If you marry her, you'd both own the ranch. Then we wouldn't have anything to worry about."

Lance straightened. "Marry?" He looked toward the house. Stan was right. She wouldn't sell the ranch if he married her. Damn it, what the hell was he thinking about? That bordered on him being a gigolo.

"You're crazy, Stan."

He shrugged. "Worth thinking about."

"No, it isn't." He tossed the bridle he was working on across the fence and went inside to get a pair of needle-nose pliers. He'd never heard of anything so damn foolish.

So he liked the way she looked, the way she laughed and smiled, the way she could look so intense when taking a picture of a deer, the way she'd been unconcerned with "you show me yours and I'll show you mine." Damn, she was brazen, sexy . . . but marry? He didn't think so. But when he exited the barn, his gaze went straight to the house.

Three years. Anything could happen.

Nina skimmed past pages of writing about the ranch, the early days. Pages she wanted to revisit because Pete shared all his dreams about how he would make the ranch profitable.

She read about Pete's marriage to Penelope Witherton, his excitement over the birth of his son, Drew.

"If only you'd known he'd turn out to be such an ass you might not have been quite so thrilled," she murmured.

She flipped through the pages, past his divorce. Was that what changed him from a caring man to someone so insensitive he didn't even want to get to know her?

There was less written in the ensuing years—until she came to Juliet. He'd wanted to meet his granddaughter.

Nina sat forward, skimming the passages. Drew said Juliet's mother didn't want to have anything to do with the Maddocks. Pete had sent money instead, even though it was apparent his heart was breaking.

She set the book on her lap, keeping her place. The pieces of the puzzle were falling in place. Why hadn't she guessed? But then, she knew the answer. Her father had poisoned all their minds.

Anxious to read more, she flipped through the pages. Then she found what she was looking for—what he'd written about her. Her grandfather said he'd wanted to see her, but again, Drew hadn't encouraged visitation, in fact, had discouraged it, so he'd stayed away, only giving Drew money to help with her support.

Braces when she was ten. What a joke. It was a good thing she'd been blessed with good teeth because her mother hadn't had money for food sometimes, let alone braces. She read on. Health insurance, private school, clothes . . . even her first car!

That was hilarious. She'd worked after school to buy her first clunker, then worked her way through college. She knew exactly where the money had gone—into Drew's bank account.

But now she had to rethink how she felt about her grandfather. He *had* cared. But damn it, now she'd never know him.

She pulled the picture from her pocket and stared at it.

"How can a man as smart as you have been so blasted stupid? I would've loved knowing you and not for your money." All she had was this ranch. A place without memories . . . at least for her.

Her bottom lip trembled. She didn't care that tears were sliding down her cheeks.

Okay, this wouldn't do. She wiped her hands across her cheeks and jumped to her feet, replacing the diary in the drawer. This was no time to get maudlin. She couldn't erase the past, and if she was going to stay here, she might as well make the most of it.

And stay she would. Through his diary, Nina felt as if she'd met her grandfather. The ranch was his baby, and maybe through it, she'd get to know him a little better. Maybe that's what he'd hoped for.

First things first. She needed a darkroom. She couldn't function without one and her joy in life was still her pictures. And with the money she now had, she could afford one. A really nice one.

With a little help from Maxine, she found the perfect room on the first floor. It wasn't too large or too small, and it had a sink for her chemicals. She went to Pete's study and was delighted to find he'd owned a computer. She only felt a moment's trepidation using her credit card, but the time to be frugal was in the past. She was going to buy the best!

After making her on-line order, she went to the front porch, her gaze slowly roaming over the barns and outbuildings. Tingles of excitement washed over her. Pride filled her at all that her grandfather had built. Now this was hers—all hers. She was a rancher. And she'd probably never have to worry about money again.

"You surveying your land?" Lance said as he came around the side of the house.

She jumped, then frowned. She'd been having an I-can't-believe-this-is-happening moment. "And if I was?"

He didn't answer as he took the steps two at a time and joined her, half sitting on the cedar rail that ran the length of the porch. Then he stared long enough that she started to get a little uncomfortable.

"What? Do I have a wart on my nose?" she asked.

"No, but you look different."

"It's the country air."

He shook his head. "No, I don't think so. Could it be that I noticed just a little pride?"

She raised her chin. "What if you did?"

"I'm not complaining. Just wondering why the change."

She sat down in one of the rockers and pushed it into motion with her foot. "I found his diary."

"Whose?"

"My grandfather's."

He raised his eyebrows. "Pete kept a diary? Doesn't sound like him. He hated writing letters. Usually talked me or Maxine into doing all his business correspondence." He paused. "So, you must've read something you liked."

She nodded. There was nothing that said she had to tell him a thing. So why did she feel the need to confide? Because he was easy to talk to, that's why.

"He gave money to Drew. Drew was supposed to give it to my mother, only he didn't. I've hated my grandfather for a long time. This sort of puts a different spin on what I've always believed." It was her turn to stare. "You don't seem surprised."

"Pete always believed there was good in everyone. I'm not surprised he thought Drew was helping with your support and certainly not surprised he wasn't. Like I said, I met your father a couple of times."

She leaned her head against the back of the chair. "I

don't really think of him as my father. I never have. He wasn't a part of my family. Neither was my grandfather. We scraped by without their help. Then my mother married Adam, when I was seventeen. He was the closest I've ever had to a father figure."

"But Pete would've liked to be a part of your life."

"Yeah, but I still can't help thinking it was too little too late. He could've contacted me after Drew died."

"Maybe he didn't know how."

"I wasn't that hard to find."

"No, I don't mean a physical address. How do you go up to someone you've never met and introduce yourself as a long-lost relative? I'd think it would be pretty hard."

"I guess I'll never know since he died before I had the chance to meet him." Damn, all that wasted time.

Silence reigned for a few minutes, each lost in their private thoughts.

"Hey, come on, I want to show you something," Lance said, and some of the tension dissipated.

Nina cocked a sassy eyebrow. "I've already seen it."

Heat flared in his eyes and for a second she wished she had kept her smart mouth shut for once. Especially since that same heat was flaring inside her.

"Trying to talk your way into my bed, boss lady? I'd say that bordered on sexual harassment."

She opened her mouth, then snapped it closed.

"Nope, you won't have your way with me quite so easily next time."

"You're so funny I can't stop laughing," Nina said, with more than a touch of sarcasm, but, at the same time, giddiness tickled all the way down her spine, then back up again.

He grabbed her hand and pulled her out of her chair. "Just because you're the boss doesn't mean you can get lazy."

"Where are we going?"

"Do you always ask this many questions?"

She thought for a moment. "Yes, I do."

"Well, just trust me."

"Hmm . . . if I remember correctly, the last time I trusted you and let you take my picture I ended up naked."

"Not my fault. You started it with 'show me yours and I'll show you mine.'"

He was never going to let her forget. Not that she ever wanted to forget a second of the delicious sexual experience they'd shared.

"Okay," she grumbled. "I'm right behind you." As if he didn't already know that, since he still held her hand. She had to admit she liked the way his warmth transferred to her. If she wasn't careful, she could really start to like this cowboy.

As he pulled her inside the barn she had to wonder exactly what his intentions were. Wicked thoughts filled her mind. She'd never had sex in a barn. Would someone walk in on them? She wasn't sure she liked that idea. Threesomes were not her thing.

"Here, come closer," he whispered.

She probably shouldn't trust him. After all, she still didn't know *that* much about him. She only knew he had a great smile, and he seemed really nice, and he was funny some of the time, and he was good at sex. Really good.

But she did as he asked and peered over the gate. "Oh," she said, with more than a touch of awe, as she looked at the newborn colt standing on pencil-thin legs. "When was it born?"

"Last night. It's a little filly."

The mare looked up and nickered, then bent her head to check on her baby.

"What's her name?"

He shook his head. "Don't know. You'll have to ask the owner."

It took a few seconds for her to comprehend. This was her colt. The filly, and the mare, for that matter, belonged to her. That odd giddy feeling swept over her again. She actually owned something. Other than her car or camera equipment.

"What are you thinking?" he asked.

"How strange it feels to own a ranch, let alone a horse and her newborn. I don't think I really felt a sense of ownership until I read my grandfather's diary."

"It's because he's not just a relative you've never met anymore. He's given you a greater gift than this ranch—he's given you roots."

She thought about it for a moment. "Yeah, I guess he has. But that doesn't mean I won't sell the place after the three years are up."

"We'll see."

Yes, they would see. She had a life outside of this ranch and she damn well planned to return to it. She should be able to find enough cowboys in Silver Gulch whom she could photograph so that Mica would be satisfied.

And there was still Lance. She *would* get him to drop his pants and pose. Only this time she'd make sure she held on to the camera. There'd be no more "you show me yours and I'll show you mine"! At least, not until she had her centerfold picture. Her grin was more than a little devilish.

Eight

The next afternoon Nina hurried to the porch when she heard a truck lumbering up the drive. UPS. Her stuff was here.

She refrained from jumping up and down and clapping her hands. She was the owner of a ranch. She should act the part. Okay, maybe a small jump.

Stuffy was just not in her nature.

Finally, she'd have a darkroom to develop her film. She'd taken pictures all over the ranch yesterday: Maxine rolling out a piecrust, Lance talking to another cowboy, the new colt, Lance carrying a bale of hay—she'd taken a lot of pictures of Lance.

The UPS truck came to a rocking stop and the driver got out and went to the back of the truck. Everything seemed to move in slow motion. She kept telling herself only a few more minutes and she'd be tearing into boxes.

The doors creaked open, and then he disappeared inside and returned with a dolly. After loading it down with boxes, he pushed it toward the house. She signed for her stuff and began carrying the boxes inside, attempting to stay calm, but it felt too much like Christmas.

"Is that the stuff for your picture-developing room?" Maxine asked, wiping her hands on her apron as she grabbed a box and followed Nina.

"It's called a darkroom. And, yes, it is."

"If it's a darkroom, how are you going to see?"

Nina laughed. "I'll use a safe light, a low-intensity red light. It'll provide just enough illumination that I can work, but not so much that it will damage the pictures." She set a box down and went after another one, but when she got to the porch Lance was examining one of her purchases. He looked up when she stepped outside.

She took the box from him. "I'm taking over part of the mudroom and turning it into a darkroom," she explained. "If I'm going to be here for a while I'll need a place to develop my film." She raised her chin, waiting for him to argue.

He picked up another box. "You'll probably need a partition to separate it from the back door. That way you won't have someone inadvertently opening it and ruining your film." He looked at her, giving her that crooked smile that warmed her from the inside out.

"I was going to hang a dark blanket on a rope." Lord, why did she sound so lame?

"I can have a partition up by the end of the day."

"Thanks." She watched as he walked past her. This wasn't good. She was starting to like Lance the more she was around him. It would be harder to convince him to do something she knew he'd regret.

But as the morning moved into late afternoon, she couldn't help relaxing more and more. And true to his word, he had a wooden partition up in very little time and had even framed in a door.

She surveyed her small space and liked what she saw.

"Looks like you're ready for business," Lance said as he came up behind her.

Her space just got a whole lot smaller as it filled with testosterone. She took a deep breath and faced him. Her head told her that had been a bad move, but if it was so bad, why did being this close feel so damn good?

He brushed back behind her ear a lock of hair that had escaped her ponytail, his fingers trailing down to cup her chin.

He's going to kiss me.

She tried to swallow, but her mouth was suddenly dry as powder. Goose bumps spread over her arms. She wanted him so bad her body trembled with need.

There was nothing to stop them. Why not enjoy a little late afternoon sex? Maxine had left a few minutes ago. They had the house to themselves. He could strip her right here if he wanted.

Her nipples tightened as a deeper ache spread across the lower part of her body. Her eyes fluttered closed. *Take me,* her mind screamed as she leaned toward him.

Pounding on the back door jarred her eyes open.

"Hey, Lance. You in there?"

Lance's sigh washed over her. "Yeah, I'm here. What do you need, Stan?" he called back but was still looking at Nina as if he were memorizing every one of her features. "This had better be good," he mumbled.

"Bulldozer plowed through the fence to the Pattersons' place."

"Bulldozer?" Nina asked.

"One of your bulls," Lance explained.

"He's trying to breed old man Patterson's cows. You know how pissed Mr. Patterson got the last time. Thought you'd want to know," Stan continued.

"Damn," he cursed under his breath. He'd be glad when the crusty old rancher found a buyer for his place. A frown turned his lips downward but just as quickly they curved upward. "Seems like that bull and I had the same idea." His gaze swept over her. "Hold that thought until I get back."

If he thought she would twiddle her thumbs until he . . .

He swiftly lowered his mouth to hers. His kiss was quick, but it had the desired effect. So maybe she would have a few fantasies about him while she waited for him to return. "Hurry," she said as he reached the door of her darkroom.

Desire flared in his eyes. "I'll shoot the damn bull if I have to."

She laughed, knowing he wouldn't. When she stepped to the back door, Stan took off his hat and crushed it between his large hands. "Ma'am." He nodded.

Nina barely had time to return his greeting before they were gone. With a sigh of regret, she turned back to her darkroom, eager to start developing her pictures since sex was now out of the question. But Lance had told her not to lose her train of thought. She frowned. How did he know what she was thinking? Was it that obvious? She smiled wryly. Probably.

She poured chemicals into the appropriate developing trays and went about the process of turning negatives into pictures. She felt like a mother giving birth. Excited over the thought that what she'd waited for was about to come forth. Would it be like she expected? Would other people see what she saw?

Some people might say she was crazy taking her work so seriously, but it was much more than just taking pictures. Her camera was an extension of herself. Taking her pictures was who she was and she couldn't not take pictures even if her life depended on it.

She held her breath as the first negatives began to develop. Lance riding the horse. Sweat trickling down the sides of his face. She drew in a shaky breath. Lance with his shirt off. She'd been so right knowing he would take a great picture. He was the quintessential cowboy.

She worked steadily, developing negative after negative and hanging the pictures on a cord to dry, slowing only when she came to the pictures of when they went riding. Lance with his shirt off, then his pants, wearing only briefs. Strong, lean thighs. Her mouth began to water.

The next pictures caught her off guard. For a moment she'd forgotten he'd taken the ones of her. She looked wanton, her hand touching her bare breast, eyes half closed as she waited for her lover. Then completely naked, legs open in invitation.

Her nipples tightened, and her hands shook as she hung each picture. She didn't notice the door opening just enough that someone slipped inside, but she heard the intake of breath and whirled around, heart pounding.

"Lance, you scared me!" When he didn't speak, she wondered if something was wrong. "Lance?"

"My God, these are magnificent."

He reached toward the hanging pictures, but she grabbed his hand. "They're . . . uh . . . still wet." And they weren't the only things feeling a little damp. When she realized she was still holding his hand, she let go and took a step back, but because of the small size of the room, she couldn't go very far.

"That's some camera you have there," he said.

She looked at the pictures of her touching herself, partially nude, just a strip of scarlet panties, then completely nude. "Maybe they're ready to come down now." The small space was closing in on her.

This time he grabbed her hand, pulling her against him as he turned her around. Her back fit snugly against his front, against the bulge in his pants.

"You're so damn sultry looking. Like a woman begging for hot, dirty sex." He cupped her breasts, his thumbs scraping across her nipples. She almost groaned when he moved his hands away, but it was only to move to the hem of her T-shirt. His hands caressed her bare midriff before slowly pulling the shirt up and over her head.

"I like the one where you're touching your breasts," he said close to her ear. His hot breath tickled her neck. He unfastened her bra and let it fall to the floor. Taking her hands in his, he brought them up to her breasts.

She drew in a sharp breath as her palms caressed her sensitive nipples. The ache inside her grew, burning.

"Don't stop," he told her as his hands moved lower, unfastening each silver button on her jeans. "Tell me what you're feeling as you touch yourself."

"My breasts are throbbing."

"Squeeze your nipples. Roll them between your finger and thumb."

She hesitated.

He was in the process of pushing her pants down, but as if he sensed she'd stopped, so did he.

"Do it," he whispered. "Don't ever be ashamed or embarrassed because you find pleasure with your body."

She squeezed, gasping as the tingles shot over her abdomen and settled between her legs.

"That's it." He shoved her jeans over her hips, her thong following.

She kicked out of them and stood in the middle of her darkroom completely naked, touching herself in a way that she'd never touched herself when someone else was in the room, and she felt damn good doing it.

He turned her around until she faced him. "God, you're so fucking beautiful with the red light glowing around you."

He knelt in front of her. Slowly, he slid his hands up her legs. She closed her eyes, letting the pleasure wash over her as his hands caressed her ankles, up her calves, all the way to her thighs.

"Spread your legs." He nudged her legs open. "That's it," he breathed, the softness of his breath against her curls causing her to whimper. "You like that?" Before she could answer, he was blowing softly across her sex again.

"Yes," she said. Tremors of pleasure erupted inside her.

He stroked the inside of her thighs. "What else would you like me to do?"

A blaze of heat engulfed her. "Taste me," she whispered, but he heard and parted her lips.

She grabbed his shoulders to steady herself as his tongue found her sex and glided over it. Her whimpers turned to cries as the ache inside her grew. He sucked her into his mouth while his finger slipped inside her.

"Ahh, God, Lance. Please, don't stop." She couldn't think; she couldn't breathe. Yes, this was good. So damn good. "Oh . . . yes . . . I'm coming . . . oh, damn . . . it feels . . . ahhh." Spasms of pleasure wracked her body.

She couldn't say when his mouth moved away from her, but she was vaguely aware of hearing the tearing of a foil packet and then he was sliding inside her as she leaned against the wall for support. She grabbed his shoulders as he filled her. The heat began to build again. He brought her legs up and she wrapped them around his waist. He slid deeper. She heard his groan, but she was already lost in her own haze of passion.

Her body tightened as another orgasm convulsed over her. Lance growled from low in his throat, his body jerking forward. Their ragged breathing filled the tiny space.

This was what sex was all about, she thought to herself. Odd that in all her years of living, she'd never experienced this heady rush of such exquisite gratification.

Nine

Later that night, Nina carefully rolled over and eased from
Lance's bed. As she stood, she stretched her arms high in
the air. It felt good to be alive. Grabbing one of Lance's
shirts from his closet, she slipped her arms into the sleeves
and buttoned the two middle buttons.

Making love with him had been hot, and for the first
time in her life she felt complete. Sleeping curled up against
his warmth had been pure heaven.

With a deep sigh trailing after her, she padded softly toward the door, but halfway there, something on the floor
caught her eye. Frowning, she bent to pick it up. Her hand
closed over the crinkled cellophane.

She straightened, her gaze slowly moving over the man
sleeping in the bed. Could she be that wrong about him?
Was he trying to scare her away? Or seduce the ranch from
her? Scattering signs there was a ghost in the house or
sweet-talking his way into her life until he was married to
her?

He groaned and turned onto his side. Lazy lids opened to
stare at her. "I miss you."

She crumpled the cellophane in her hand and smiled. She

was being foolish. Lance's character was exactly as it appeared and nothing more.

"I haven't gone anywhere," she told him.

"You're not lying next to me." His gaze slowly trailed over her. "You look better in my shirt than I do," he commented.

"And I'm starved. We skipped dinner."

"You're right." He charged from the bed, coming straight at her in all his naked glory, and grabbed her.

She screamed but threw her arms around his neck as laughter bubbled out of her. "I'm hungry," she said, moaning when he nuzzled her neck.

He swatted her bottom. "I suppose we have to eat if we want to keep up our strength." He strolled back to the bed and scooped up his jeans. "I'll meet you in the kitchen."

Damn, he was magnificent to watch. Every muscle rippled. With a sigh, she went to the kitchen, tossing the wrapper in the trash. Who was to say that Lance didn't have a sweet tooth, too?

She searched the refrigerator until she found the ingredients for omelets. By the time he joined her, she had it all on the counter, ready to put together. He slid a bowl closer and began cracking eggs one at a time. She glanced his way, wondering what he was thinking. Her gaze moved downward until it reached his jeans. Okay, so maybe she didn't have to wonder. It was nice to know she had that effect on him.

After they'd eaten, they slipped out to the back porch and sat in the double-seated rocker. It was late, the darkness enveloping them. She inhaled, drawing in the fresh country air as she leaned against him. Yes, it would be really easy staying here after the three years were up.

"What are you thinking?" he asked, his voice breaking into the silence.

"That I'm beginning to like your country air."

"Told you so."

She could feel his grin without looking up.

Time passed as they sat there. Maybe she was falling in love with the land. She had a feeling she was falling for more than the land. Could love happen this fast? A sudden breeze sent cold shivers down her spine.

"Cold?"

Cold, apprehensive . . . and needing time alone to sort through her feelings. She uncurled herself from his warmth. "It's been a long day. I think I'll go up to my room." As if he knew she needed time by herself, he stood, lightly kissing her on the forehead.

"See you in the morning."

"Night," she said and slipped back inside.

But when she got to the top of the stairs, she noticed the door to her grandfather's room was ajar. She reached to close it but opened it instead and flipped the light switch. Light flooded the room. Her gaze swept the area. Everything looked as it had when she was up here earlier. Except the peppermints were on the desk and there were wrappers on the floor. She quickly flipped off the light and shut the door.

Once inside her room, she turned the lock and leaned against the door. "I do not believe in ghosts, I do not believe in ghosts, I do not believe in ghosts." She checked the lock again. "Yeah, right, like that will keep a vapor-filled specter out of my room."

Okay, either someone was trying to drive her crazy or her grandfather's ghost was hanging around. That was the only explanation. She'd heard people talk of . . . dead people not being able to let go, but she'd always brushed it off as vivid imaginations.

She laughed, but it sounded shaky.

"There are no such things as ghosts," she said in a loud, commanding voice, as if to prove to herself that she wasn't afraid of repercussions. Lord, she hoped there were no such things as spirits. She couldn't see herself living with a ghost for the next three years.

But she couldn't live with the other explanation, either: that Lance was behind some elaborate scheme so he could get the ranch—one way or another. Of course he wasn't. Hadn't he told her that money wasn't that important?

What the hell was he doing? Lance leaned against one of the cedar posts that braced the back porch. He felt as if he were stepping off into something he knew nothing about. Sure, Nina was fun to be around. He felt comfortable with her. That is, when he wasn't panting after her like a dog in heat. Hell, she probably thought he was trying to seduce the ranch out from under her or worse.

He stepped off the porch and walked out to the barn. The moon was bright enough that he didn't need any other light. Besides, he knew every inch of this ranch like the back of his hand. His horse whinnied when he stepped inside. He ambled over to Biscuit's stall and rubbed her forehead.

"Go to sleep, girl," he whispered, gave her one last pat, and left the barn.

Once outside, he took a deep, cleansing breath. His gaze strayed to the house and up to the second floor. Her light was off. Was she already asleep or lying there, thinking about him?

He smiled, remembering the darkroom and seeing the pictures he'd taken. He wasn't too bad, but then, he'd had a great subject. He got a hard-on thinking about her lying back against the rock, her eyes filled with passion, legs open, beckoning him to come closer.

He shook his head, drawing in a deep breath. Walking around hadn't helped clear his head. Hell, he wanted her again.

There was only one way he would ever have her and just

the thought of what he had to do scared the hell out of him, but there was no way around it.

His gaze moved over the land in front of him, and a feeling of peace calmed his edginess. Damn, he loved this place as much as Pete had. With heavy steps, he trudged up to the house, dreading what he had to do, but it was the only way he could prove to Nina he didn't want her because she owned the ranch.

It was time he bought his own spread and left the only place he'd ever cared about. The money he'd saved, and the money he could make if he posed naked, would be just enough for a down payment on the Patterson ranch. Damn, he was going to be the laughingstock of Silver Gulch but he had to have more money to make this work.

"I'll pose for your magazine," Lance said.

Nina almost jumped out of her skin when he spoke from behind her. She whirled around. "Don't you ever warn people you're right behind them? You could kill someone." Oh, Lord, had she just uttered those words? She didn't really think he would intentionally scare anyone to death.

He twisted his hat in his hands and looked everywhere except her face. "Exactly how much money would I get to pose for your magazine?"

Was he serious? She studied him. He looked serious. He'd just about destroyed his hat by crushing it between his hands, and he was shifting his weight from one foot to the other. Yeah, she had a feeling he was dead serious.

Damn, she'd thought he'd be different. His values had made a deep U-turn.

She squared her chin. Isn't this what she'd wanted, though? From the minute she'd laid eyes on him, she knew he'd make a great centerfold. She should be happy. Yeah, she felt like jumping for fucking joy.

Get over it, she told herself. This was business and she never let her personal life interfere and she wouldn't this time. "A centerfold gets more." She named a figure. "Will that be sufficient?"

He nodded. "When can we get started?"

"I can have a crew . . ."

His face took on a bright rosy hue. "Does there have to be a crew?"

Why was he doing this? He certainly didn't act like someone who wanted to pose naked for a magazine layout. Was there some reason he needed the money? She knew what her grandfather had paid him so surely he couldn't be hurting that much.

Nina didn't want to face the truth and she knew it. Drew had squandered money that should've helped her mother. Most of the men she'd photographed had dollar signs in their eyes. Lance was no different.

Then why the hell did she feel embarrassed for him? It was crazy, but she did. "I can do the shoot without a crew." They could touch up any flaws. Besides, if she did most of the shoot outside it would look more natural.

"Tomorrow?" Could his face get any redder? "Are you sure this is what you want to do?" she asked, to make certain.

"I'll meet you here at eight in the morning."

"Tomorrow at eight," she confirmed.

He jammed his crumpled hat on his head, mumbled something about getting back to work, and strode toward the barn like she had a contagious disease and he hadn't been vaccinated.

Something was going on. She wasn't sure what, but Lance had acted really odd. She had a feeling tomorrow would be a very interesting day.

Ten

Lance was stiff. Nina had never seen a man this stiff. It was very aggravating. Where was the naturalness? But then, he hadn't really been posing the other day when she'd snapped his picture. She drew in a deep breath.

"Just relax. Pretend I'm not even here." She zoomed in on his face. Oh, yeah, pure terror, that would really turn women on. It wouldn't be so bad, but he was still fully dressed. It wasn't like there was anyone out here in the middle of nowhere. "Lance?"

"Yeah!" He jerked his attention to her.

She set the camera down and he visibly relaxed. "Why are you doing this? If you need money . . ."

"No. I don't want your money unless I've earned it." He straightened from the tree. It was supposed to have been a casual pose—it wasn't.

She had a feeling she wouldn't get any more out of him than what she had right now unless she could make him relax. She boosted herself up on a rock, her camera beside her.

Damn it, she shouldn't take pity on him. He was doing it

for the money, no matter what he said. But she did feel a twinge of something.

Get over it, Nina. You're a professional and you can get him past his nervousness.

"Tell me about the ranch, the first time you saw it," she said, changing the subject.

He leaned back against the tree as he looked at the land around him: the gently rising hills, the towering oaks, tall cedars, and scruffy mesquite trees.

A slight curving upward of his lips told her he'd forgotten she was there as he let the breathtaking beauty of the landscape wash over him. She picked up her camera and snapped the first picture.

"I fell in love with it that first day. I think that's why Pete hired a green kid as a ranch hand."

She continued to snap pictures as he talked. This was what she looked for when doing a layout. He raised his hat, ran his hand through his hair, and put it back on his head. A simple motion but so damn sexy it curled her toes.

"Unbutton your shirt."

He looked startled for a moment, but then his hands moved to the buttons and began undoing them one at a time.

She smiled. "Do you know how damn sexy you look right now?" She snapped his bashful look. The women would eat that one up. "Your chest is rock solid. No one will be able to resist it."

"Compared to the professionals?"

"Even better." She slipped off the rock and moved past him until she was behind the tree. Sure enough, he peeked around the old oak and she took his picture. He raised an eyebrow because she'd tricked him and she got that one as well.

It was a little harder getting him to lose his jeans. Longer to get him to relax. As he lost each article of clothing, she grew hotter, not sure if she would last through the shoot.

They moved to the river and she talked him into losing his boots and hat, then walking out into the water. She snapped him exploding to the surface, raining droplets of water everywhere. When he stepped from the river and back to the bank, his briefs were plastered to his skin and she had no doubt he'd been watching her as well.

"Take off your briefs and lie down," she managed to tell him.

He hesitated, then removed the last of his clothes. He looked resigned. She couldn't send pictures to Mica that looked as if he was forced into doing the shoot.

She snapped some more pictures, knowing these wouldn't work. She had a plan, though. "I love how you look without a stitch on. Sexy as hell. It makes me so frigging hot." She set the camera down, removed a rubber band, and shook out her hair. Next, she pulled her cotton shirt over her head. His eyes widened and his nostrils flared. All that covered her breasts was a wispy piece of white silk.

She picked up her camera. This was what she wanted to capture on film. The look of a man ready for sex . . . needing sex. She snapped a few more pictures, then set her camera down and strolled over to him. "Raise your leg and bend the other one just slightly." She swallowed past the lump in her throat as she positioned him.

Resist, her mind screamed. She was the type who didn't resist very much of anything. She stroked his length, her hands trembling.

He quickly sat up and unsnapped her bra, letting it fall to his thigh before she could blink. God, had he practiced that move as a teen and perfected it as an adult?

"I wanted to see you," he rasped.

She straightened and went back to her camera. Her legs

barely held her as she snapped picture after picture. Lord, he had a nice body.

After a few more pictures he stood and ambled toward her while she snapped even more. He took the camera from her and set it on a rock.

"I want you," he said. "My body aches to see you completely naked, to touch the softness of your skin." He unfastened her jeans and inched them over her hips.

She kicked out of them. Her thong followed. She longed for him to take her into his arms, their bodies melding against each other, but he stepped back instead, his gaze moving slowly over her. It was all she could do to breathe.

"Nice." He brushed his fingers across her nipples.

She reached out, wanting to do a little of her own exploring. She touched one nipple, circling it before scraping her fingernail lightly across the nub. He drew in a sharp breath. Oh, so he liked that, did he?

Leaning forward, she flicked her tongue across one nipple, then the other, while her hands roamed his body. He quivered when she caressed his erection. Suddenly, she was filled with a sense of power, of being the one in control.

She moved to her knees in front of him and licked up him, then back down. Nice and slow.

"Damn! Woman, you're driving me to the edge."

A wicked smile curved her lips. She liked the idea that she could push him that far. And if she nudged him a little more? What would he do then? She was about to find out. She took him into her mouth, swirling her tongue around the head of his cock, then sucking him deeper inside her mouth.

He gasped, grabbing her head. "Son of a . . ."

She closed her eyes, reveling in the knowledge she was giving him so much pleasure. Not that she wasn't enjoying herself, too. She loved the feel of him inside her mouth, the texture and smoothness against her tongue.

All too soon he was reaching beneath her arms and pulling her up, his mouth covering hers, his hands sliding over her body, cupping her butt, pulling her closer.

Through passion-glazed eyes, she watched him move away, grab his pants, and pull a condom out of the pocket. She slid her hands over her breasts, then down to grasp her thighs. Her body cried for release that only Lance could give.

He turned her around, nudging her to bend over, entering her from behind. She gasped as he slid inside the heat of her body. Not her favorite position, but as hot as she was . . .

He moved his hands to her sex and began to caress her with one hand while the other hand moved to her breast. He squeezed her nipple, rubbing the hard nub between his thumb and forefinger. She cried out, shaking as an orgasm flooded her entire body. He jerked, groaning as he followed right behind her.

For a moment they didn't move; then he eased from her body, turning her until she was resting in his arms. "I don't think I would ever get tired of making love to you." He kissed the top of her head.

Her heart nearly exploded inside her chest. Funny how a few words could make her feel so alive.

"Yeah, he certainly couldn't get enough of me, all right."

Nina turned from the window after watching him drive away. She'd finished the shoot a few days ago and Lance had made himself scarce. At first, she'd thought he was embarrassed.

There was always some excuse. Things needed to be done on the ranch that only he could do. His excuses had begun to run thin. And the last straw? He'd taken to sleeping in the bunkhouse.

She'd given him a check for the photo shoot, but he'd only crammed it into his pocket and mumbled a thank-you before taking off once more. What was wrong? What had she done?

She'd have her answers today. Except the day had dragged by and still no Lance even though she'd left word she wanted to talk to him.

By nightfall, she could spit nails she was so mad. She paced up and down the porch, waiting for him to return. One way or another, she'd have it out with him.

She froze when she saw the headlights coming down the road. Lance's pickup. Rather than go to the bunkhouse, as had been his norm, he passed it and drove straight to the house. She stiffened her spine, not saying a word as he climbed out and walked to where she stood.

Just looking at the way he walked, the way he smiled at her made her realize just how much she'd missed him. How much she cared about him. That probably pissed her off more than anything.

"Hello, stranger." Damn, she'd wanted to play it cool, as if she didn't care, but her words were hard and crisp. Anyone with half a brain would know she was ticked off.

"Hi."

His gaze moved slowly over her, warming every spot he touched. It was all she could do not to fling her arms around his neck when he pulled her against him. She felt his sigh, the kiss he brushed across the top of her head. Some of her anger left.

"I quit," he spoke softly.

It took a minute for his words to sink into her brain. He'd spoken the words almost as if they were an endearment.

She reared her head back and glared at him. "You what?"

"I quit."

She shoved away and stormed to the end of the porch. He quit. What the hell did that mean? She whirled around, hands on hips.

"You quit?"

He nodded.

Betrayed. Of course. Why hadn't she realized this would happen? Lance couldn't stand the thought that she'd been given the ranch. He'd posed so he could leave town, have a new start somewhere else, and . . .

"I bought the Patterson ranch," he said.

"You bought the ranch next to this one?"

He nodded. "Well, me and the bank. I was able to scrape together enough, along with the check I got from"—he downed his head, cleared his throat, and met her gaze again—"from posing and what I had in savings."

She shook her head. "I don't understand. Why?"

"Because I like you—a lot. I know you've had your doubts about me. That I wanted the ranch more than you. I figured the only way we were going to have any kind of a chance was if I bought my own place. I didn't want you to think I was seducing the ranch out from under you."

"Pfft . . . I'd never, ever . . . I mean . . ."

"It doesn't matter now. The Patterson place is a nice spread." He grinned. "You won't even have to worry about me getting mad when the bull jumps the fence."

But she liked having Lance at her ranch. He was right, though. If he had his own place, she'd have no doubts about his intentions toward her. She had no doubts he'd be hanging around—because he was interested in her.

"You don't have to move out tonight, do you?" she asked. "I mean, it's getting late and there aren't any streetlights or anything. I'd hate for you to get lost."

His grin widened. Before she could say another word, he'd scooped her up in his arms and was carrying her inside. She had a feeling they'd be doing a lot of sleepovers.

Her glance fell to the floor when the light bounced off a piece of cellophane. She sighed. Just her, Lance, and her grandfather's ghost. As long as Grandpa stayed out of her bedroom, she'd be quite content.

She wondered if she should mention to Lance that she hadn't sent any of the pictures to Mica that bared his bottom half. There were just some things she refused to share with other women.

But when Lance set her feet on the floor and lowered his mouth to hers, there was only one thing on her mind.

Tomorrow would be soon enough.

COME TO A
BAD END

Dianne Castell

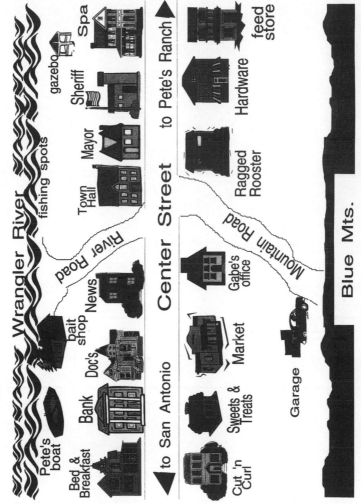

Silver Gulch

Wrangler River

fishing spots

Spa

gazebo

Sheriff

Mayor

Town Hall

River Road

Pete's boat

bait shop

News

Doc's

Bank

Bed & Breakfast

to Pete's Ranch

feed store

Hardware

Ragged Rooster

Center Street

Gabe's office

Mountain Road

Market

Garage

Sweets & Treats

Cut 'n Curl

to San Antonio

Blue Mts.

One

How the hell could a spa get a sleepy little town like Silver Gulch, Texas, so totally pissed off . . . at least the male half? John Snow sat behind the sheriff's desk as Rusty Pierce growled, "I'm telling you right now you got to close the place down. Every man here's had enough of this Lillie June person and her fancy ideas. My Betty's done taken me off fritters and cream gravy, burns smelly candles night and day, and feng shuied the damn chicken coop."

Lucky Freemont added, "My Dorothy's doing yoga, bending herself around like some pretzel, and dishing up Special K for breakfast. I'm here to tell you the only thing special is that it tastes like crap."

John stood and held up his hand to stop more complaints. "Okay, okay, I get the picture. I'll try and sweet-talk Mizz June into making some changes, but opening a spa is not against the law."

"Appeal to her feminine side and get her to change the place back to a hotel," Rusty added.

Lucky Freemont hooked his thumbs into the waistband of his jeans, doing the *I'm a tough cowboy* routine. "Sheriff

Parker would have put an end to this. He picked a god-awful time to go on vacation. We want things back to the way it was before June showed up. You hear that dang hammering and sawing next door? Bet her granddaddy is flipping in his grave with her turning the Silver Bullet Hotel into the Silver Springs Spa and Healing Center. If we're in need of healing we go to Doc Shelton's or grab a bottle of whiskey and drown what's ailing us."

Rusty stomped his way to the door and left, his cronies following as deputy Jimmy Morris came inside. The door swung shut and Jimmy slid his weathered gray Stetson to the back of his head and grinned, making him look years younger than fifty. "Let me guess, the band of grumpy-ass men is here about the spa. It's all the talk at the Ragged Rooster."

John paced the office. "Why can't everyone just get along till Parker returns? I'm not exactly the favorite son, and I don't need to be stirring up more problems."

Jimmy hung his hat on the rack. "People in town holding a grudge has more to do with your daddy embezzling that money from the bank than you personally. Even if it did happen fifteen years ago and your grandmother paid every cent back, folks don't forget the name Snow no matter who wears it. And as for Parker, he doesn't handle squat. He just ignores problems hoping they go away by themselves or someone else does the work for him."

He nodded at the calendar on the wall. "You've been here two weeks now, how much longer is that police chief in Dallas making you do penance filling in as sheriff before he gives you back your cop job there?"

Jimmy tried to stifle a laugh but didn't succeed. "Damn, boy, did you really hold that guy out the thirteenth-floor of a Dallas hotel window till he fessed up to where he hid the money he conned out of those senior citizens? I'd think they'd give you a medal, not toss your fanny back to the Gulch."

John paced. He was afraid this would happen . . . not the part about him and the thirteenth floor and people finding out or even the good citizens not treating him all that great, but Lillie June. She was the real problem with her blazing hair and dancing eyes that he had to keep hell-and-away from. "Being here is more about me getting it on with the mayor's twin daughters than the con." He froze. Oh, shit. Did he just say that out loud? He should think before opening his big mouth.

Jimmy's brows arched to meet his receding hairline. "Twins? Didn't know about twins. You sure are full of surprises."

John ran a hand through his hair. "Look, I didn't know they were sisters. They don't look alike and I sure as hell didn't realize their daddy was the mayor till one sister got serious and started picking china patterns, the other sister flipped out, and there was a fight in Tiffany's that cost me five grand in smashed dinnerware. I'm a paper plate kind of guy, dammit—made that clear right up front. The girls got sent to Europe till this blows over and I got sent here."

Jimmy laughed and slunk into an oak office chair. "Twins? The mayor? What a hoot. Nothing like that happens around here."

"Thank God." John rubbed the back of his neck where his headaches always started when he thought of the twin fiasco. "I'd better do something about the spa before Rusty calls Dallas. His brother-in-law as chief of police sucks and I sure as hell don't need any more trouble, especially women trouble." And Lillie June had trouble written all over her. What a babe.

John snagged his Stetson from the coat rack and tramped across the worn hardwood floor to the front door. "Ah, fuck."

"I'd forget about that if you want your cop job back."

"Mizz June's not my type. I like 'em tall and blond, not petite with red hair." He turned back to Jimmy. "Think it's naturally red?"

"Not your type, remember, sheriff?"

John frowned and nodded. "Right. Got it. Don't know what came over me."

Like hell he didn't know! What came over him was a big fat lie. Blondes weren't his thing; redheads were, especially ones with green eyes and freckles on their cheeks—the very reason he'd stayed far away from that damn spa and Lillie June until now. Did there have to be a now?

Jimmy got his own hat. "I'm coming with you."

"The spa's next door. I won't get lost and I've busted everything from meth labs to dognapping rings. I can handle a spa."

"Meth labs don't have curls down to their waist and have you wondering about naturally red."

John closed the door behind them and pulled his hat down on his head to shade his eyes from the late July sun. "I'm thinking your tagging along has nothing to do with me and something to do with that gal who's been setting up the spa for Lillie June before she arrived on the scene. What's her name? Belinda." John glanced at Jimmy. "She has nice . . . eyes. Hell, go for it."

"Her name's Melinda and I don't remember how to go for anything but a beer."

"It'll come to you." The hotel used to be painted mudhole brown with a dandelion yard and boards for windows. Now it was slate blue and framed with Texas bluebonnets and yellow columbine. Water splashed in a white stone fountain as they entered the picket gate and stepped onto the porch. John started to knock but Melinda bustled out the door lugging two bags. She stumbled into him.

"Oh, I'm so sorry," she said, looking flustered. "I've got

to get these to the post office before it closes. We're running a special to attract the men in the area to the spa."

John took the bags and handed them to a speechless, blushing, staring Jimmy, who seemed mesmerized by Melinda's pink T-shirt with "I ❤ Silver Springs Spa," or maybe it was what was under that shirt that had him staring. Jimmy hadn't forgotten squat. John said, "I'm sure the deputy will be glad to lend a hand with this, ma'am."

"Me?" Jimmy muttered as Melinda said, "I can manage on my own."

John gave his I-know-best smile. "Ah, but we're here to serve and you have fifteen minutes to get the mail in. The post office waits for no one."

That propelled Melinda into action and she grabbed Jimmy's arm. "Time's a wasting, deputy, get a move on."

John watched the two hustle off down Center Street. It was not exactly love at first sight but a good start. And when he turned back and saw Lillie June framed in the doorway, he knew that was a start of something too, and it wasn't good.

He hadn't seen her up close, only walking around town. Watching her from a distance had driven him crazy enough: the sway of her hips, the tilt of her head, her hair—incredible hair. Today it was long and loose, nearly reaching her white skirt. She wore a green blouse that dipped in the front, showing a hint of cleavage. He didn't need cleavage. He needed a buttoned collar and a sack over her head. Lillie June was the temptation of both twins rolled into one dynamite package.

He swept off his hat to give the appearance of doing something besides ogling as she said, "And what brings the town sheriff to my spa? Lessons on meditation? A book on nutrition? The men in town complaining about my evil ways of leading their women astray?"

He followed her into the cool hallway, the plants and

adobe walls a welcome relief from the blast furnace outside, the scent of lavender and something else . . . peppermint? . . . in the air. "I'm here on business."

"To get rid of your headache?"

He paused. "You know I have a headache?"

"Clouded eyes, drawn face, wrinkles." She touched his forehead. "Here."

He felt dizzy, off center and he never felt that way before. He doubted it came from the headache but thought it had a lot to do with Lillie June.

She continued, "You look the way I used to when I worked for an advertising firm in Chicago." She held up a jar she'd been carrying. "A touch of this new lavender ointment at the temples helps, and you can sit in a chair and let me work on your neck and shoulders."

Another touch from Lillie June would be like eating a second cheese doodle—he'd want more, lots more, and not be satisfied till he had the whole damn bag. He stepped back. "The women in town are different since you came here and the men like things the way they were before."

"Well, of course they do." A frown pulled at her full lips, which he'd wanted to kiss since the first time he saw her getting out of her red Jeep with the name of the spa on the side door. "Most of the women in Silver Gulch assume full care of family and home—what man wouldn't like that?—but they need a little time to themselves."

"All I'm asking is for you to soft-pedal your ideas, let the men adjust."

"Or maybe I should just turn this place back into a hotel?"

"That works. You can sell some makeup and perfume on the side, like one of those boutique places in the city. Men around here like the women to look nice for them."

"I wasn't serious, Sheriff Snow." She parked her left hand on her shapely hip, where he suddenly wanted to park his hand. "My spa isn't just about looks. It's doing things differently to feel better and live longer and stay active and healthy, and the men around here would realize that if they'd give this place a chance."

"Well, I can tell you right now the men part of your plan is never going to happen and we're all living fine around here so you can—"

"Pack up my snake oil and go back where I came from?" Her eyes went beady.

"Okay, the snake part might be a little over the top but—"

"*Might?*" Her voice rose to a screech, bringing other women into the hallway.

Outnumbered about twenty to one. He didn't want a confrontation; he just wanted the men off his back and Lillie to . . . go away. "All your creams and candles and whatever else you have here are quick ways to make a buck, lots of bucks. Like potions that get bald men to grow hair, water that makes people feel young. If folks want to feel better they should go to a doctor, a trained professional, not—"

"A charlatan?"

"I didn't say that."

"You were thinking it."

Guilty.

"You arrogant ass." The women applauded. "I've gone to school for aromatherapy, massage therapy, nutrition, yoga, and a host of other modern health solutions for men and women. The men don't get it and that includes you."

"Or we see through your scam. In Dallas I do criminal investigations and—"

"Now I'm a criminal?" The women hissed and booed, and a wadded-up towel went flying by and grazed his head.

"You're a glorified con artist." A little strong but the men would hear about this battle and that would appease them for a while. And, since Lillie June looked as if she'd like to punch out his lights, there's no way he'd ever get together with her.

This was good. He'd just gotten rid of two problems at once and that beat the hell out of a dish fight at Tiffany's. Except Lillie June was such a delicious problem.

She pointed to the door. "Out!" She closed her eyes for a second. "See what you've done? You made me raise my voice and you're ruining my karma."

"I'm the sheriff—I can ruin whatever I want." He turned for the door. "Good day."

"It damn well was until you showed up, John Snow," she yelled after him, then moaned, "I haven't ranted in two years and here I am sounding like a blasted—"

"Fishwife? And you do it very well." He glanced back. "Try not to bilk the good ladies of Silver Gulch out of too much money. This isn't a rich town, and there are no hard facts that spas do anything except make people poorer."

He closed the door behind him, narrowly missing the jar she'd been holding as it flew through the air and crashed against the wall, shooting that karma Mizz Nuts-and-Berries was so worried about right to hell.

He considered going for a beer at the Rooster to celebrate how he'd handled the situation but his head throbbed. He should be feeling better, dammit. Lillie June was out of his life and that's exactly what he wanted, right?

Lillie slammed the door shut, spun around, and faced the women gathered behind her. She hadn't been this fuming angry since she was aced out of a promotion at Liming and Rodgers two years ago. She'd gone to the spa to get over it, dragged her secretary Melinda with her and neither ever went back to the office. Lillie pictured a thousand doves flying from her soul, leaving peace and harmony behind and obliterating all thoughts of John Snow. "Who the hell does that son of a bitch think he is?" So much for flying doves and harmony.

"For starters he's Mr. January in the Dallas police department's calendar," Betty Pierce said, with a laugh, the other women looking at her in astonishment. "Hey, it was for a good cause, to raise scholarship money for the Dallas inner-city kids, so I bought a calendar . . . just to help a charity. But I got to tell you January is my favorite month. Oh, Lordy." She did the hand against the forehead fake swoon. "You should see that man with his shirt unbuttoned. A sprinkle of dark curly hair, great muscles, six-pack abs to die for. I'll bring the calendar in for you all to see."

The gals who'd gathered in the hallway giggled, but not one protested Betty bringing in Mr. January. Lillie said, "So, John Snow's a sucker for charity, is he? Well, that's probably the only thing he has in his favor."

Betty snorted, "Honey, that man is dangerously handsome, on and off a calendar. Weren't you watching him stroll around here like he owned the place?"

"This is *my* place."

"But he's such a hunk."

Lillie took the towel from the floor and whipped up the broken jar, feeling disgusted with herself for putting a dent in the new wall. "He's arrogant and pigheaded and narrow-minded. His hair's too long, and he thinks he's God's gift to the world and all women should fall at his feet."

"Well I'll be—you *were* watching," Betty said, with a tease.

Lillie dropped the pieces in the trash. "Just an observation, nothing more."

If only that were true. Why did the most handsome man she'd seen in years also have to be the biggest jerk in the universe? She'd broken up with the second biggest jerk a year ago. Did that make her a jerk magnet? Something she inherited from her mother, with five failed marriages, and no doubt the reason marriage held no appeal for Lillie. Why couldn't she have inherited her mother's five-foot ten-inch pencil-thin frame instead?

Lillie checked her watch and shoved John Snow and all men from her brain. She had another situation to deal with right now. "Well, ladies, that's it for the day. Soon we'll have the place open for overnight guests, and with the steam room and whirlpools and saunas already in place it shouldn't be long. I have a meeting so I'll see you all tomorrow. Remember to do deep-breathing exercises." She demonstrated the slow in-and-out breathing. "Do them before you sleep and, remember, good sex makes for good circulation, keeps you looking young."

If that were true she should look about ninety by now. How long had it been since she'd followed her own advice? And why did the only man to get her thinking about circulation have to be John Snow?

Lillie followed the women outside, most from Silver Gulch and some from the surrounding towns. She'd helped a few with arthritis creams, two with back troubles, and a young mother find how to relax and not stress out over kids. Although all this was good she needed the male half of the town to sign up at the spa. The revenue would keep the place solvent till she attracted customers farther away.

But today the lord-high sheriff showed up and added to the antispa campaign. Now the only way to get men here would be to hogtie them to her Jeep and drag them one by one.

She passed the neat, white frame building that was Gabe Rankin's law office, the man who'd set up this meeting at Sweets 'n Treats with her sisters. Oh, boy. *Sisters.* Nina and Juliet. Lillie's steps slowed and her stomach crunched. What do you say to sisters you didn't know you had till a few months ago? Nice genes? That was really pathetic.

As she pushed open the pink door of the sweet shop, her gaze connected with two women sitting at the little round table in the corner. They looked a bit younger. Sundaes melted in the dishes instead of being eaten, and nervous energy radiated clear across the room. Least she wasn't the only one a wreck over this. All her life she'd wanted someone to connect to as Mother moved from husband to husband, house to house, bank to bank, the accounts getting larger and larger.

Mother first married Drew Maddock and brought Lillie into the world but never repeated the birth experience. No more stretch marks for Mother. Lillie slipped into the wire-backed ice cream parlor chair and smiled. "I guess I'm sister number three."

The sister with curly brown hair down her back smiled in return and held out her hand. "I'm Nina." She nodded at sister number two, with short red hair and green eyes. "This is Juliet and we're both happy to meet you. Offering any family discounts at the spa? We'll be your best customers." She winked and laughed, the awkwardness fading.

Lillie said, "Well, we don't look a lot alike but Juliet and I have the red hair and green eyes and Nina and I wear our hair long, so we think alike." She glanced at the two dishes of ice cream. "And I like hot fudge sundaes without whipped cream, just like you two."

Nina said, "I'm a photographer. Juliet worked in an art gallery."

Lillie added, "And I'm a graphic designer, so we're all artsy-fartsy." She couldn't hold in the sigh. "Why didn't our father—who only came to see me twice in my whole life— at least tell me about you? I always wanted sisters, least he could have done was tell me I had you two."

"Dad didn't visit me at all and Juliet only once," Nina said as she pushed an old book and clipped-together papers across the table. "We definitely got the booby prize in dads.

But we got first prize in Grandpas. Wait till you read this. It's Grandpa Pete's diary that I found at the ranch and receipts that Juliet came across at the Rooster. From what we can piece together our grandparents divorced, and little Drew and Grandma Penelope went back to Connecticut and the country club set. Drew, our Daddy Dear, never had anything to do with Pete till Drew needed money. But the real shocker is that he didn't pay for anything for us—child support, education, you name it. Grandpa Pete picked up the tab. It seems Drew told Grandpa we didn't want anything to do with him."

Lillie's jaw dropped. "But Dad told *me* Grandpa Pete didn't want anything to do with me."

Nina and Juliet nodded in agreement and Juliet said, "That way Drew could skim money from the payments before passing them on, and in Nina's case he never passed anything on, just kept all the money. If we didn't know each other we couldn't compare notes and catch him."

Nina fiddled with a napkin on the tabletop. "The only thing important to Drew Maddock was the happiness of Drew Maddock and that was usually in some woman's bed . . . till that irate sheik found him messing with one of his wives. There wasn't even a funeral."

"Too dangerous. Too many hostile husbands." Juliet shrugged. "And I don't think they even found the body . . . least not all of it."

Lillie eyed the beat-up diary. "What a mess. Wish I'd gotten to know Grandpa Pete. I could have thanked him for what he did, or tried to do."

Juliet said, "This may sound a tad off, but sometimes I do have the feeling Grandpa's spirit is still around the Rooster, like he's with me, watching over me."

Nina sighed. "I get that feeling too. You know, we should do something for Grandpa Pete, like have a memorial of some kind. Everyone liked Pete. It would be a fitting good-bye to a fine man from his long-lost granddaughters. What about a wake at the Rooster? Tomorrow night at eight?"

Lillie nodded. "Great idea. I like it. We'll all chip in for a few kegs of beer and food and do it up right. We'll invite the town. I have a copier at the spa, so I'll make flyers and look around for memorabilia about the town, his life and what he did here. If we can get people talking, I bet they'll have Pete stories and we can get to know Grandpa that way."

Nina held her sisters' hands. "It took a while but finally we're together. Grandpa Pete's girls."

And by the time Lillie left Sweets 'n Treats and her sisters two hours later, she felt more positive than ever that she and Nina and Juliet would always stay in touch and be there for each other no matter where they lived. That's what Grandpa Pete would have wanted. That's why he left them the ranch, the Ragged Rooster, and the old hotel. It brought them together at last. They were family.

The sun set behind a bank of clouds gathering on the horizon as Lillie headed for the spa. Rooms on the top floor were converted into apartments for her and Melinda, with the guest rooms on the second floor. The spa was on the first floor and would be finished soon along with a gazebo and grotto out by the hot spring in the back garden.

She crossed the street, dotted with couples and families out to enjoy the summer evening, and passed in front of the sheriff's office. *Don't look, don't look. John Snow is a jack-ass.* Least that's what her business side said. But her female side made her look anyway. How pathetic to be ruled by hormones and basic lust.

And John Snow was there all right, head on the desk and rubbing the back of his neck. She should just walk on by and that's what he'd want, too, except she could help him with that darn headache. And if she did help, maybe he'd tell the other men and they would change their opinion about the spa and give it a chance. Going to see John was all about advertisement, good public relations, nothing more.

Yeah, right. Who the heck was she was kidding? Public relations, ha! She wanted to get her hands on John Snow and right now any reason would do just fine.

TWO

John's head throbbed. Aspirin had little effect. The door to the office opened and he growled, "Whoever you are, no one's here. Go away."

"In a minute."

Lillie June? What the hell was she doing here? He bolted upright, making his head pound worse than ever. "What do you want?"

"An endorsement."

"From me?"

"At the moment you're the best I've got." She walked toward him, her hair pulled back into a clip, her eyes greener than ever. No headache in the world could keep him from noticing. But she didn't stop at the desk; she went around and stood behind his chair.

He watched her over his shoulder. "You're going to wring my neck for trying to shut your spa down?"

"Tempting as that is, no. I need you to talk." Then he couldn't remember what he intended to say in response because she began rubbing his shoulders and the base of his neck, lessening the ache that was like an ice pick stabbing into his brain.

"I'm going to get rid of your headache because that's what we charlatans do."

His head drooped forward. "Damn, that feels great."

"Your muscles are hard as a rock."

And getting a hell of a lot harder and not the ones in his neck.

"And as payment for this fine treatment you can go over to the Rooster and tell the other men how this helped you and they'll come to the spa, and I won't go bankrupt before the paint dries on the walls."

Except he couldn't walk right now if he wanted to. Telling Lillie to stop wasn't a good idea because his headache was really going away and, God, he liked her hands on him. Warm, firm, pushing into him, and suddenly that's exactly what he wanted to do to her. *Think of something else besides Lillie!* "You should know that a reference from me won't do any good around here. My daddy stole money from the bank years ago. I'm the black sheep by association."

"That's why you decided to become a cop? Compensate for his wrongdoing?"

"Mostly I wanted to drive a car with flashing lights and a siren."

"Is your dad living here in town?"

Town? What town? He couldn't think about anything but Lillie. "He lives in the Hamptons. Wrote *Confessions of a Con,* a *New York Times* best-seller for months. That's why he and Mom are living in the Hamptons." And right now he wished he was visiting them there instead of being tempted beyond all reason by Lillie here.

Enough! He reached around and grabbed her hands. If he got any more turned on he'd implode. Except now he held her slim wrists in his fingers and felt her pulse racing, the rate nearly matching his. Being turned on was tough.

Both of them turned on at the same time was downright dangerous.

He let go and walked around the chair and faced her. He intended to tell her to go away except her eyes darkened to jade. Why didn't she just deck him for trying to close the spa? It would make things so much easier. "What are you really doing here?"

"Drumming up business." Her breasts nearly touched his chest. He could imagine how they'd feel, all firm and round and . . .

"Buy an ad in the paper."

"I did. It flopped." He framed her face in his palms and kissed her warm, sweet lips. Maybe this one simple kiss would be enough to get Lillie June out of his system and he'd stop obsessing over her. Not needing everyone in town to see them and without breaking the kiss, he backed her behind the file cabinet. Except how could he stop kissing a mouth that opened so nicely and didn't suggest he leave at all . . . until he heard the door open and Rusty Pierce call, "Hey, anybody here? John? I brought you a piece of peanut butter pie from the bed-and-breakfast. I have to sneak it because Betty won't make it anymore. She fixes those damn granola bars. A man's gotta have pie and you deserve it since you went head-to-head with that Lillie June gal."

Rusty Pierce, the kissing police! Well, damn. The words were like getting doused with a bucket of cold water, and Lillie must have felt the same way because kissing her was now like kissing a pickle. She stepped away and gave him a we-must-be-nuts look, then tossed her head, smoothed her hair, and strutted around the file cabinet as John followed.

"Hello, Rusty," she said. "Having a nice evening? I sure am. John and I were just necking in the back room. He's a fair kisser but I've had better. See you around."

Rusty gave a rough laugh. "I heard about the scene at

the spa, Lillie June. You were throwing things at John. That sure doesn't lead to necking in the back room."

Lillie opened the door and called over her shoulder, "Believe what you want, but I doubt that John wears Sundance Peach lipstick and he sure is wearing some now."

Crap! John swiped the back of his hand across his mouth to get rid of the lipstick before Rusty turned back and said, "That is some woman. What a first-class pain."

Pain? John could relate. His erection pressed against the zipper of his jeans, his only salvation being that standing behind the sheriff's chair hid his condition. Difficult to convince Rusty that the local sheriff was butting heads with Lillie when he sported the biggest hard-on of his life.

Rusty plopped the pie on the desk. "So, was Mizz June here to tell you she's closing the place down?"

"Not exactly."

"Well, dang. She's a hard nut to crack."

Except *she* wasn't the one with hard nuts!

Rusty added, "You just keep at her, boy—she'll give in. Besides, how can she make it financially? She doesn't have that many clients."

Rusty left and John eyed the bag. He didn't want to be scarfing down pie. He wanted another taste of Lillie and he wanted it to last a hell of a lot longer than a thirty-second kiss on the run that made him hornier than a Dallas traffic jam. Lust rode him hard till he remembered Lillie's "I've had better" comment that referred to his kissing ability.

What was that all about?

His dick shriveled. He was a great kisser, dammit. Ask the twins. They broke dishes over his kisses. How could Lillie June not agree? What was wrong with that woman? What was wrong with him?

Lillie stormed into the spa and tramped her way up the refinished hardwood stairs, past scaffolding, and over paint-splattered tarps. How could she kiss John Snow? Was she completely out of her flipping mind? He wanted her to turn the spa back into a hotel, said she was a quack, a criminal . . . and then she went and kissed him with enough force to suck the Wrangler River dry as dust.

But the sucking was over and done with and wouldn't happen again, especially after that bad-kisser crack. A true stroke of genius on her part, true inspiration . . . even if it was a big fat lie. The important thing was, she needed to keep a clear head and not salivate over John Snow, spa enemy number one. Knocking a man's kissing was a guaranteed way to get rid of him.

She rapped on Melinda's door and got no answer. Where was she? With that Jimmy guy? After a divorce from hell, Melinda did not need another man in her life even though she always thought she did. Well, there'd be no gab session tonight to get Lillie's mind off a certain sheriff. She needed something—*anything*—to divert her thoughts, so she headed for the door at the end of the hallway and took the rickety gritty steps that led to the attic. Cobwebs, spiders, bats, and a hunt for memorabilia were a poor substitute for necking with John Snow.

Melinda said she'd stored junk there that looked too interesting to throw out. Maybe there was stuff about Grandpa Pete up here. A flashlight sat on a wooden barrel next to a milk glass oil lamp. This was her rendition of Chicago girl does old Western attic. Except this Chicago girl would much rather be doing John Snow. *Forget John Snow!*

The place creaked, no doubt caused by the air-conditioning kicking in. Moonlight spilled through the end panes that faced the sheriff's office. She clicked on the flashlight and opened the window, allowing the night breeze to cool the suffocating interior. Tables, chairs, lamps, books cluttered the area, and a humped trunk that looked like something the pioneers dragged across the plains sat in the corner next to a faded rocker with stuffing poking through the seat.

She lifted the trunk lid to newer, neatly folded men's clothes, and the scent of cedar and peppermint. Grandpa Pete's things? She imagined he'd smell of cedar and peppermints—didn't all grandpas? Maybe he lived here for a while. Sadness washed over her. She'd give anything to have known him, a real grandpa, someone who cared, really cared about her. To Mother and her husbands Lillie was an acquisition, something that helped them keep up with the Joneses. Like a Mercedes in the garage: *Look, we have one too!*

Lillie touched a shirt, then picked it up. Something dropped from the pocket, and as she bent to retrieve it she was shoved hard from behind, making her fall headfirst into the rocker.

She screamed and the chair flipped over, taking her into an unplanned somersault. The flashlight skidded to the corner, footsteps raced across the wood floor to the stairs, and from the sounds of stumbling and cursing, the pusher tripped down the last part. Served the bastard right! "Damn you, whoever you are! I hope you got bruises."

Leaning back she put her hand to her chest to keep her heart from beating right out of her body. *Breathe, Lillie, breathe.* Search for your calm place, inner peace, beauty and tranquility. Falling water, a cool stream, her hands around the intruder's neck. She needed to work on this inner-peace thing.

Again running footsteps sounded on the stairs, revving her heart back to panic mode. What the heck? Things like this never happened in Chicago, and Chicago was crime central.

Scurrying over the chair, she spotted a pile of books and prayed the top one was a nice thick copy of *War and Peace.* She stood and swung at the silhouetted figure that crossed in front of her, but he grabbed her arm before she connected. "Lillie?"

Holy Lord, the bad guy knew her name. Terror sliced through her, fogging her brain, and she pushed with all her might but lost her balance and fell against him, sending them both over the trunk. He held her tight and she landed on top of him with a solid *oomph.*

"Let me go! Let me go!" She squirmed and elbowed him in the gut. "I have connections. I know the sheriff."

"Dear God, so do I! Will you hold still!"

She stopped dead, her heart still racing. "John?" Turning in his arms she peered at him through the darkness. "What are you doing here?"

"Will you just hold still so I can let go of you without fear of bodily harm? And why were you screaming like a stuck pig? You scared the hell out of me, girl."

"I do not scream like a pig." He let go of her but she didn't move. Strong arms, terrific body, sexy guy . . . archenemy. She ignored the last part, the first three things making that pretty easy. "Someone was up here and he pushed me, then took off running, and then you came along—not that I knew it was you—and I grabbed a weapon."

John rubbed his gut and closed his eyes. "If the guy ran away, Lillie, why would he return?"

She rolled to the side, propped herself up on an elbow, and studied John as he lay stretched out on the floor, moonlight falling across his naked torso. Naked and torso went really well together when referring to John Snow. "Maybe they forgot something, like my head on a platter. How the heck should I know? I'm new to this attic stuff. I didn't even have an attic in Chicago. Mrs. Wilson lived above me, eighty years old and drove a pink Cadillac and had a schnauzer named Pookie and why aren't you wearing a shirt?"

He lifted one eyelid. "I was taking a shower." He pointed to the window behind him. "We're right next to each other and I'm staying in the upstairs apartment and it doesn't have air-conditioning. When I heard you bellow I grabbed my jeans and . . . and . . . well, I *am* the sheriff and it's my duty to check things like this out and . . . ah, dammit all, Lillie June, why couldn't you just stay in Chicago with Mrs. Wilson and Pookie and the Cadillac?"

"What the heck's that supposed to mean?"

Both of his eyes opened and he reached for her, threading his fingers through her hair and he said in a husky voice, "You're just too damn beautiful for your own good, for *our* own good." Then he cupped the back of her head, his touch one of possession, as if laying claim to her.

Okay, this was the part where she was supposed to jump up and run away because she and John were adversaries and talking about her being beautiful and thoughts of possession didn't fit with being adversaries.

Slowly he brought her face to his and inch by inch she leaned to him till their lips touched, the connection like a gulp of hot chocolate warming her all over. And she wanted more, lots more, and not just kissing. She didn't care how arrogant or pigheaded or closed minded he was or that he thought she screamed like a pig. She placed her hands against his chest—bare, muscled, tight, so male—and kissed him back.

His arms curled around her and he slid over her, not breaking the kiss as she wound her fingers into his wet hair, glistening with moonbeams. His erection pressed hard against the juncture of her legs and she parted them, letting his body sink down into hers.

Thank God she didn't stay in Chicago and miss this. Smoothing her hair from her face he kissed her temples— one, then the other—her ears, and behind them, driving her nuts. "You smell like heaven," he whispered, in a ragged breath.

She tucked her thumbs into the waistband of his jeans. "How fast can you get these things off?"

He stilled; his eyes opened wide. "You sure about this?"

"I shouldn't be, but I am. Bet I can get these jeans off you pretty fast myself. Want me to show you?"

He grinned, the wolfish kind that said this suited him just fine. "Well, damn. I had no idea."

"Yeah, well I did and it won't go away no matter what I do. And believe me I've tried."

He stood and peeled off his jeans, least he tried to. He grunted and yanked one side, then the other, not making much progress. "Never dress when you're wet. I think these jeans are glued to my skin."

Her one great chance to get laid by a really hunky guy and he has glued-ass problems. She kicked off her sandals, gathered her skirt, slid her panties over her legs, and flipped the bit of lace off the end of her toe into the darkness.

He watched, mesmerized. "I think you're the sexiest thing I've ever seen."

She scooted up onto the little table across from where he stood and crooked her finger at him. "There's more."

He glanced down at his jeans around his thighs. "I look ridiculous."

She eyed his erection. "Ridiculous is not the word that comes to mind, and I'm sure not complaining about your looks." Her heart beat in her throat, and the juncture of her legs felt soft and wet. "But we need to hurry."

"Before we change our minds? I really don't want you to do that," he said in a strained voice, as he took a condom from his wallet. She watched as he slid it on.

Oh my stars! He was hers, all hers, every wonderful inch, and she hadn't seen inches like this in a really long time . . . probably never. Chicago inches weren't the same as Texas inches.

He cradled one thigh in each hand, his sure touch an incredible turn-on. Then he pulled her to the end of the table and spread her wide. Her legs straddled his bare hips, skin to skin, heat to heat. He peeled back her skirt, giving him a full view. He smiled, his eyes liquid fire and his breaths shallow, erratic, making her want him all the more. "You're so beautiful."

"You're so big."

Her hands embraced his neck, then trailed to his nape as he sucked in a quick breath. "Oh, honey."

She locked her legs around him. "God, I want you."

"I'm glad this isn't one sided." And he cupped her hips and slid into her in one long, continuous stroke.

She gasped, the intimate connection more powerful, more complete than she'd imagined, taking her to the brink of passion . . . then beyond. In one quick, unexpected flash she climaxed, the world spinning out of her control, and John with her, his body shuddering with hers.

As she clung to him the pulsing orgasm tore through her, filling every need, every desire, every fantasy. She never had fantasies this good. And never this fast! Darn!

He held her against him, every muscle taut, his skin sleek, hot, damp. "You're fantastic," she said, in a shaky breath, as she rested her cheek against his stubbled one.

"I wasn't ready for something like this," he whispered in her ear.

"Trust me, you were ready. I saw the evidence. Heck, I felt it but it was over too quick."

He grinned, his teeth white against the dark. Then he kissed her forehead. No arrogance or pigheadedness now. Just a man; just a woman. She said, "That was some sex for two people who don't much like each other."

"Except some parts of us like each other a lot."

"I wonder why?"

"Maybe because we fit together so well. Animal magnetism."

'Yoo-hoo," came Melinda's voice from the hallway

below. "Lillie? Are you in the attic? What are you doing up there? The front door was wide open. Everything okay? Lillie?"

"Does anyone in this whole blasted town know how to mind their own business ever?" John whispered as he slid off the condom. Lillie stood up and found her kicked-off panties, snatched them from the floor, and handed them to him, nodding at the condom. He wrapped it inside, not looking too pleased about that but not having any choice. He stuck the panties in his pocket and zipped his jeans as Melinda's footsteps sounded on the creaky stairs.

"Lillie?"

"I'm over here and Sheriff Snow's with me."

"Don't you have a flashlight and why is the sheriff in our attic?" Melinda lit the oil lamp and held it high, casting around a golden glow. "And with his shirt off no less?" Melinda added with a grin. She puckered her lips. "Well, well, well. Anything you two want to tell me about? The attic is rather ingenious for a rendezvous. A little hot and dusty and cluttered but it'll do. I'm great at keeping secrets." She made the zip and lock gesture across her mouth.

Lillie said, "You're gossip on parade and you know it, but this time there is none. I came up here to find mementoes about the hotel or Grandpa Pete for the memorial we're having for him over at the Rooster tomorrow night. Someone shoved me and I screamed and John came running and he'd just gotten out of the shower. We were looking for clues as to who was up here and why. Any ideas?"

"Oh, girl, do I have ideas, but I think you have better ones." Melinda cut her eyes from Lillie to John. "You two got a thing for each other and don't want it to get out because it won't look good—that's it, isn't it? The men will think John's wimping out on his duty to shut down the spa because he's got the hots for the babe who runs it, and the women will think Lillie's caved in to John and she'll turn the spa back into a hotel. That's why you're in the attic, least I hope so."

Lillie parked her hands on her hips. "There was someone up here and that's the truth."

"Maybe, but it isn't *all* the truth. I can tell. I know men and women and sizzle when I come across it. I can feel it in the air." Melinda fluffed her hair. "Besides, you both have your shoes off and this isn't the beach."

"John was in the shower."

"And what's your excuse, missy?" Melinda flashed her best "gotcha" grin and aimed for the stairs saying in a sing song voice, "I'll be leaving you two alone now to find more burglars. There's just so much to steal in an old attic. Burglars must be waiting in line to get their hands on dusty books and photos and musty furniture. Have fun you two."

Lillie rubbed her forehead to ease the tension as Melinda's words trailed off. "How'd she know?" she asked John, in a low voice. "I'm never going to hear the end of this. I give her lectures about hooking up with the wrong kind of guy and now I have."

"Your flattery overwhelms me, but she does have a point. There's nothing of value up here, so why *would* someone break in?"

"A valuable piece of whatever that we didn't realize we had? What else could it be?"

"This place has been boarded up for a year. Anyone could have broken in anytime, so whatever brought them here has to be something recent not something that's been here all along."

The dim light silhouetted John's fine physique as he leaned against the table where she'd sat minutes ago. He was exquisite . . . and virile as all get-out. Her belly tightened at the memory, and it was suddenly hard to breathe. Maybe she should bronze that table in dedication to the very best sex she'd ever had.

"I'd bet the break-in has to be related to Pete's death in some way," John said, snapping her back to the moment, even if she didn't want to be snapped back and was enjoying her memory just fine.

He continued, "That's the only thing new around here and from what I've heard everything associated with Pete's demise is a little off. How could a man who's fished a river all his life drown in it? Why would he go out in a flood in a little rowboat? He wasn't senile, more like smart as hell and yet . . ."

John stroked his chin. "Pete being gone sure set this town on its ear in a lot of ways. Changed a lot of people's lives, like Lance Colby and Rod Carter. I've known them all my life. We grew up together and they're the only two guys in town who didn't stop hanging with me when Dad went to prison. Lance thought he'd inherit Pete's ranch till Nina came along, and Rod assumed he'd take over the Ragged Rooster but then Juliet showed up."

"Grandpa Pete had the properties in trust for me and Nina and Juliet, and that lawyer, Gabe Rankin, was to notify us about the trusts if anything happed to Grandpa. That's exactly what Rankin did and we inherited the properties."

John stared off into nothingness as if deep in thought. "So that means things got better for you and your sisters after Pete died. You all got your own business and some start-up money, right?"

Lillie's spine stiffened. She smelled a big rat, and this particular rodent had dark hair and a great body and had just had incredible sex with her on an old wobbly table. "Your point being?"

"Did Pete really die in an accident? I've been thinking about this since I got here. And now with this break-in . . ."

"Hold on I don't like the way this is going. You're really suggesting that Nina and Juliet and I had something to do with Grandpa Pete's death? Are you out of your mind? Do I look like a murderer?"

"I didn't say that."

"Well, you might as well have."

"I'm simply speculating."

"Simply heck." She poked him in the chest, not caring one bit that he was strong and male and delicious and she could still taste him on her lips and feel his arms around her. "For your information Juliet, Nina, and I hadn't met till a few hours ago at Sweets 'n Treats. We didn't even know each other existed till a few months ago after Grandpa passed."

"Unless . . . something else was going on, like one of you learned about Pete and the trust before and—"

"And decided to help things along so we or she or whoever you have in mind could get their hands on the property and money? Okay, Sherlock, why would that person be in my attic tonight?"

"Making sure there weren't papers or letters hanging around that would connect her to Grandpa before he died. Especially now if she knew you'd be hunting for memorabilia for the wake tomorrow night."

"Or, I've got a better idea. Maybe I faked the whole blasted break-in tonight and there wasn't anyone here at all and I wanted to keep suspicion off myself because I killed Grandpa and am trying to throw the blame on my sisters because we all have a motive."

"That doesn't wash. If you wanted me up here you wouldn't have told Rusty I'm a rotten kisser then seduce me—"

"*I* seduced *you*?"

"Well somebody sure as hell seduced somebody tonight. How else do you explain what just happened between us? I

don't think it was our instant camaraderie or brilliant intro-
duction that brought us together."

"Stupidity. Pure, blatant, unexplainable stupidity is what
got us here. Mixed with basic lust. You're trying to close my
spa and throw me and my sisters in jail." She shut her eyes
and slapped her palm to her forehead. "I think this makes it
official. I *am* truly the biggest jerk magnet on the planet."

"I deal in facts and the facts are that no one else benefited from Pete's death but the three of you. That gives you
a good connection."

"Sometimes called motive, and here's some facts for you,
buster. You said Lance and Rod thought they inherited the
saloon and the ranch. Maybe they offed Grandpa Pete to
get what they thought they had coming all along—what
about that?"

"No way."

"Yes way. Facts, remember. If you're suspecting my sisters of doing in Grandpa Pete then you have to include Rod
and Lance."

"I know *them*. I don't know Nina or Juliet."

"And you don't know me."

He leveled her a heated look that suggested otherwise
and let out a deep resigned breath. "How the hell did we
ever get to this point from where we were fifteen minutes
ago?"

"That's a really good question, sugar lips, because this
sure ain't afterglow."

Three

John ground his teeth as he clambered down the attic steps and turned for the first floor. He should write a book called *Endless Ways to Really Fuck Up Your Life*, because he was a damn pro on the subject. Not only was he screwing around with the one gal in town he disagreed with on everything, but she just might have knocked off her own grandfather and gotten away with it, until now.

John yanked open the front door to find Jimmy on the other side. "What in the hell are you doing here?"

"Uh . . ."

John stepped out onto the porch and closed the door behind him as Jimmy added, "What are *you* doing here?"

"Business. What's your excuse?"

"Well, Melinda and I had dinner over at Mizz Jones's bed-and-breakfast. Then she asked me in for coffee—Melinda, not Mizz Jones—and I stopped at my place and got some chicory—you know how I like chicory in my coffee—and . . ." Jimmy stopped and a sly grin spread across his face. "Business? As in getting a personal after-hours tour of the place?"

"Chicory my ass," John said, not able to keep the tease

from his voice. "You've shaved, got yourself all spruced up, and you smell good, not like the sheriff's office."

Jimmy reddened. "It's Old Spice, and what do you mean I smell like the office, and I still don't know why *you're* here, and don't try to change the subject."

John lowered his voice. "There's something going on with Pete's death—I can feel it—and Lillie and her sisters are involved."

Jimmy grinned. "That's the only reason you're here at this hour? To talk with Lillie June about Pete? You really expect me to believe that?"

"It's complicated." And getting worse every time he looked at Lillie. "Did you find anything besides the overturned boat when Pete went missing?"

Jimmy pushed his Stetson to the back of his head. "Complicated and women go together like ham and eggs but women are a darn sight prettier." Jimmy shrugged, then added, "And they taste a whole hell of a lot better and—"

"The accident?"

"Yeah, right, the accident. All we found was Pete's overturned rowboat on the shore about two miles downriver from the bait shop. We searched the riverbank for weeks, didn't find hide nor hair of Pete. That's pretty much it. Real sad. He was a good guy. We all miss him. Now can I get my damn coffee?"

"You didn't find his tackle box or his vest? He never went fishing without his lucky vest. And doesn't it seem convenient that he dies unexpectedly, no body found, and his granddaughters come into a boatload of good fortune?"

Jimmy eyed the door behind John and shifted his weight from one foot to the other. "Juliet and Nina are really nice, just ask Rod and Lance. I think there're wedding bells in their futures, and I think Melinda's expecting me right now, and people die all the time, John. Give it up."

"Maybe I'll have a little talk with the granddaughters three."

Jimmy pulled a frown. "Gabe Rankin will be totally honked off if you pester the girls. He treats them as if they were his own, and since he and Pete were like brothers I can understand that. Besides, what could they know? They got here after Pete died."

"Pete gave me a job sweeping out the saloon and doing dishes at the Rooster after Dad got convicted. I owe it to him to figure out what happened and I'm not convinced we got all the facts."

"You're barking up the wrong tree, boy, if you think those girls had anything to do with their grandfather's death. It was an accident pure and simple, nothing more. What's Lillie June think of your cockamamie idea?"

"That maybe Lance and Rod did the deed because they thought they'd inherit the ranch and the saloon."

"Well, piss up a rope." Jimmy chuckled. "This is getting to be a real mess. You accuse Lillie and her sisters and she accuses your friends. Doesn't sound like a match made in heaven."

"No kidding." Except Lillie felt like heaven in his arms. "Tomorrow I'm going to drive downriver and look around where you found the rowboat. You never know what can get caught in bushes along the bank. Now that the river's low and more of the bank is exposed I might come across something that wasn't there before. Can you cover for me?"

"And you can cover for me tonight, or at least get the heck out of my way." Jimmy stepped around John. "Right now I've got coffee waiting for me." He gave John a little salute and a man-to-man look. "See you in the morning, sheriff."

John watched the door close behind Jimmy. *What the hell.* Jimmy was in for a night of chicory and a lot of other tasty things while John Snow headed for a night of tossing and turning and thinking about Lillie June. Not that he wanted to, but the kind of sex they had just had wasn't the sort you walk away from and forget.

He went inside the office and up to bed. Too many questions about Pete and his granddaughters and not enough answers. And there was also his unexplainable attraction to Lillie June to deal with.

And by the time the six A.M. alarm went off—which he didn't need because he'd been staring at the damn ceiling all night—he still couldn't come up with an answer for either problem. Beauty? Sex? He'd had both before. So what made Lillie so special? John stood and looked out the window through the pearl gray of early morning to the spa across the alleyway. A light came on in the second floor and someone moved about. Lillie. He could tell that much just from her silhouette on the lace curtains.

He'd so much rather be waking up beside her or in her than across the alleyway. His dick swelled and got damn uncomfortable. How much longer did he have in the Gulch before going back to Dallas? A week or so? Too damn long to live with a permanent erection. Least he'd be gone all day and out of sight of Lillie; that would give him some rest.

He showered and dressed and tramped down the stairs, and from the back hall he spotted Lillie sitting in the big oak sheriff's chair. Long green skirt, yellow jacket, coffee in hand, looking sexy as hell. She lifted her coffee in greeting. "Morning, sheriff. Up bright and early I see."

He was *up* all right. "What do you want?" He already knew what *he* wanted!

"I ran into Jimmy last night, having coffee with Melinda, and he said you were going out to look for clues or whatever on the riverbank today. Since my sisters and I are your number one suspects, I think it's in our best interest for me to tag along on your fact-finding mission."

"What if you're not invited?"

"It's a free country and I want to see what you find first-hand." She stood. "We'd better get a move on. The weather station says we could get rain, and running around in the mud doesn't sound like much fun."

"Then maybe you should stay here and keep dry." *Fuck.* After not sleeping all night because of her, he didn't need her around all day to distract him more. He'd be thinking about kissing her, holding her, getting into her pants—he was always thinking about getting into her pants. He wouldn't find a damn thing but trouble if Lillie came along.

She held up a basket. "Hope you like vegetarian fare. I have lunch."

He didn't move. The farther away he was from Lillie the better. From here he couldn't smell her herbal fragrance mixed with her own feminine scent, which made him crazy. He couldn't feel the warmth of her petite body or be tempted to touch her hair, pulled back into a band. "Isn't there a wake for Pete tonight? Don't you have to work on that?"

"Juliet and Nina are taking care of preparations for the wake; I'm taking care of you." She swallowed. "I mean following you."

She dug into her basket as if she needed a diversion after that last crack. "I found old photos of the Silver Gulch Hotel and some of the guests. Did you know Buffalo Bill stopped by Silver Gulch? Did you know he really hunted buffalo? Why would anyone ever hunt a buffalo?"

She was rambling. Good. Least he wasn't the only one affected by last night. She handed him the pictures. "I brought these—thought you might be interested since you grew up here. Look, here's Bill standing in front of the hotel."

She flipped to the next picture and smiled, a genuine one this time. "And look at this. Here's Pete with his new bride, Penelope, from back East . . . least that's what it says on the back. Pete's happy enough but Penelope looks as if she has swallowed a lemon. Small wonder they got divorced. Grandpa said in his diary that Penelope never belonged in the West. It sounded like she married him on a lark, wanting to get back at her parents for not sending her to Europe for the summer with her girlfriends. Seems it wasn't the proper thing for an unattached lady from back East to do."

Lillie seemed to lose herself for the moment. She was so excited about finding information about her family that it touched his heart. The one thing they shared was love of family. His grandmother saved his family; Lillie's grandfather brought her family together.

So, how could sisters so enthused with finding each other polish off their grandfather? Sometimes he really hated being a cop, made him too damn suspicious. Maybe today he'd find evidence that supported the accident theory and get everyone off the hook—except with Lillie following along evidence would be the last thing on his mind.

She handed him more photos and his fingers connected with hers. Her gaze met his and he'd never felt a bond like that to anyone else. His heart pounded and his lungs constricted as if he couldn't get enough air when the real problem was he couldn't get enough of Lillie. He touched her cheek and her eyes went to jade. Then he scooped her into his arms and kissed her.

Backing her to the desk, he sat her on the edge, dropped the pictures on the top, and slid his hands under her soft T-shirt, connecting with the smoothest skin on earth. He trailed his hand up her sides to her bra and tucked his fingers underneath to the warm swell of her breasts, making him want all of her right then. But this was the sheriff's office, public place number one.

He stepped away. Her eyes were glazed and her breaths shallow. His head was spinning. "Jimmy will be here any minute. I don't want him to find us like this. And someone could look in the window or come in."

The old clock on the wall ticked out the seconds and she nibbled at her bottom lip. "I should care about those things but I don't know if I do or not."

His blood surged. "Hell, Lillie, did you have to say that?"

"You want me to lie and say I don't want you?"

"Oh, yeah. Definitely. That would help us stay apart and we need all the help we can get."

"Because you think I'm a murderer?"

"Because I have no idea what the hell's going on and I can't think for squat with you around except that I want to have you."

The back door opened and Jimmy sauntered into the room. "John? Lillie?"

"Morning, Jimmy," John said, with more calm in his voice than he thought possible under the circumstances. "Lillie and I are going out to look for clues along the river-bank about Pete's drowning."

She gave him a bright smile of appreciation for including her, but he so didn't deserve it for what he was about to do to her.

"You wait here and I'll get some flashlights and some rope. You never know when you'll need rope. Then we'll take off."

What Lillie really wanted to take off was John's clothes and have her fill of him. Could that ever happen? She sat in the chair and Jimmy parked behind his desk by the window. He said, "You sure got yourself here bright and early this morning."

If Jimmy was looking for an update on what was going on between her and John, he was asking the wrong person. Not only wasn't it any of his business, but she didn't know. "I want to find out what happened to Pete as much as John does. Nina, Juliet, and I had nothing to do with his death and we don't need anyone in the Gulch thinking we did. This is our new home and being accused of murder is no way to make friends. Do you realize Pete thought we didn't want anything to do with him and we thought he didn't want to see us? Isn't that sad? My father was a donkey's butt."

Jimmy played with a pencil on his desk and asked in a nonchalant voice that didn't fool her for a moment, "And the fact that you wanted to spend the day with John didn't enter into you being here?"

A little . . . maybe . . . maybe more than a little. Being with John was like eating a gallon of ice cream: not good for her but she'd pick up the spoon and dig in anyway. "You wouldn't ask that if you'd been around for our little argument last night. John's a cop head to toe." Though there were some pretty impressive parts in between.

Lillie checked her watch. "Wonder what's taking John so long? He went to get flashlights and"—she glanced outside and jumped up—"damn that man. We don't need flashlights—it's daylight. And why would we need a rope? It's a riverbank, not a cave."

She kicked the trash can across the office. "He left me behind, that dirty rotten creep."

Jimmy's eyes widened. "Well, I'll be a monkey's uncle. I think he did."

And to think she'd compared John to ice cream. She loved ice cream. She should have compared him to anchovies. She hated them. "Where'd he go?"

"For what?"

Lillie went to Jimmy's desk and leaned over, bracing her arms on the top. She growled, "Do not mess with a messed-over woman. Spill it. Where's John gone off to looking for clues?"

Jimmy sat up straight and folded his arms. "I will not be intimidated. If John wanted you to stay behind you should do it and stay out of harm's way."

"I'll tell Melinda you're seeing that cute little blonde over at the Rooster."

Jimmy's eyes widened. "But that's a lie."

Lillie smiled too sweetly. "These are desperate times."

"No kidding. Dang." He leaned back in his chair and bunched his shoulders in resignation. "We found Pete's boat capsized downriver from the bait shop." He pointed toward the back of the office. "Bait shop's that way next to the picnic grove."

Lillie grabbed her basket and raced out the back door. John Snow was and always would be a pain in the butt on many levels and this time he'd outfoxed her. Well, she could fox with the best of them. The advertising world had taught her that much. She'd catch up with Sheriff Snow and tag along whether he wanted her to or not.

But an hour later, with sand in her shoes and bug bites and a storm bearing down on her as she waded along the riverbank, she still hadn't found John. Where the heck was that man? And where were clues about Pete?

Thunder rumbled in the distance and clouds collected overhead. A gust of wind swayed the treetops. She should have paid more attention to the weather than the bank. So far she'd found driftwood, two frogs, a turtle sunning himself—or maybe it was herself—on a rock, fishing lures dangling in trees from lines cast too close to shore, and a butter-colored dog that looked part Lab but mostly indiscriminate heritage that had followed her for the last twenty minutes. Though, truth be told, she was probably following the picnic basket.

"Since you're out here," she said to Butter, "you could be more helpful. Like find one of Pete's boots or something. Don't dogs do that sort of thing? Where do you live, girl? Are you someone's pet? You look well fed."

A big fat raindrop splashed in front of her, sending ringlets out into the still river. Butter danced in circles and splashed into the water as if this were paradise. "Crazy dog, you got me all wet."

Not that it mattered because the gray sky suddenly opened, drenching her and everything in sight. The trees on the shore offered more protection than the open river, so, hooking the basket over her arm, she grabbed an exposed root to help climb off the shore . . . except the root *moved?* And it had a tail and a head and looked pissed as hell.

Snake! Oh, God, she'd grabbed a snake! She had snake cooties. She screamed, let go, and jumped back, landing in the water butt first. Butter studied the snake as it slithered under a boulder and then she darted up the bank. "Fair-weather dog."

Lillie pushed herself up. She looked like a statue in a fountain . . . a really ugly statue. Splashing every step, she trudged her way to the sandy bank, then crawled her way up the side, this time taking special care where her hands went.

When she got to the top and into the trees, Butter barked and nudged her arm. The rain beat harder, the trees not offering as much protection as she'd hoped. She stumbled through the woods following the dog. With luck she'd lead her to a road where she'd flag down a ride—probably from Jack the Ripper, the way her luck was going. But instead she spied an old fishing cabin that looked as if one good gust would knock the place flat.

Praying no Jack the Ripper was there, she ran for the cabin, Butter at her side. Together they leapt onto the crumbling porch, Lillie shouldered open the door, they darted inside as lightning cracked, and she slammed the door shut. She turned and looked straight at John Snow sitting by a fire, bare feet propped up on the hearth, Butter already lying down there, a perfect Norman Rockwell moment. And John was drinking something steamy in a mug and he was dry! The no-good rat didn't have a wet spot on him! "You!"

"You?"

She lunged at him full force, knocking him and the mug out of the chair and onto the floor, without Butter moving an inch.

"Ouch," he said from under her. "What the hell was that for? And you're getting me all wet and where'd you get the dog?"

"I grabbed a snake, damn you. A real live one with a mouth and beady eyes and it wiggled, and I'm soaked to the skin, and the dog found me, and this is all your fault, and where in the heck are we?"

John paused, and the only sounds were the crackle of the fire and dog snores. He touched her cheek, his fingers warm against her chilled skin, a soft smile suddenly at his lips. Then he rolled over, trapped her beneath him, and kissed her. "I think we're in big trouble."

"What are you doing?" she mumbled with his mouth on hers. "You think I'm a murderer and you're a sheriff. Isn't there a no-kissing-the-killer rule? Why did you leave me at the office and not take me with you?"

"Oh, honey, I want more than kissing and I left you because when we're together all I think about is you and me and like we are now and I don't think you murdered anyone. You're too busy finding stuff out about Pete and enjoying it to want him dead. It doesn't fit."

She framed his rough chin in her hands and pulled his head back a bit. "You're just saying all those things to get me to spread my legs."

"Would I do that?"

"Oh, heck yes."

"Maybe, but actually I'm telling you the truth—I swear. I don't know what it is between us . . . lust at first sight?"

He nuzzled her neck and kissed her throat and she swallowed a gasp. "How do you know I'm not just faking all that enthusiasm for Pete and for you just to throw you off?"

He smoothed her hair from her face. "You have enthusiasm for me?" He grinned and she couldn't resist stroking her thumb over his lower lip—smooth, sensual, very kissable. His eyes smoldered. "You don't fake anything, not even the color of your hair."

He kissed her again, this time his tongue slipping between her lips. He tasted warm and sweet and of coffee mixed with brandy. He tasted male and that was the best taste of all. She wound her arms around his neck and kissed him back, her mouth opening so easily to his.

"You're shivering. You're cold. You need to get your clothes off."

"Is that lame excuse number two or three for getting a woman naked?"

His eyes looked deep into hers as if deciding what to do. She didn't think a guy like John needed directions, so what was he thinking now? He sat up and let out an audible sigh. "Your lips are blue and your teeth are chattering. You bit my tongue and that wouldn't be bad except I got a feeling it wasn't on purpose."

He ran his hand over his face. "I thought about you the whole blasted night, Lillie June, and as much as it kills me to say this—and trust me, it really does kill me—I'm going to get you out of your clothes and warm you up and it's not going to have anything to do with sex or lust or whatever's driving us crazy. I owe Pete and getting you sick isn't how to repay him. I might die of pent-up frustration but that's the way it's got to be."

She stared at John, the most handsome man God had

seen fit to put in her life. Not only did he want her, he wanted what was best for her. A unique situation for Lillie June. "Wanna bet, big boy?"

"Bet what?"

"You're about to find out."

Four

John held up his hands and leaned back as if warding off some threat as she grabbed the front of his shirt and kissed him. "Don't do this, Lillie. A man only has so much self-control and you are Pete's granddaughter and you need to get dry and . . . and . . ."

Lillie scooted from under him and stood, her eyes dark, a hint of devilment lurking deep inside. She tucked her hands into the waistband of her skirt. "You want me to get dry? I can do that." Slowly she peeled the wet cotton over shapely hips, exposing creamy skin and damp green panties clinging to every crevice of her feminine body. "See, just like you want."

The skirt fell, and his breath caught as the damp cotton pooled at her ankles and the firelight gave her body a shimmering glow. He didn't need glow—he needed wrinkled and gray elephant skin, though, truth be told, he'd probably be attracted to her that way too.

He needed to escape . . . except escape meant running out into a damn monsoon. He had to choose between a rain storm and Lillie. No contest! But he had to keep his hands and every other part of his body from hers. How could he conduct an investigation if he didn't? "Blanket. I'll get a blanket."

"Make it big enough for two."

He stood, then shoved his hands in his pockets so he wouldn't reach out and grab her to him and take her in some kind of Neanderthal lip-lock. At thirty-one, that he had such little control over himself was damn pathetic. He headed for the bed. If he could just think of something besides Lillie stripping nearly naked and this bed!

He went for diversion. "My dad and grandfather built this fishing shack when Dad was just a kid. A lot of people around here have them. Pete has one by Small Creek around the next bend. The cabin is pretty much a mess. I think he left it to Gabe. They used to go fishing and . . ."

And when he turned back Lillie was right in front of him in a green bra and panties but cold. Shivering cold. She snapped the blanket from his hand, flung it around her body like a cape, held it tight with one hand at her neck, the other grabbing it closed at her middle, as she ran back to the hearth, then sat and scooted as close to the fire as she could get without sitting on the dog or becoming charbroiled.

She pulled her legs under the blanket. "Got any more of that coffee and brandy? I'm freezing."

Not exactly what he expected. "What happened to *wanna bet?*"

"Seemed like a good idea at the time, but I think it's a window of opportunity missed. Coffee? Brandy? Hurry."

"You look like a tent with a head."

"I feel like a Popsicle."

He felt horny as the town bull. "Being noble sucks," he mumbled to himself as much as to her.

She laughed and even that sounded shaky. He cleaned up the spilled coffee from when she'd charged him and knocked him flat, then got a mug from the open cupboard. He poured coffee from the pot hanging over the fire, his body so close to hers he could smell the scent of lilac still clinging to her wet hair. Rain hammered the old tar-papered roof, making the leak in one corner a steady plink into a metal bucket. Lightning split the sky. He added brandy and handed her the mug. Her hands shook and teeth chattered against the metal rim as she sipped.

"Tastes great."

He needed another diversion from Lillie. "What's the dog's name?"

"I call her Butter. Must live close by. She led me here. Finding her was a real stroke of luck."

Stroke? That's what he wanted to do with Lillie. Stroke his hands over her firm breasts, feel her flat abdomen quiver under his palms, touch her warm, wet sex that was hot just for him. He could imagine his fingers plunging into her, pleasuring her, making her ready for—

"John?"

"What?" he yelped as his head snapped up, jarring his brain. *Good!* Something had to get his mind off Lillie.

"You were a million miles away."

Oh, how he wished that were true. Instead he said, "I was thinking of . . . the dog."

"She needs a good rubdown with a big towel. Got anything like that around here?"

"Butter will be fine, but I have a towel you can use."

He could picture himself rubbing Lillie with some of that lotion she had at her spa. Down her smooth back, over the firm rounds of her buttocks, her thighs to the backs of her knees. He loved the backs of women's knees. And then kiss her there and work his way up, driving her crazy . . . just like all this fantasizing was driving him crazy.

"John? I keep losing you."

If only he could quit thinking about Lillie, and that was not going to happen with her almost naked under a blanket right in front of him. He wanted her so much he had a headache—actually his other head ached more and he had no idea what to do about either.

Suffer! He took the bottle of brandy and gulped. Alcohol was a sex inhibitor . . . so why wasn't it working now?

"Do you always drink from the bottle?"

"Seemed like a good idea."

The fire spit and crackled behind the rusted wire screen as she raked her hands through her hair to dry it, letting it catch the firelight. He wanted to run his fingers through her curls, but then what? Where'd he and Lillie go from there? A fling? She didn't seem like a fling sort of woman, and there was the Pete factor to consider. Pete would haunt him to hell and back if John had a fling with his granddaughter. John took another drink from the bottle and Lillie watched him, her eyes liquid, her face flushed. His desire for her faded not one bit.

Then, as if reading his mind, she pulled him down, making him sit beside her. She slid the bottle from his hand, their fingertips touching, his heart racing. She took a sip from the bottle.

"Are you still cold?"

"I'm going to get a heck of a lot warmer."

"Thanks to the brandy?"

She gave him a siren's smile. "I think that window of opportunity's opening back up."

"We haven't known each other that long and—and this is getting involved. Maybe we're moving too fast."

"I lived with a guy for two years and it ended badly. We can't do worse than that. Time isn't everything." She brought her delicious mouth to his in a searing kiss that melted his insides. If he got haunted by Pete, he'd deal. How bad could a ghost be?

He took Lillie into his arms as she tangled hers around

his neck. The blanket slipped from her slim shoulders, falling around his arms. Her fingers stroked his nape and he leaned back on the stone hearth, sliding her torso on top of him as she planted kisses along his jawline to his ear. She nipped the lobe and desire roared through him at lightning speed. Holding on to her he tipped them from the hearth to the floor, his free hand breaking the short drop as he braced himself over her.

Looking up at him with dreamy eyes she said, "Hey, I liked things the way they were before."

"Not much room up there and this way I'm on top." His nose touched hers. "I want to unwrap you from this blanket."

"Then I get to unwrap you."

"I'm not wearing a blanket."

"I'll improvise." Her eyes held a twinkle that made his stomach flip and he kissed her again, lips to lips, then to her chin. He could feel her heart beating fast against his tongue as he licked the indent between her breasts.

She wanted him. A lot. This was the biggest turn-on of all, and he captured her left breast through the thin material, the nipple hardening as he suckled the sensitive bead. "Oh, honey," he breathed on a sigh, "you taste like heaven."

"John, you're driving me crazy."

"Good." Then he hooked his fingers under her bra and slipped it up as he looked his fill. "You're perfect."

"An A cup. You don't need to feed me lines to get a roll in the hay. At this point I think it's a given."

He stilled. "That's no line, I swear." And he meant it, every word. She *was* perfect. "Are you nervous? We've done this before."

"In a dark attic and there wasn't time to think and sex was more of a reaction and my last boyfriend said I was perfect too, then left me for Ms. Jugs at Murphy's Bar and

Grill and I think I have a complex." She let out a long breath. "I don't do well at this thought-out sex thing. I'm more of a fly by the seat of my pants sex partner."

He gave her a wicked laugh. "You need reassurance. I'm really good at reassurance." And not just because he wanted to have sex with her more than he wanted air, but because she deserved better than getting dumped for Ms. Jugs. Hell, any woman did.

He cupped Lillie's left breast in his palm and ran the pad of his thumb over the nipple, causing the pink nub to bead. "See?" he said, gazing into her wide eyes. "You're perfect. Trust me, honey, more than a mouthful is a waste."

She laughed and he lowered his head and gently licked the taut tip. She gasped again, louder this time, and her fingers tangled in his hair.

"John," she said, on a breathy sigh, and her legs widened as she opened herself to him. He licked her other breast, taking his time, his tongue tracing paths over her heated skin.

"You're too good."

And it wasn't just sex—he wanted her to enjoy this; he wanted to give her pleasure. Right now it was all about Lillie. He took her hands in his and held them to her sides as he nuzzled his way over her flat stomach to her navel. He kissed the gentle notch, then went on, stopping at the waistband of her panties.

Taking the elastic in his teeth, he dragged the lacy bit of green down—down was so very nice—exposing her soft patch of curls. "Lovely."

She raised her head, looking at him. He could feel her eyes on him. "John?"

"I'm right here, sweetheart." Then he slid her panties over her thighs, over her knees, and to her ankles, then off. He knelt at her feet and looked his fill. "You're incredible."

"You still have clothes on."

He winked. "I know. I like it that way, at least for a while."

He could see her blush even in the firelight. Had anyone ever *really* made love to this woman? It excited him to be the first and not because it was some conquest but because he did it for her, and that mattered.

He kissed her ankles, the inside of one knee, then the other, then spread her legs . . . least he tried to. Lillie whispered in a self-conscious voice, "I don't know if this is such a good idea."

He whispered back, "It's a great idea trust me." Then he lay between her legs—what a fine place to be. He kissed her silky thigh, her legs trembling as he pressed them farther apart still, revealing her intimate secrets.

"John?"

Without answering he kissed his way to the soft, damp folds of her sex, making her body shudder.

"*Oh, God, John,*" she hissed, and then her words morphed into raw moans of sexual pleasure as his tongue stroked and plunged into her wet heat, building her pleasure till he pressed his mouth to her swollen clit. Her body trembled in climax, making him feel more complete and satisfied than he ever had before when making love.

He brought his face to hers and kissed her closed eyes and smoothed back her tousled hair. "Making love to you is an incredible experience."

Making love . . . and it was that, he realized. Something beyond mutual gratification. He cared for Lillie and what happened to her and it wouldn't end when they walked out of this cabin.

She said, "This is a little one-sided, you know."

"Sometimes one-sided is good."

She lay there for a minute catching her breath as he lost his. He'd never seen a more beautiful woman. Finally she managed, "But it's selfish." And before he knew what had happened she'd flipped him onto his back and sat on his chest.

"How'd you do that?"

"Summoned my inner strength. I think I'm better at inner strength than inner peace." She gave him a sassy half smile. "Especially when I've had three cups of coffee—the extra caffeine just kicked in. Besides, I think you were distracted."

"That was some kick. And you always distract me."

"I can do better, and I have to do something to pay you back for getting me over the Ms. Jugs dump. I didn't realize how much it affected me till now." She bent down and kissed him. "In fact, think I'm cured."

"Glad I could help. But you don't need to repay or do anything but—"

His words were lost as she sucked his bottom lip deep into her mouth, then let it go. "Oh, but I do," she purred. "I feel refreshed, new. I feel liberated and I need to demonstrate."

She sat up and ran her hands through her hair, flipping it in all directions, the firelight turning it gold and burgundy, and then she bent to kiss him again, with the gorgeous mane flowing forward, surrounding them as her mouth consumed his.

Desire pulsed through his body and he fisted his hands in the blanket under him to gain control. "Lillie," he panted, "you're doing me in, honey."

"Oh, I hope so." She bunched up his shirt and stared at the crisp curly hair scattered across his muscled chest. "You are so well built."

"I'm so turned on."

She scooted back, his erection grazing her sex. "I can tell." She sat on his thighs and undid his belt. "And I think we need more liberation, this time yours."

She unsnapped his jeans, his erection swelling as much from the extra room as from the fact that she had her hand on him. "You're different now, not the same as in the attic."

"Sex in the attic"—she looked at him and laughed, the

contagious sound filling the cabin—"sounds like a bad sit-com. But for me it was more pent-up frustration then."

"Horny?"

"That pretty much covers it. But now"—she glanced back to his briefs, then slid them over his erection—"it's more." Her voice was a whisper as her fingers stroked his shaft, nearly sending him over the edge.

He gripped the blanket tighter and ground out, "Lillie, I can't do more."

He fished his wallet from his back pocket and took out a condom. "I'm sorry," he said, in a ragged voice he barely recognized. "I want you too much."

With shaky fingers he covered himself, the scent of sex mixing with pine and smoke. Her eyes shone dark and full and bright and he snagged his arm around her middle and tucked her neatly under him.

His skin burned hot as the glowing grate, every muscle aching, throbbing. She arched to meet his thrusts again and again, her legs at his waist, fusing her body to his. His climax came in a flash that knocked the air from his lungs and every thought but Lillie from his mind. She clung to him, calling his name, her sweet, sweet body convulsing in completion with his.

He collapsed on top of her, barely able to keep his weight on his arms for fear of squashing her flat. He didn't want to let this moment go. Too intimate, too perfect, so filled with Lillie. He never felt that way before. Sex was sex and he always gave as good as he got. But not this time. As much as he tried to please her and make it good for her, she was the one who made it perfect for him. She gave him her body, her mind, and a bit of her soul. "Dear God, woman, what you do to me."

"We just met," she said, breathless. "How can we . . . Why?"

With supreme effort he brought his head up and gazed at her. "Basic sexual chemistry."

"But we have issues. We have so many issues I can't imagine why I'm here."

He kissed the tip of her nose. "Honey, chemistry doesn't give a rat's ass about issues. Besides, there's more. We're connected through Pete and because our grandparents cared for us more than our parents ever did, and you're loyal as hell to your sisters and I feel the same way about Rod and Lance."

He flopped on his back like a landed fish. Not too suave but he was completely wiped out. "The last part of that might be common ground but it's also what's tearing us apart. The big question is, where do we go from here, Lillie June?"

"You're headed back to Dallas so that sort of answers our question."

And when he didn't respond, she sat up and looked him in the eyes, the magic of a moment ago fading. "Why do I have a feeling things between us are worse than ever? What's happened? What did you find on the riverbank? You have to tell me. This is my family we're talking about."

He stood, disposed of the condom, and reclaimed his briefs and jeans, and when he turned back she'd wrapped herself in the blanket as if protecting herself against . . . issues. Damn the issues.

"Must be something important since you're getting dressed, sort of like putting on your armor for doing battle?"

"I don't want to do battle with you."

She arched her brow. "But . . . You've got that *but* look in your eyes."

He went to the coat hooks anchored to the wall, took down a vest and brought it back. "I found this on the riverbank. It's Pete's; everyone knows it."

Lillie took the vest. "Guess this puts an end to wondering if Grandpa Pete was here. So what's the problem?"

John sat on the hearth and braced his elbows on his knees, the warm glow of the fire turning his skin golden. "That vest didn't go through any flood, Lillie. It's not washed out enough or beat-up enough to have been exposed to the elements for four months. It was planted there recently. Someone threw a little mud on it and swiped it through the water a few times, but only recently. There's no gravel in the pockets, like you'd find if it was tumbled in a flooding river. No rips from getting dragged over rocks."

"Meaning?"

"Someone wanted this vest found right now. I drove here because I wanted to scout downstream but I didn't have to go that far. The vest was on the shore almost directly in front of the cabin. Hell, if it had had a neon sign over it and an arrow directing me it couldn't have been any more visible. The only ones who knew we were here are you and me and Jimmy unless . . ."

"I'm not going to like the next part am I." It wasn't even a question.

"You said Nina and Juliet were getting things ready for the memorial. I'm guessing you told them you were going with me today to look for clues about Pete. Right? Finding the fishing vest now proves Pete was here when I'm suspicious about his death. It's too convenient. It was planted to reinforce the accident, which makes me all the more certain it wasn't a fishing accident at all but something more, something planned."

Lillie stood. "Nice try, John, but Juliet and Nina probably told Rod and Lance and *they* could have planted the vest. What do you think about that? Every time you find a piece of evidence that implicates my sisters in Pete's disappearance, Rod and Lance are in that pot too because they thought they were inheriting the bar and the ranch."

She glared. "How could I have a sexfest with the man who thinks my sister, or sisters, are murderers?"

"Sexfest? That's all this was to you, nothing but sex?"

"That's all it can be, John." She stood and tossed her hair, wishing she could toss her feelings for John right along with it, but she couldn't. "We are the most incompatible people I've ever known, and in case you missed something, our situation is not improving with age."

"I'll show you what's improving." He snagged her into his arms and kissed her. "We are. You and me. And it's not just sex no matter how many relatives and friends and spas come between us. We connect and it's too bad if it's inconvenient because it's the truth. Now we're going to find a way to make it all work."

Five

Even though it was still raining, the Ragged Rooster was packed for the memorial. Lillie, Nina, and Juliet sat on bar stools as Jimmy played his guitar and sang about Texas and bluebonnets, the state that Pete loved and the flowers that grew there.

Melinda stared at Jimmy all goo-goo eyed, swaying to the tune, their gazes never leaving each other, even after the song ended. The owner of Sweets 'n Treats stood, cleared his throat, and told how Grandpa Pete bought the kids candy and ice cream. Doc Shelton took the floor and reminisced about how Pete picked up the tab for more than one family who couldn't afford medical care. An old-timer with a full beard, an oversized Stetson, and a ragged voice choked with emotion told how Pete loved the town and the people in it and thought of them as family more than friends.

Lillie stood along with Nina and Juliet. The three held up their longnecks—longnecks is what Juliet said beers in a bottle were called in Texas. Nina said to the crowd, "To Pete Maddock for bringing us together."

Juliet said, "We love you Grandpa."

Lillie added, "To a wonderful man we never knew."

And a bleary-eyed Rusty Pierce chimed in with, "And we hope you're not flipping in your grave over your hotel being turned into a sissy spa."

Everyone froze and Betty slammed down her beer and glared at her husband. "There you go, you old fool. You had too much to drink and you had to open your big yap and ruin this nice affair."

Rusty's eyes didn't quite focus. "Hell, damn it, woman, it's the truth."

"And you just used two cusswords at the same time, proving just how sloshed you are," Betty huffed.

Lucky Freemont said, "Well, I'm sober as a judge and I know what Rusty's saying is true enough. The spa should be closed. It's not what Pete would have wanted at all and now's as good a time as any for getting the truth out."

The men nodded in agreement and Betty faced Rusty and the other women in the saloon faced the men they were with. Betty said, "So it's come to this, has it? Well, you have your saloon, Rusty Pierce, and I get my spa."

"But you come to the Rooster," Rusty countered.

"And you can come to the spa," Betty said.

"Fat chance that. Besides, John here was supposed to have the place closed down by now. That was the agreement. Said he'd sweet-talk Lillie June into changing it back into a hotel."

Lucky added, "Said he'd appeal to her feminine side. He was supposed to make things peaceful here so he'd be sure of getting his job back in Dallas. Looks like that sweet talking didn't work for squat."

Lillie's gaze met John's across the saloon. "It's not what you think," John said. "It might have been at first but things changed. *We* changed."

"Sweet talk? Feminine side? Eat dirt and die, John Snow." Lillie straightened her spine, anger eating at her insides. "I'll be going to my spa now. My spa that's going to stay a spa and no sweet talking is ever going to change that."

Betty stood and glared at Rusty. "And the sooner you understand that, the sooner you get me and your bed back instead of sleeping every night on the living room couch. So there."

The women followed Betty and Lillie out the saloon door, the men staring dumbfounded.

The little parade got to the porch of the saloon, rain still coming down in waves. Lillie said, "Thank you for your support, and the spa will be open tomorrow first thing, like always."

The women cheered and Betty said, "And we'll be sleeping alone fine and dandy till our men come to their senses."

Lillie smiled as she waved to the women as they left, but deep down inside she felt wretched. Her spa was causing tension, breaking up homes, doing the exact opposite of what a spa should do. Spas were designed for peace and harmony, and there sure wasn't much of that in Silver Gulch tonight, thanks to the Silver Springs Spa and Healing Center.

She should leave. She'd caused enough problems in town and there was the John Snow factor to consider. She was involved with a man who suspected her sisters of doing in Grandpa Pete and had played her like a well-tuned fiddle so she'd close down the spa and keep the menfolk of Silver Gulch happy, all to secure his job back in Dallas.

Could she pick men or what! If she ever considered marriage she should be shot. It was doomed from the start. She had the flawed marriage gene just like her mother.

To avoid getting soaked Lillie kept to the covered porches of the shops and made her way to the spa. She climbed the steps to the third floor. Sleep, she needed sleep. Solid male footsteps sounded on the stairs and Lillie called out, "If that's you, John Snow, you'd better run for the hills, because I intend to strangle you dead and cook your sorry ass in the hot tub."

"And your sisters will be more than happy to help," John said as he pulled up in the kitchen doorway, looking like a drowned rat.

Nina and Juliet appeared behind John, both huffing and looking equally wet. Nina said, "He outran us, Lillie. We tried to stop him from coming up here but he wouldn't listen."

John gazed at Lillie. "I came to straighten things out between us. What happened in the cabin today had nothing to do with this spa and getting you to close it down or me keeping my job in Dallas. It was between you and me and it was special. You're special and if you don't believe me there's not one damn thing I can do about it. I don't lie to women, never have and I don't intend to start now." He took her into his arms and kissed her hard, then turned on his heel and left.

Lillie felt stunned like she always did when John kissed her fast and hard like that. Nina put her hands to her hips. "Well, he is something." She laughed. "Reminds me of Lance."

"And Rod," Juliet chimed in. "Men of that sort do put on quite a show." She took Lillie's hand. "So, what do you plan to do now, dear?"

Lillie closed her eyes for a moment. "Jump out the window, but first I'm getting you towels to dry off."

Lillie got robes from the new stash she'd ordered for her customers, and Juliet filled a teapot and put it on the stove. "Bet you have some chamomile handy. We'll brew it up and sit and talk and forget about men." She kissed Lillie on the head. "It's a time for sisters to be together."

Nina put out cups and napkins. "But I must say that John has a point."

Lillie scoffed, "The one on the tip of his thick head?"

Juliet grinned as she located the cookie jar. "Nice try, dear, but we know you're crazy about the man. He's just gone a bit astray." She sobered. "But there is something very strange going on with Grandpa Pete's death. For a while I thought it was his ghost and, don't laugh," she rushed on, "it seemed to fit because I wanted to meet him. But now I think something else is cooking and it's of this world. Things were moved about in my office, and I found mint wrappers on the floor."

"Me too," added Nina. "And I found a sandy footprint on a floor I'd just cleaned at the ranch and no one was home but me."

"And someone was in the attic here," Lillie said. "And there was sand on the steps that lead to the attic."

Both Nina and Juliet gasped and Nina said, "You never told us."

"I didn't know what to make of it until now." The sisters exchanged looks and Lillie continued, "We all think there's something amiss—good Lord, I'm starting to talk British." They laughed and Lillie said, "John thinks so too, and even if he is a jerk he probably has good cop instincts."

Juliet poured tea. "Everything seems to lead straight-away to the riverbank: the overturned boat, the fishing vest, the sandy footprints."

"Grandpa Pete has a cabin there," Lillie said as she stirred her tea. "I think we should take a look inside. Maybe there was a scuffle there. Maybe someone did in Grandpa and the scoundrel is hiding out there and keeping tabs on us to make sure we don't find him. We have to find out why someone would kill Grandpa Pete. We need to start looking somewhere and I say the cabin is the best place. We'll meet here at eight and hope for dry weather."

They were quiet for a moment, as rain beat on the windows. Juliet said, "I thought I left all this rain back in England. Perhaps tomorrow it will let up a tad."

But at eight, as Lillie, Juliet, and Nina headed toward Grandpa Pete's cabin on the back gravel road in Lillie's Jeep, the sky was gray and rain continued to fall. Nina looked out the window at the dripping landscape. "There's no one out here but us. Maybe we should have told the men where we were going. Lance thinks I'm getting my hair done at Betty's and having lunch with you two."

Juliet said, "I conveyed the same to Rod. If the men knew the truth they would have pitched a hissy." She glanced from one sister to the other. "Do Texas men pitch hissies?"

Nina laughed. "They do something, just don't think anyone's put a label on it."

The tires slid on the loose gravel and Lillie slowed the Jeep to a crawl and headed down a dip. "The river is starting to rise. If we don't go now we could be cut off and anything we might find that could lead us to Grandpa Pete's killer might be lost."

She pulled to a stop and Nina gasped, "Holy cow! The road's gone."

Lillie nodded. "Small Creek isn't so small at the moment. It's flooded over the road. We'll have to walk in. I think John said there was a footbridge in the woods. Hopefully, that's still standing and we can get to Grandpa Pete's cabin that way."

Juliet flipped up the hood on her rain jacket and stepped out of the car. Lillie zipped her yellow jacket and followed, as did Nina. Lillie pointed through the dripping woods. "There's John's cabin, so the little bridge must be—"

"Ouch," Juliet yelped and crumpled to the ground. Nina and Lillie rushed to her and Lillie asked, "What happened?"

"Twisted my blooming ankle. Rabbit hole, I'd say."

Or snake hole, Lillie thought but kept it to herself. "You two head back to town and I'll go on."

"Not in this lifetime," Juliet protested, as she held on to Nina and Lillie and righted herself. "You're not staying out in these woods by yourself with a potential evildoer scurrying about."

Lillie said, "I know, you two stay at John's and I'll look around at Grandpa Pete's cabin. If I see anyone I'll come back. I'll be fine. I swear I will not confront anyone on my own. Okay?"

Nina exchanged looks with Juliet. "Bloody poor idea if you ask me, but we're out here now and need to get the job done," said Juliet.

Lillie and Nina got on each side of Juliet and Lillie nodded toward John's cabin. "Just up ahead."

Juliet hopped on one foot, and when they got to the cabin Lillie lifted an old log—making real sure it was a log before touching it—and located the key John had used to lock up the place when they'd left. She opened the cabin door and helped Juliet inside. "There's a fire ready to be set. John built it before we left yesterday."

Nina giggled. "Oh, if these walls could talk."

"I'm not answering that one," Lillie said. "But there's half a bottle of brandy to get you warmed up."

"Something you didn't need yesterday, I bet," Juliet quipped as Nina and Lillie helped her into a chair by the hearth. "Just how long were you here?"

Lillie sighed. "Long enough to get into trouble." She headed for the door before either sister could ask more questions. "I'll be back soon."

Juliet said, "Nina should go with you for protection."

"You're the one with the bum ankle. I can run like the wind if I need to. Lock the door behind me."

Lillie left before her sisters could protest again and made her way to the creek. This was probably just like the day Grandpa Pete drowned. A lump lodged in her chest at the thought. What she wouldn't give to have known him, talked to—

Barking snapped her back to the moment and Butter darted through the trees, jumping in little circles. "Yeah, I'm glad to see you too. What are you doing out here? You ran off last time without even exchanging e-mails."

Butter ran and came back and did it again, just like yesterday, when she led her to John's cabin. "Okay, where are we going this time?"

She followed Butter toward the creek. She could hear the water rushing, then spotted a log bridge with a chunk of it gone and a cabin like John's in the distance, smoke curling from the chimney. Someone was in Grandpa Pete's cabin? Gabe Rankin? He was the one Grandpa left the cabin to or—

"Help! Lillie! Over here, girl!"

She spotted an old man clinging to a fallen tree half submerged in the water. It wasn't Gabe Rankin but he did look familiar. From the wake last night?

She raced to him as he yelled, "Get help. I fell off the dang bridge. My leg's caught. Can't budge it and this here tree is the only thing keeping me from getting washed out into the dang river."

She waded into the water and held out her hand. The man shook his head. "I'll just pull you with me, girl. We need a rope and some muscle. My strength's just about ate up from the cold. Been out here since daybreak and this here creek's getting deeper by the minute."

He was ashen and looked weak. "Were you a friend of my grandfather and staying in his cabin?"

"Hell's bells, girl, I *am* your grandfather."

John leaned across Melinda's desk at the spa. "Where is Lillie? Where are Nina and Juliet? Are they all together?"

Melinda folded her arms across her ample chest and tipped her chin. "I'm not at liberty to say. In fact, Lillie will string me up if I tell. You honestly think she and her sisters

did in their granddaddy? If that isn't the most asinine thing
I've ever heard in—"

"It's raining like mad, Melinda. The river's on the rise
and I've got Rod and Lance helping people to evacuate right
now. Lillie wouldn't take off unless she was up to something, and I don't know what happened to Pete but something's not clicking and I'm going to find out why."

Jimmy came up behind John. "Hello, beautiful."

Melinda blushed and fluffed her hair. "Well hello, handsome."

John did a mental eye roll and swallowed a groan.
"Melinda?"

"Oh, all right, all right. But I'm only telling you because
Lillie and her dear sisters are down by the river and I'm
starting to get worried sick. Never seen so much rain before
in my life."

John felt as if someone had smacked him upside the head
with a two-by-four. "What are they doing at the river?"

"That's all I know. She didn't tell me any more. Said she
had a hunch and everything pointed to the river."

"Her hunch is going to get her killed." John swallowed a
string of curses. "When the evacuees from the flood come
into town put them up here."

Melinda sucked in a quick breath. "This is not a hotel,
John Snow, in spite of what you want."

"It will be a hotel forever if you don't do what I say. I
don't have time to sit here and explain, but get this place
working at full tilt: hot tubs, sauna, massage rooms, yoga,
health food, the works."

He turned to Jimmy. "You're going to help get people
settled in here and keep records of who's here so we don't
leave anyone behind who needs assistance."

Jimmy nodded. "Got it, but where in blazes are you
going at a time like this?"

"Fishing." John left the spa and turned his collar against

the rain as he headed for his truck, parked on the street. When he found Lillie he'd wring her neck . . . after he kissed her. Messing around by the river was not good during a flash flood, and with a day's hard rain here and even more in the mountains, the Gulch was ripe for a flood, something a Chicago girl knew zip about. Except she did have one thing right: everything about Pete led back to the river. John revved the engine and headed out of town toward the cabins.

Even though the sisters benefited from Pete's death it would have taken a lot of planning and privileged information from Gabe for them to realize they inherited property on his death. Gabe would never betray Pete, and John could find no proof that anyone besides Gabe knew anything about Pete's trusts or his will. So, what else had changed since Pete's death? Nothing. His granddaughters came to Silver Gulch, period.

John slowly smiled to himself. And isn't it just too damn bad old Pete isn't around to enjoy them. "Well, I'll be damned."

Three miles wasn't far but gravel and water washing across the roads slowed him down. He shifted into third gear to give the tires more traction, and as he rounded the bend in the old gravel road that led to the cabins he spotted Lillie's red Jeep.

His blood ran cold. Three city gals out in this rain with flooding all around was not good. John killed the engine and got out. "Lillie," he yelled into the woods. No response except Butter running his way. She jumped in little circles and yelped. *Dog talk for follow me, dumb ass?* Hell, he didn't have a better idea.

Butter took off in a run with John right behind. She headed for the creek, which was no doubt a small river by now, and in the distance he saw a yellow splotch of cloth in the water. Lillie's jacket? Oh crap! "Lillie?!"

She turned and waved and he felt as if their gazes met across the distance. "John?!" she yelled back. "Here! Hurry!"

Hurry? Hurry was never a word of reassurance. He tore through the underbrush, ignoring the more roundabout cleared path, till he got to her, waist deep in the water. "Thank God you're here."

She was holding on to someone. "Howdy, Pete!"

"Me and my granddaughter are getting mighty wet. If she hadn't come along I'd be fish food by now. And you're not acting all that surprised to see me."

"I'm not." John waded into the racing water, the current swirling around his thighs, then up to his waist. He said to Pete, "I'll get you off this log then hand you to Lillie, and she'll get you onto the shore."

John grabbed Pete around the waist, bracing him from the back so the current wouldn't sweep them both away. He got to the edge and Lillie grabbed her grandfather's arm, smiling, her eyes shining. "I can't believe you're really here and we're all safe." She leaned forward to kiss him . . . except her foot slipped and she tripped forward, splashing into the churning water.

John held Pete with one arm and snatched Lillie's wet hand but it was too wet and she slipped right out of his grasp. Terror ripped through him as her body swept into the fast current, her terrified eyes big as softballs as she disappeared around the bend. Pete yelled, "Go get her, boy! That's my granddaughter out there! I can take care of myself!"

John scrambled up onto the shore, hauled Pete onto the bank, then ran along the bank. A yellow splash of color bobbed in the water, then was lost around the next bend. John ran faster, jumped a log, took the curve, and spotted Lillie clinging to a rock for all she was worth . . . and he realized that to him Lillie June—entrepreneur, courageous granddaughter, loving sister—was worth more than the sun, moon, and stars all rolled into one. He splashed into the water and grabbed the waistband of her jeans tight into his fist. "You scared the hell out of me."

Still clinging to the rock, she glanced back at him. "I'm moving to the desert."

Securing each footstep, he inched back toward the shore, hauling Lillie with him. With one hand on her thigh and the other on her very nice rump, he pushed her out of the water. Then he grabbed a log to hoist himself out, but it let loose and he tumbled backward till Lillie's hand snatched his wrist, giving him a second to regain his balance. "You should move to the desert with me."

And suddenly that sounded like the best idea he'd heard in ages. Not just because of the water but because he wanted to be with Lillie no matter where they were.

They sprawled on the bank in the weeds, catching their breaths. Lillie said, "I'm wet in places I didn't know I had."

Grinning, he rolled over and cupped her head in the palm of his hand and kissed her, her warm lips making him feel more alive than ever.

"Pete," she said, snapping him back to the moment, "we'd better get to him."

"Right. Pete." They ran back to the bridge, where Pete was sitting on a log, with Butter licking his face. "I fished Goldie here out of the creek three months ago and she went and returned the favor by getting you both here and saving me. This is some dog."

Lillie hugged Pete tight and said in a ragged voice, "I'm so glad you're here."

"Me too, girl. Me too." He patted her as if comforting a child—his child. John let them have the moment. Pete went to a lot of trouble to make this happen and he'd succeeded. But he'd been in the chilling water a long time and needed to get warm.

"Hey," John said, "I'm cold as a snake's belly and damn tired of being rained on. Let's get out of here."

Lillie smoothed back Pete's silver hair. "Guess what? Nina and Juliet are at John's cabin."

Pete's tired eyes brightened. "Well, hot damn. You mean all my girls are here together in one place because they came looking for me?" He slapped his knee and laughed hard. "Looks like my little plan worked sweeter than apples in August."

"Wait," Lillie said, holding up her hands, studying her newfound granddaddy. "Plan? What plan?" She folded her arms. "Why aren't you dead, like you're supposed to be? Not that I'm complaining, mind you. What in the world did you do?"

Six

Nina stood by the fire and Juliet had her leg propped up on the hearth as they stared speechless at Pete in the doorway.

"This really is our grandfather," Lillie repeated for her sisters' benefit as much as her own, because it was still hard to believe.

The brandy bottle slid from Juliet's fingers and John snagged it midair before it hit the floor. She croaked, "G-Grandpa?"

Pete stood tall and proud. "It's me, girl. In the flesh. And I'm thrilled to pieces you're here."

Juliet's mouth opened and closed and opened again but no words came out. She blinked as if clearing her vision. "Grandpa Pete?"

He laughed deep as he kissed Nina on the head, then Juliet on the cheek. "Well, I've got to tell you that this isn't exactly the way I had our little reunion planned, but it'll do just fine and dandy, yes it will."

John wrapped a blanket around Pete, and Nina got him a chair by the fire. John got a blanket for Lillie and himself and they all faced Pete, as if making sure he wasn't a figment of their imagination and was about to fade away like smoke up the chimney.

Juliet licked her lips, rubbed her eyes, and finally managed, "I don't bloody believe this. You're alive. But . . . But"—she put her hands to her hips—"we mourned for you, you know. We even had a wake for you."

Pete nodded. "And a damn fine one it was, too. I appreciate it to no end."

Lillie couldn't contain her gasp. "Oh my God, you were there. You were the old guy in the beard."

"I gave myself a pretty fair eulogy, if I do say so. Damn near made myself cry."

Nina took the brandy from John's hand and threw back a long swig from the bottle, then handed it to Juliet, who took a drink and passed it on to Lillie, who took a sip that made her eyes water, then asked, "What's going on?"

John propped his foot on the hearth. "My guess is that Pete wanted you all exactly where you are right now and faking his death and leaving you property was the easiest way to make that happen."

Lillie pointed at John. "You knew all along?"

"Got a hunch on the way here. Other than his granddaughters, Pete was the only one who gained anything from his own death. And since no body was found, it fit."

Pete added, "You all got a chance to get to know each other without me in the mix." He grinned like a little boy on Christmas morning. "And from what I've seen, I'm a blooming genius. You got a chance to bond and act like the real sisters you are."

This time Nina gasped. "You've been spying on us, haven't you? The candy wrappers, things moved around in the Rooster's office, they were all from you snooping."

"Guilty." Pete beamed. "I kept my eye on you all. Stayed in the attics at the Rooster and the hotel or outbuildings at the ranch when I wasn't out here. Didn't count on Lillie coming up to the attic night before last. Nearly found me out."

Juliet smiled. "You're pretty sneaky for a grandpa."

Nina stood. "Rod and Lance are going to be tearing up the countryside driving everyone nuts if we don't get back to town." She studied Pete for a long moment. "Did you plan on me and Lance falling in love and Juliet and Rod?"

Pete's eyes sparked with devilment. "Would I do a thing like that to my own granddaughters and two of the best men I ever met? Course Lillie and John here were a bonus I didn't count on."

John carried Juliet to Lillie's Jeep, with Lillie, Nina, and Grandpa Pete following and Pete telling how he fell in the creek. Lillie listened but mostly she just wanted to be Juliet. She wanted to be the one in John's arms, feel his strong, muscled chest next to her, talk to him about what happened today and hear about what was going on in town and how *he* figured this all out.

John sat Juliet in the front seat and Nina and Grandpa Pete climbed in the back. John backed his truck around and Lillie followed him into town as Nina said, "Well, Lillie, are you going to be stone quiet forever or are you going to tell us what's going on with you and John?"

"Not much to tell. There's nothing between John and me. He's going back to Dallas to a job he loves, and I'm staying here and probably filing bankruptcy or turning the spa back into a hotel, like everyone wants. It's caused too much trouble."

Grandpa Pete scoffed, "Give things a chance, girl, for the spa and John. Mighty fine boy. Had a rough go of it when his daddy went to jail, but John is not his daddy and he needs to realize that and so does this town. They need to see him for the man he is."

Lillie considered that. "Oh, he's handsome enough. And he is a good cop, but his plan was to talk me into closing down the spa because that's what the men in town wanted. How can I trust him after that?"

Lillie pulled up in front of the spa—least that was her plan—but there were cars and trucks everywhere and people coming and going out of the spa like Grand Central Station. Pete asked, "What's going on? Did you have a special or something?"

"I sent out coupons for a free massage."

Nina laughed. "That must have been some coupon."

"Except there are men and women and kids. Family memberships are the best but why this, why now?"

Juliet pointed. "There's a parking place on the next block."

Nina added, "And Rod, Lance, and John are flagging us down. And a lot of people are looking at us."

Lillie chuckled. "They're looking at a ghost, Pete Maddock." She pulled into the parking place and people gathered around the Jeep.

Rod elbowed his way through and opened the door. "Well now, Juliet, you just had to go and mess up your ankle." His eyes danced. "And that's just fine by me because now I can carry you everywhere."

Lance hooked his arm around Nina. "Leave it to you to find your dead granddaddy alive and well." Lance patted Pete on the back. "Welcome back."

Pete laughed. "You all head over to the Rooster. I'm getting a change of clothes and I'll be there to tell you all about it and how I'm such a smart old guy."

The crowd followed Pete but Lillie stayed by the Jeep, mostly because John was there. He said, "You should change."

"Why do I have a feeling that all these people being at my spa has something to do with you?"

He leaned against the side of the Jeep, the afternoon sun breaking through the clouds. "Think of it as an apology."

"For . . . ?"

He took her hand. "For being an ass. The first time I met you was to close your place down so I could keep my job in Dallas. Now I realize I don't want either. I put up the folks who had to leave their homes because of flooding here. I knew if the men were exposed to hot tubs and massages and saunas and the like after all the stress of fighting the flood they'd be hooked, and they'll spread the word. What did you call it? An endorsement?"

"You did this for me?"

His eyes went black. "And me. I apologize for thinking you or your sisters could harm Pete. You'll sell enough memberships to keep you going for a while and then the word will spread and you'll make more money. I want you to stay in Silver Gulch, Lillie. I want to pick out china with you."

"China?"

"I'm going to run for sheriff. I did a pretty good job of organizing the evacuations of the families flooded out and getting them settled. People remember things like that. I want us to have a chance together, Lillie. I want to start fresh and have you with me. I love you. I want to marry you. I know you don't trust marriage but I'm not my dad and you aren't your mother. We're us together, at last. We can make it work, Lillie. What do you think?"

She threw her arms around him. "I love you. I can't believe in three days I've fallen hopelessly in love this way. You're willing to give up your life in Dallas for a chance to be with me, wanting nothing in return but my love? How could I not love you, John. You make me the happiest woman on earth."

Epilogue

Pete fidgeted in the back of the jam-packed church. A lump the size of Texas lodged in his throat as he took in his three granddaughters all in sparkling white wedding dresses. "I get you all here together only to be giving you away," he joked.

Nina fussed with his tie. "Three granddaughters and three grandsons-in-law. We have a big family now. Next week is Thanksgiving. Just think how crowded the table will be."

Pete sighed. "A man can't wish for more than that. I was wanting you with me for so many years and now you're all here happy and lovely as can be."

He faked concern. "So let's see if we're all ready. You have the something new with your pretty dresses, something old—that's me and mighty lucky to be here—something borrowed . . ."

Juliet laughed. "We lent each other hankies in case we cry."

Pete patted his own pocket. "Me too. So that leaves us with something blue."

Lillie said, "We have blue garters."

Pete shrugged. "But nobody can see those." He reached in his pocket and took out three little blue boxes. He handed one to Lillie and kissed her on the cheek, handed one to Nina and kissed her, and then handed a box to Juliet and kissed her. "Well, go ahead and open them. Can't know what's on the inside by staring at the outside."

The girls took off the lids and smiles spread across their faces. Lillie said, "It's a Texas bluebonnet."

"On a silver chain," Nina added.

Juliet sighed, "It's so lovely."

Pete felt the biggest smile ever spread across his face. "You are my beautiful bluebonnets, my family."

The organ music kicked up a notch and the first chords of the "Wedding March" sounded. "I think they're playing your song, ladies."

Nina, Juliet, and Lillie hooked arms and Pete felt tears sting his eyes. "To sisters."

"To grandfathers," Lillie said and Nina and Juliet nodded.

Pete hitched his chin toward Rod, Lance, and John, standing in the front of the church. "And if I don't get you girls up there right quick, there are three men coming to get you."

Pete faced the aisle and the three men in front gave him the thumbs-up sign. Pete returned it, then led his granddaughters to the happiness he'd wished for them all their lives.

Don't miss this sneak peek at
Shannon McKenna's
HOT NIGHT
coming in October 2006 from Brava . . .

Abby was floating. The sensual heft of Zan's black leather jacket felt wonderful on her shoulders, even though it hung halfway down to her thighs.

They'd reached the end of the boardwalk, where the lights began to fade. Beyond the boardwalk, the warehouse district began. They'd walked the whole boardwalk, talking and laughing, and at some point, their hands had swung together and sort of just . . . stuck. Warmth seeking warmth. Her hand tingled joyfully in his grip.

The worst had happened. Aside from his sex appeal, she simply liked him. She liked the way he laughed, his turn of phrase, his ironic sense of humor. He was smart, honest, earthy, funny. Maybe, just maybe, she could trust herself this time.

Their strolling slowed to a stop at the end of the boardwalk.

"Should we, ah, walk back to your van?" she ventured.

"This is where I live," he told her.

She looked around. "Here? But this isn't a residential district."

"Not yet," he said. "It will be soon. See that building,

over there? It used to be a factory of some kind, in the twenties, I think. The top floor, with the big arched windows, that's my place."

There was just enough light to make out the silent question in his eyes. She exhaled slowly. "Are you going to invite me up, or what?"

"You know damn well that you're invited," he said. "More than invited. I'll get down on my knees and beg, if you want me to."

The full moon appeared in a window of scudding clouds, then disappeared again. "It wouldn't be smart," she said. "I don't know you."

"I'll teach you," he offered. "Crash course in Zan Duncan. What do you want to know? Hobbies, pet peeves, favorite leisure activities?"

She would put it to the test of her preliminary checklist, and make her decision based on that. "Don't tell me," she said. "Let me guess. You're a martial arts expert, right?"

"Uh, yeah. Aikido is my favorite discipline. I like kung fu, too."

She nodded, stomach clenching. There it was, the first black mark on the no-no's checklist. Though it was hardly fair to disqualify him for that, since he'd saved her butt with those skills the night before.

So that one didn't count. On to the next no-no. "Do you have a motorcycle?"

He looked puzzled. "Several of them. Why? Want to go for a ride?"

Abby's heart sank. "No. One last question. Do you own guns?"

Zan's face stiffened. "Wait. Are these are trick questions?"

"You do, don't you?" she persisted.

"My late father was a cop." His voice had gone hard. "I have his service Beretta. And I have a hunting rifle. Why?

Are you going to talk yourself out of being with me because of superficial shit like that?"

Abby's laugh felt brittle. "Superficial. That's Abby Maitland."

"No, it is not," he said. "That's not Abby Maitland at all."

"You don't know the first thing about me, Zan."

"Yes, I do." His dimple quivered. "I know first things, second things, third things. You've got piss-poor taste in boyfriends, to start."

Abby was stung. "Those guys were not my boyfriends! I didn't even know them! I've just had a run of bad luck lately!"

"Your luck is about to change, Abby." His voice was low and velvety. "I know a lot about you. I know how to get into your apartment. How to turn your cat into a noodle. The magnets on your fridge, the view from your window. Your perfume. I could find you blindfolded in a room full of strangers." His fingers penetrated the veil of her hair, his forefinger stroking the back of her neck with controlled gentleness. "And I learn fast. Give me ten minutes, and I'd know lots more."

"Oh," she breathed. His hand slid through her hair, settled on her shoulder. The delicious heat burned her, right through his jacket.

"I know you've got at least two of those expensive dresses that drive guys nuts. And I bet you've got more than two. You've got a whole closet full of hot little outfits like that. Right?" He cupped her jaw, turning her head until she was looking into his fathomless eyes.

Her heart hammered. "I've got a . . . a pretty nice wardrobe, yes."

"I'd like to see them." His voice was sensual. "Someday maybe you can model them all for me. In the privacy of your bedroom."

"Zan—"

"I love it when you say my name," he said. "I love your voice. Your accent. Based on your taste in dresses, I'm willing to bet that you like fancy, expensive lingerie, too. Am I right? Tell me I'm right."

"Time out," she said, breathless. "Let's not go there."

"Oh, but we've already arrived." His breath was warm against her throat. "Locksmiths are detail maniacs. Look at the palm of your hand, for instance. Here, let me see." He lifted her hand into the light from the nearest of the streetlamps. "Behold, your destiny."

It was silly and irrational, but it made her self-conscious to have him look at the lines on her hand. As if he actually could look right into her mind. Past, future, fears, mistakes, desires, all laid out for anyone smart and sensitive enough to decode it. "Zan. Give me my hand back."

"Not yet. Oh . . . wow. Check this out," he whispered.

"What?" she demanded.

He shook his head with mock gravity and pressed a kiss to her knuckles. "It's too soon to say what I see. I don't want to scare you off."

"Oh, please," she said unsteadily. "You are so full of it."

"And you're so scared. Why? I'm a righteous dude. Good as gold." He stroked her wrist. "Ever try cracking a safe without drilling it? It's a string of numbers that never ends. Hour after hour, detail after detail. That's concentration." He pressed his lips against her knuckles.

"What does concentration have to do with anything?"

"It has everything to do with everything. That's what I want to do to you, Abby. Concentrate, intensely, minutely. Hour after hour, detail after detail. Until I crack all the codes, find all the keys to all your secret places. Until I'm so deep inside ya . . ." his lips kissed their way up her wrist ". . . . that we're a single being."

She leaned against him, and let him cradle her in his

strong arms. His warm lips coaxed her into opening to the gentle, sensual exploration of his tongue. "Come up with me," he whispered. "Please."

She nodded. Zan's arm circled her waist, fitting her body against his. It felt so right. No awkwardness, no stumbling, all smooth. Perfect.

Here's a look at
OUT OF THIS WORLD
by Jill Shalvis
available now from Brava!

"What the hell happened?" he demanded. A few drops of water fell off the tip of his nose onto my face. "Why are you lying on the ground? *Are you okay?*"

Was I okay? Hmm, wasn't that the question of the hour? Trying to figure out that very thing, I looked back up into the sky, watching the raindrops coming down, one by one. Wow, it was really beautiful.

Every part of everything around me seemed deeper, more colorful, richer . . .

More intense.

"Rach?" Kellan tossed aside his glasses and leaned over me, protecting me with his body, stroking my hair from my face. "You're silent. You're never silent."

A bird flew overhead, and when I concentrated on its body, its wings flapping, I found I could see its heart pumping, beating . . .

Oh.

My.

God.

"*Rach.*"

"I think I broke a nail," I whispered.

He stared at me. "Tell me you're kidding."

"I'm kidding." I lifted my hand and studied my plain, trimmed-by-my-own-teeth nails.

"You're scaring me, Rach. Here, can you sit up?" He took my hand to pull me upright, then steadied me, his hands firm on my upper arms. "Are you all right?"

Without his lenses, his eyes were so clear and blue, I could have just looked at him all day long.

Wow. Gorgeous.

I wobbled, then set my head against his chest. Beneath the drenched shirt, his heart beat a bit fast but steadily, and he was warm, deliriously warm. Sturdy and solid and always-there Kel.

He extended his arms, pushing me back, so he could peer into my face. Man, he was cute. I smiled up at him dreamily, thinking I'd no idea just how cute . . . and while thinking it, a shiver wracked me. Probably it was the cold, but it might have been the totally and completely inappropriate surge of lust I was experiencing.

Kel kept his hands on me, drawing me back against his warm body, making me all the more aware of him, of his sweet but firm touch, of the strength that allowed him to easily take on my weight. I sighed in pleasure.

"You're scaring the shit out of me, Rach."

"Did you know you have the most amazing eyes?"

They narrowed on me. "Huh?"

"Seriously," I said, reaching up, touching his face, which was wet from the rain. "I could drown in 'em. Anyone ever told you that?"

"Uh, no. You're the first. Hold on there, champ," he said when I tried to get up, holding me down with a hand to the middle of my chest. "Don't move."

Good idea, since everything had begun to swim. I put my hands to my head. "What happened to me?"

"That's what I was going to ask you."

He was so cute with all his worry that it made me smile. "Kel? How come we've never gone out?"

"Out?"

"Hooked up."

He went still, then lifted two fingers. "Okay, how many?" he demanded.

"I'm fine," I insisted.

"I thought we were erasing that word from the English language."

I tried to stand up on my own. "Whoa." I reached for him, because maybe I wasn't so okay after all. "Hey, stop the world, would ya? I want to get off."

"You're dizzy?" He gripped my shoulders. "What the hell happened? Did you fall?"

I closed my eyes. But just like on the plane, that only made it worse, so I opened them again. I focused on a tree. Again, I saw right through the tree, as if I had X-ray vision, meaning I could still see the long line of carpenter ants making their way through the trunk. I followed their line down to the ground, where they emerged from a hole only a few inches from me.

One crawled out near my foot, and I would have sworn on my own grave that it craned its neck and glared at me for being in its way. I stared at it, stunned. "Uh . . . Kellan?"

"Jesus," he breathed, and for a minute my heart surged, thinking he could see through stuff, too, but he shook his head and pointed at my clothes.

They were smoking.

"You were hit by lightning," he said, and looked into my face. "My God. Are you okay?"

His eyes still seemed luminous and filled with far more worry than before. I dropped my gaze from his, and then gasped.

Like with the moon, like with the tree, I could see through him. As in *beneath his clothes.*

Um, yeah, I was definitely different.

"I can't believe it," he said. "I mean, what are the chances?" Leaning in again, he began to run his hands over my limbs. Up my legs, over my hips, over my ribs—

"What are you doing?"

Please turn the page for a preview of
the next book in Jessica Inclán's
marvelous, magical trilogy
REASON TO BELIEVE,
a Zebra trade paperback
available in October 2006.

Rubbing her gloved hands together, she walked toward the man, slowing as she neared him.

"Hello," Fabia said softly, blinking against the street-light.

He stared at her—no, past her—his face expressionless. His face was smudged with dirt, a deep, dark red scratch running from temple to jaw, one eye blackened. Blood swelled the skin under his eye and hung in a painful purple moon over his cheek. As Fabia moved closer, she realized that his hair wasn't matted so much from the wet, dank air as from dried blood. There was a clear, perfect circle of red-dish, broken skin around his neck, and she noticed now that the dirt she'd seen under his nails this morning was ac-tually blood.

Whatever had happened, he'd fought back. Whoever he'd fought with probably looked as bad as he.

"Are you all right?"

The man turned to her, tried to look up, and then took a deep breath, his mouth trying to move. He was trembling, his arms tight against his body now, his black eyes filled with fog and sadness. Again, she tried to reach for his mind, but the iron wall was still there, planted solidly.

What do you think? Fabia asked Niall without even meaning to.

All that blood, Niall thought. *Maybe it's not his. Moyenne are messy murderers.*

He hardly looks capable of a right killing, Fabia thought.

True. He didn't do his level best, there. So he might be on the lam. Injured from the barbed wire he crawled under, Niall thought. *Just call the police.*

Fabia stared at the man, ignoring Niall for a moment. Maybe she couldn't read the man's mind, but there was something about him. Something kind even in his quiet, painful desperation.

Bloody bleeding heart, Niall thought. *But just be ready to escape. Be prepared to step into the gray, okay? Hop back to your flat.*

Yes, sir, Fabia thought, shaking her head. But Niall was right. It was easier to extend this kindness knowing that if the man grew strange or crazy or even dangerous, she could disappear in an instant, traveling through matter to the police station where she could report the crime she'd just escaped. The *Moyenne* she worked with at the clinic were always amazed that Fabia would go to flophouses and tenements and dark alleys looking for clients. What she couldn't tell them was that she was protecting them by doing so, keeping them away from danger from which they might not be able to escape.

Fabia bent down, trying to attract his gaze. But he wouldn't look at her, and she could feel the tension radiating from inside him.

"Hi, there," she said. "My name is Fabia Fair. I live at a flat just down a bit."

He didn't move his eyes, but he blinked, once, twice.

"Would you like to come with me?" Fabia said, crouching down farther and looking into the man's desperate, searching eyes. "How about a wee bit to eat?"

He licked his lips, breathing in, scanning the ground as if he'd dropped some change. *Not drunk,* Fabia thought. *Schizophrenic.*

Perfect, Niall thought. *Go from Cadeyrn to just another crazy. Get yourself into another fankle.*

Haver on, man! Would you mind affording me some space here? she thought back. *Go watch your bleeding telly.*

Fabia closed her mind to her brother and moved closer to the man. He was shaking, his knees hitting together. Again, he moved his mouth, but then shook his head, tears streaming from the corners of his eyes.

Fabia watched him, trying everything she knew to get inside his mind, but there was no opening, as if the block was put there on purpose. And not by the man, who clearly was in no shape to create or even maintain a block, even if he were *Croyant,* magic, like her. And there was something about him, even with his quaking gaze and his long, thin, dirty body. Fabia couldn't read his mind, but she could feel . . . kindness.

"All right," Fabia said. "That's it. Please, come with me."

She stood up straight and held out her hand. The man breathed in, looking at her hand and then her face, her hand, her face, and then slowly, he lifted his dirty palm from his knee, studying his movements with surprise as if he'd never moved before. His fingers quivered, shook, and Fabia took them in her small gloved hand, feeling how cold he was even through the leather and wool.

Take a look at Diane Whiteside's
THE SOUTHERN DEVIL
available now from Brava!

The mantel clock began to chime.

Jessamyn's head flashed around to stare at it before she looked back at Morgan.

She forced back her body's awareness of him. "I needed him as my husband, you fool! For two hours, starting now."

"Husband?" Jealousy swept over his face.

"In a lawyer's office," she snarled back. "I have to be there with a husband in fifteen minutes, or all is lost. Damn you, let me go!"

The clock chimed again.

His eyes narrowed for a moment then he pulled her up to him. His grip was less painful but just as inescapable as before. "A bargain then, Jessamyn. I'll play your husband for a few hours—if you'll join me in a private parlor for the same span of time afterward."

She gasped. A devil's bargain, indeed.

"Nine years ago, before you married Cyrus, I promised you revenge for what you did—and you agreed my claim was just. Two hours won't see that accomplished but it's a start," he purred, his drawl knife-edged and laced with carnal promise.

Her flight or fight instincts stirred, honed by seven years as an Army wife on the bloody Kansas prairies. She reined them in sternly: No matter how angry he'd been, surely Morgan would never harm a woman, no matter what preposterous demands he'd hurled nine years ago when she'd held him captive.

Her fingers bit into his arms, as she tried to think of another option. But if she didn't appear with a husband, she'd lose her only chance of regaining Somerset Hall, her family's old home . . .

The mantel clock sounded the third, and last, note.

She agreed to his bargain, the words like ashes in her throat. "Very well, Morgan. Now will you take me across the street to the lawyer's?"

Morgan escorted Jessamyn across the street with all the haughtiness his father would have shown escorting his mother aboard a riverboat. It was a bit of manners ingrained in him so early that he didn't need to think about it, something he'd first practiced with Jessamyn when she was five and their parents first openly hoped for a wedding between them. Such an ingrained habit was very useful when his brain seemed to have dived somewhere south of his belt buckle as soon as she'd agreed she owed him revenge.

What was he going to do first? There were so many activities he'd learned in Consortium houses: How to drive a woman insane with desire. How to leave her sated and panting, willing to do anything to repeat the experience. More than anything else, he needed to see Jessamyn aching to be touched by him again and again.

A black curl stroked her cheek in just the way he planned

to later. He smiled, planning, and reached for the office door.

Ebenezer Abercrombie & Sons, Attys. At Law announced the sturdy letters on its surface.

Morgan stiffened. Her lawyer was that Abercrombie? Halpern's friend and Millicent's godfather, with whom Morgan had dined last night? Who'd beamed approval as Halpern and his wife had shoved Morgan at their daughter and he'd made no mention of a wife?

Damn, damn, damn.

Jessamyn, who'd never been a fool, caught his momentary hesitation and glanced up at him.

He shook his head slightly at her and put his hand on the doorknob. Suddenly it turned under his fingers and swung open to frame Abercrombie's well-fed bulk. The man's eyes widened briefly as he took in both of his two visitors.

Jessamyn leaned closer to Morgan and squeezed his arm, with all the assurance of a long-married woman. God knows he'd seen her do it with Cyrus before.

Morgan shifted himself so she could fit comfortably, as he'd seen his cousin do. She settled easily within a hand's-breadth of him and tilted her head at Abercrombie expectantly. The entire byplay took only a few seconds.

The lawyer's eyes narrowed and his mouth tightened, before a polite professional mask covered his face. "Good afternoon, Evans. What an unexpected pleasure to see you here today."

Morgan smiled with all the smooth charm he polished as one of Bedford Forrest's spies. "The pleasure is entirely mine, Abercrombie. I've the honor of escorting my wife. Jessamyn, my dear, have you met Mr. Abercrombie?" He could have kicked himself. His Mississippi drawl was slightly heavier than usual, a telltale sign of nervousness.

Jessamyn took Abercrombie's hand, with all the charm

of her aristocratic Memphis upbringing. "Yes, Mr. Abercrombie was my uncle's lawyer for years. I've known him since I was a child. Hello, sir."

Abercrombie kissed her cheek. "My dear lady, I'm so glad you were able to bring your husband." His eyes flickered to Morgan but his countenance was impassive. "Your cousin Charles and his wife are seated in my office, waiting for the reading of the will to begin. Please come with me."